*To
Best wishes to a great teacher and friend*

KEYS TO MURDER

OPENS THE DOOR TO BETRAYAL, REVENGE, AND MURDER

M. HARMON HALL

This book is a work of fiction. Names, characters, businesses, organizations, places, events, and incidents either are the product of the author's imagination or are used fictitiously. Any resemblance to actual persons, living or dead, or locales is entirely coincidental.

Copyright © 2015 M. Harmon Hall
All Rights Reserved
Library of Congress Cataloging-in-Publication Data is available.
ISBN 13 – 978 - 1507682807
ISBN 10 – 1507682808
Printed in USA

Dedicated to

*My beautiful daughters, Jennifer and Lauren, and son-in-law Dustin
And their sweet Emma James,
And to my wonderful wife, Gloria*

Keys to Murder

CHAPTER 1

It's not the fall that kills you, it's the sudden stop. Detective MacArthur Nowlin was so excited about the prospect of sharing a long weekend with his girlfriend, Marilyn. After all, it had been weeks since they had any time to enjoy each other's company alone. MacArthur was convinced that this time off was well deserved. He was in a great mood as he was headed home around 7:45 on Friday night August 8th, 2005. He had one stop to before heading for his apartment. Marilyn had asked him to pick up some clothes at the cleaners. His slightly off key rendition of *My Girl*, was interrupted by the ringing of his phone. Chief Aldridge was on the line. *I probably shouldn't answer it*, MacArthur thought.

"MacArthur, we've got two dead bodies with gunshot wounds."

"Chief, I'm on my way home; who else is on duty?"

"You are! Now get your ass over there now; the address is 1250 Logan Drive."

Damn, this can't be happening! I knew damn well I shouldn't have answered the phone. How am I going to explain this to Marilyn? She's not going to understand, MacArthur thought correctly.

He reluctantly called Marilyn to break the news to her, "Honey, I've got a problem – the Chief just called, there are two dead bodies across town. He wants me to work the case."

"How convenient, this is the third time in the last six weeks, MacArthur," Marilyn protested. You know MacArthur, I am trying real hard to be the understanding significant other, but I don't know how much more I can take," Marilyn warned. "I wish I had known what your ex already knew. Your damn job comes first in your life and everything else, including the one you say you love, is left to barter for your time. You don't have a clue when it comes commitment. To you it's just a word you use when it's convenient," Marilyn said, as she began to cry.

"That's not fair, I don't like it either, but it's what I do," MacArthur countered.

"That's exactly my point MacArthur. You don't get it, do you? Go ahead and do what you have to do, you're going to anyway. You don't give a damn what I think. When you are done playing detective, call me. We need to talk."

Blue lights were flashing everywhere; black and white units circled the two story house with its three-car garage and fine trimmed lawn. Upstairs, Detective Tim Killingsworth was already taking notes and pictures of the crime scene.

"MacArthur, what are you doing here? I thought you were headed out of town with that hot girlfriend Melissa?"

"It's Marilyn, you jerk. Killingworth, you really want to know the real reason I'm here. It's because somebody has to go behind you so that the investigation is done right," MacArthur said with a smirk on his face.

"Yeah, yeah, we've got work to do. Some of the guys in blue are questioning the neighbors now to see if any of them might have seen or heard anything." Killingsworth countered.

"What do we have here?" MacArthur barked out.

"It looks like a case of murder/suicide," Killingsworth said confidently. This address belongs to Samuel and Ida Sprayberry. Dr. Sprayberry is Dean of the English Department at Liberty College over in Pelham. Mrs. Sprayberry is the counselor here at Wilcox High School. Don't know much about them at this time; but Officer Peavey, is doing a complete background check on them. They look to be in their mid to late fifties. We should know more about them in the morning," Killingsworth reported to MacArthur.

Detective Killingsworth continued laying out the facts that were known at the time. "It looks like the man shot his wife while she was in the bathtub and then walked back into the bedroom sat on the edge of the bed and shot himself. There doesn't appear to be any signs of a struggle."

Killingsworth added that there was a suicide note written on a standard 8 by 11 inch sheet of white paper that was found on the night stand on the same side of the bed that the male victim was found. The note had been placed in a plastic evidence bag. He also told MacArthur that two bullet casings had been found on the floor, one in the bedroom and one in the bathroom that connected to the bedroom.

"It looks like two casings, but that hasn't been verified yet. The gun found in the male's hand appears to be a nine millimeter Glock."

"Have you checked for gun residue on the male?" MacArthur asked.

Before Detective Killingsworth could answer, MacArthur asked a second question, "Have your guys dusted for prints?"

Killingsworth said he had not found any gun residue on either victim, but his team had found several sets of prints. The prints would later be identified as belonging to both Dr. and Mrs. Sprayberry. No other prints were found.

"Who reported the shootings?" MacArthur asked.

"A call came into the station around 7:20 pm," Killingsworth replied.

"Who took the call?"

"Sergeant King," Killingsworth answered.

"Get a complete report from him ASAP." MacArthur ordered.

MacArthur took out his notepad and started scribbling notes. It bothered him that there was no gun residue found on Dr. Sprayberry's hand or face. He asked Killingsworth where exactly were the casings located on the floor, in respect to the bodies.

"One was lying on the floor in the bathroom near the bathtub. The other was found on the right side of the bed, across from where the male's body was found," Killingsworth answered.

Being the experienced homicide detective he was, MacArthur also looked closely to see if the bodies of the victims had been moved by the first responders, other family members, or the "perps". He searched for signs of a struggle, as well as additional bullet holes. This called for him to examine the ceilings, walls, and adjacent rooms.

MacArthur also searched for traces of blood in other areas of the room. Next, he did a complete walk-through of the house. He went out into the backyard looking for anything that might be significant. He looked for any signs of a forced entry and found none.

"Whoever was in that house at the time of the shootings was either let in by the Sprayberrys, or had access to the entrance of the house," MacArthur shared with the patrolman. As he turned to go back in the house, he saw it.

Why would the Sprayberrys' leave a key in an exterior door? He thought.

With his gloves still on, he removed the key, and placed it in a small plastic evidence bag. After placing the bag in his coat pocket, MacArthur began to look for a laptop or desk computer that might have been used to write the suicide note. As he opened the door to the study located just off of the living room on the first floor, he saw a computer and printer sitting on an office desk.

There was plain white paper in the printer tray. He asked one of the officers to help him carry the computer and printer to his car, which he would later take to the station. Perhaps, there was something still in the computer's hard drive that might prove to be useful. He would get the tech experts to check out the computer.

MacArthur asked Detective Killingsworth to let him see the suicide note. As he began to read the brief note his mind kept going back to the key in the door. The suicide note read:

> My Beloved Sean and Susan,
> By the time you read this - we'll be dead. Both of you know I have always loved you. Please, don't hate me for what I am about to do. There is no other choice. I hope you can understand. I have done a terrible thing.
> I know this is a cowardly thing I am doing. I only hope you two can forgive me.
> With Love, You're Father

Even though he read the suicide note three times, MacArthur was still not convinced this was a murder/suicide case. The suicide note looked phony. He couldn't prove it right now, but he was sure with some digging, the evidence would support his theory.

After reading the suicide note, MacArthur asked Detective Killingsworth if the next of kin had been contacted. He told him that the deceased's son, Sean Sprayberry, had been notified. Sean and his family lived 25 miles from Wilcox, in the town of Silver Creek.

The medical examiner estimated the time of death for both victims was between 5:30 pm and 7:30 pm. The first officers on the scene stated that as they arrived they noticed many neighboring houses with lights on. Surely someone would have heard shots fired since the bedroom windows upstairs were open. Two separate neighbors stated that it was not unusual to see the Sprayberrys' upstairs windows opened during the summer and early fall.

"Make sure you guys secure the scene, and don't touch anything. Got it?"

"Yea, sure we got it," the officer in blue shot back at MacArthur.

The bodies would not be released until the coroner had officially pronounced them dead. He was overheard telling his assistant he thought this was a classic case of murder/suicide. An hour before the bodies were transported to the city morgue where the medical examiner would complete the process.

At 9:05 pm, MacArthur's work was done. His suspicious nature would not accept the fact that Dr. Sprayberry would kill his wife, then turn the gun on himself. MacArthur was confident the evidence would agree with his theory of what really happened. Now, it was just a matter of putting the pieces of the puzzle together to find the killer or killers.

Detective Killingsworth was on the phone when MacArthur interrupted him to tell him he was going back to the police station. As he spun around to see who was tapping him on the shoulder, MacArthur noticed Killingsworth had a strange look on his face, the look of a child who had been caught doing something he shouldn't. He quickly ended his phone conversation and turned his attention to MacArthur.

"Sorry for the interruption, headed back to the office," MacArthur informed Killingsworth.

"No problem Detective, I was checking in with the wife." Killingsworth replied.

Didn't sound like he was talking to his wife to me. That piece of crap probably has something on the side? MacArthur said to himself.

MacArthur went down the stairs and made his way to his car.

"Some idiot has blocked me in." MacArthur shouted at the police sergeant.

"Sorry Detective, I'll get somebody on it right away," said the sergeant.

"Why waste the time looking for someone else to move the damn car? Why don't you get your ass in the car and move it?" MacArthur rudely responded to the sergeant.

"No problem sir." the sergeant shot back.

He is such a prick, the sergeant said to himself.

On the way back to the station, MacArthur thought about calling Marilyn, but decided he would give her till the morning to cool off. He did wonder what she was doing.

Probably taking a long bath with a glass of wine and talking to her mother on the phone, he guessed.

MacArthur would never know just how accurate he had been. The only part he was wrong about was who she was talking to.

He really did feel bad about the lost weekend but, there hadn't been a murder in Wilcox for almost a year. City Hall and the citizens of Wilcox were proud of this fact. MacArthur had mixed emotions. Of course, he hated to see a son and daughter, brother and sister, and other family members lose two loved ones.

M. HARMON HALL

The only thing to do now is to catch the killer or killers and see that justice is done, MacArthur thought.

Now that there were murders to solve, Detective MacArthur Nowlin was again in his element.

CHAPTER 2

On his drive back to the station, MacArthur mulled over the fact that his and Marilyn's get-away weekend would have been great. He was actually beginning to have thoughts of a long term relationship, maybe even marriage. His history with women and commitments was one of disappointment. He was determined to get it right this time. MacArthur was finally ready to settle down, work less, and maybe even retire in five or six years. Yes, he would not make the same mistakes he had in the past.

But I do love this job, he smiled to himself.

No one saw or heard MacArthur enter the police station around 9:15 pm. He went into the workroom to check for any messages, went to the bathroom, and then to his office. His desk was covered with all sorts of clutter. There were old and new files, as well as unfinished overdue reports. On the corner of the desk was a picture of Marilyn. In the middle drawer was a half pack of Marlboros which he had given up several years back, but he kept the pack to remind himself of the terrible habit he once had. On the other corner of his desk was a cup that still had yesterday's coffee in it. He opened the notebook that had his notes from the crime scene he had returned from.

MacArthur started the tedious and time consuming process of organizing the information. As he was looking for a pen under all of the mess on his desk, he saw two tickets to last week's championship game. He had accused the rookie Detective Williams of taking them. *I should feel bad about wrongfully accusing Williams of taking the tickets, but I don't*, MacArthur thought. After all, he hadn't actually confronted the suspected thief, but only thought it to himself.

As he poured over the notes, MacArthur became absolutely convinced that this was a double homicide. *But who did this, and why?* There were too many inconsistencies with this case. One, no one heard shots being fired. Secondly, the couple seemed happy and were looking forward to going on a cruise in two weeks, according to Sam Dayton, a neighbor and close friend of the Sprayberrys. Thirdly, why would Dr. Sprayberry shoot his wife while she was taking a bath? It would have been much easier to wait until she was asleep, then shoot her. A fourth reason was the key found in the door. He didn't know just how right now, but he was sure it had something to do with the murders.

But what was the motive? MacArthur asked himself. He knew what he had to do next, convince Chief Aldridge. He was certain the Chief would agree with Detective Killingsworth. Come tomorrow morning, he was going to be in the Chief's office first thing.

MacArthur hadn't realized that it had gotten so late. It was almost midnight. He decided to go home and try to get some sleep. On his drive home, he thought about what he was going to say to Marilyn, and how he would make it up to her. He thought about the romantic weekend that was not going happen. He thought about Killingsworth's strange behavior. He thought about the key.

CHAPTER 3

An hour after MacArthur had delivered the bad news, Marilyn Hampton dialed a number she knew all too well. As she poured her second glass of wine, she waited for the voice on the other end to pick up.

"Hi, it's me. I'm sorry to call, but I need to see you tonight. I'm done with MacArthur. He's hurt me for the last time. Will you meet me in an hour?" Marilyn pleaded with a voice of desperation.

"You know I will, I've missed you," the voice on the other end proclaimed.

"What will you tell your wife?" Marilyn asked.

"Don't worry about her, she thinks I'm working late again. I'll meet you at the usual place around 10:00. Don't be late."

As Detective Tim Killingsworth hung up, the excitement of forbidden pleasures gave him a reason to smile. When she hung up the phone she called Rachel Peavey, her new friend. Marilyn had come to rely on Rachel's shoulder as she and MacArthur continued to grow apart. Rachel was always careful not to give her opinion, but just be a good listener.

Marilyn showered and then hurried to change into the pink silk blouse and short grey skirt she knew he liked so well. Forty-five minutes later, Marilyn was turning onto the dirt road that led to their private meeting place, a small cabin that was once used by hunters in the winter. Marilyn didn't see the dark colored car waiting beneath a grove of trees. As her headlights exposed the quaint cabin she had hoped Tim would already be there. He wasn't.

She parked her car and made her way on to the porch and located the hidden key tucked away in its usual hiding place. While she was getting the bottle of wine from the cabinet, she heard her secret lover pull in and turn off his car's engine. Marilyn rushed to the door, but instead of seeing the man who would hold her in his arms and make her feel wanted again, she was staring at a masked stranger. Marilyn's night of romance quickly turned into one of horror. The uninvited intruder pushed her backwards toward the sofa. She was paralyzed with fear. Her attacker held a knife to her throat, and demanded that she put her hands behind her back, as he tied them together with short pieces of electrical wire. Her instincts told her to resist with all she had, but she was no match for this monster.

    Using a knife with an eight inch blade, he methodically cut open her blouse. Slowly, he removed it, and reached around and cut her bra off as well. Marilyn could hardly breathe; afraid to move. Her attacker told her to kiss him. She did as she was told, but almost threw up when her lips met his.

    He reeked of alcohol and cigars. But, there was something familiar about this stranger. She wanted to scream, but he had put her torn panties in her mouth. He assured her that he would not hurt her if she did as he said. By now, Marilyn was faint, but she knew if she was to survive, she would have to keep her wits about her. The intruder was getting more and more excited as her fear grew. Her attacker called her a bitch and a whore.

    "You see, sweetheart, payback is hell, ain't it? The thing is, you probably like what I'm doing, being the slut you are."

    As he began to violate her, Marilyn fixated on the wagon wheel light fixture hanging from the ceiling, praying to God this would soon be over. The attacker told Marilyn he would remove the panties from her mouth, if she promised not to scream. She shook her head in agreement.

"Why are you doing this? Please, I'll do whatever you want me to, just don't kill me, please."

Marilyn was crying and continued to beg for her life.

"I won't ever tell anyone, I swear," she pleaded.

When he finished, he calmly pulled his pants up, walked over to the small kitchen, and opened the cabinet. He reminded Marilyn that she was not to move. He opened the refrigerator, and looked in the freezer section, and pulled out a cold glass mug.

As Marilyn laid back on the sofa with her skirt pulled down to her ankles and her blouse and bra laying on the floor, she became aware of the attacker's knowledge of just where to find the scotch, and especially the frozen mug. It was obvious to her that her attacker had been in this cabin before. She began to talk to him, hoping to gain his trust, in hopes of finding the right moment to make her escape. She told him again she would not tell anyone of this incident, if he would only let her go. The intruder gulped down his large glass of scotch and walked back to Marilyn.

If she thought this nightmare was over she was wrong, dead wrong! Once again, he held the knife to her throat and had his way with her. Her attacker continued his drunken invasion for a third time. Completely spent, and drunk from the scotch, he lay back on the sofa. Marilyn watched motionlessly, as he appeared to be dosing off to sleep.

Where was Tim? He should have been here by now, she thought.

Marilyn decided that this may be her only chance to get herself free from this monster. She slowly got up from the sofa, not bothering to try and put any clothes back on, except to pull her skirt up. She quietly opened the door and looked back to see if he was still asleep. She knew that if she could just get to her car, she would be free from this maniac. As she opened the door to her red Altima, she felt for the first time in the past two hours that everything was going to be alright.

But then, her heart sank; the car keys were back in the cabin.

Do I run for it or do I go back in and get the keys? With only seconds to decide, not thinking clearly, Marilyn decided the only way of getting away from her attacker was to drive out of there. If she tried to run he could probably catch up with her.

Her decision would be costly.

As she re-entered the cabin, she saw her keys lying on the counter in the kitchen. She slowly walked past the passed-out demon in a ski mask. Marilyn was so frightened, she could hardly breathe. With her keys safely in her shaking hands, she turned to leave. As she drew near the door to freedom, she never saw him lunge for her leg.

Fighting for her life, Marilyn kicked as hard as she could. In their struggle, she accidently snatched the hood off his head. Suddenly, the only thing that had kept her alive was gone. Marilyn's fate was sealed.

"Oh my God, it's you!" Marilyn screamed in desperation. The knife's blade found its first mark. As Marilyn was slowly losing consciousness, her last thought was of MacArthur. She hoped he could forgive her.

There could be no turning back now, as the attacker found himself in a frenzy of violent blows to her chest and head. He slit her throat. He stumbled back on to the chair, sitting next to the blood soaked sofa. *I have to think this out*, he thought. As he sat staring at the body of Marilyn Hampton, he became aroused again. The sight of this beautiful woman, partially naked, and covered in blood, turned him on. Without any shame or remorse, he pulled her skirt down around her knees and did the unthinkable.

When he had finished, he placed her body on the rug that was beneath the sofa, and wrapped her lifeless body in it. He took the rug and placed it in the trunk of his car, on top of the large plastic sheet to avoid getting blood on the carpet.

He went back inside and scanned the room for anything he might have forgotten to remove. He gathered all of Marilyn's clothes, her purse, and her phone and put them in a garbage bag, with the exception of her panties. This would be his trophy to re-live the excitement of what happened tonight.

Once he dumped the body, he planned on getting rid of the knife. He decided not to throw it in any of the ponds or lakes in the area, because that would be the first place the police would search. No, he was smarter than that. Burying it would be the best way of making sure it was never found. He decided on a spot underneath the hedgerow, behind the Assembly of God Church on County Road 45.

He kept telling himself he hadn't planned on killing her, but once she recognized him he had no choice. If only she hadn't tried to escape, she would still be alive. In his mind, he was convinced it was actually her fault. He decided to dispose of the body in a clearing just off of Connell Road, but first he had to get rid of her car. Because he was familiar with this area, he knew of a secluded pond that was located in a heavily wooded area one mile behind the cabin.

He placed the bag of items in the trunk of her red Nissan Altima. He drove down to the pond by way of a seldom used dirt road. When he reached the pond, he drove onto the dam, put the car in park, and got out. Just before he was about to let the car down into the water, he got her phone out of the trunk. He leaned through the driver's side window and put the car in gear, watching it pick up speed as it rolled down the embankment into the water. In only minutes, the car was completely emerged in its murky grave. He stood there until he could no longer see the car. Satisfied his mission was complete, he began the long walk back to the cabin and Marilyn's mutilated body.

When the killer returned from the pond, he went back inside the cabin to make sure he had gotten rid of anything that could be traced back to him. He had worn gloves the entire time so he knew prints would not be a problem. He had worn a condom, so he made sure the three he had used were recovered and put in a bag on the front seat of his car. He would dispose of them on his way home. He had wiped the glass mug clean, removing any traces of saliva that could have his DNA on it. He took the half-empty bottle of scotch with him as well. As he drove away, the killer was confident that he had cleaned the crime scene well enough not to leave any traces of evidence. He hadn't thought about the semen that was on her body, because of his last despicable act.

The murderer was familiar with the bike crossing on Connell Road. This area was popular among bikers with its many trails running through it. It would be only a matter of time before Marilyn's body would be discovered.

He took the mutilated corpse out of the trunk of his car and laid it on the ground. He carefully unrolled the bloodstained rug that he had wrapped the body in. His earlier plan was to dig a make-shift grave and bury the body. This changed quickly when he heard a small group of teenagers enjoying some beers and music. He laid the body facing up and covered it with fresh fallen leaves. He neatly folded the silk blouse and skirt she had been wearing and placed them near her head

Marilyn's killer returned to his car, backed out from the clearing where he had parked and started driving. He had sobered up by now and decided to stop at the 7 Eleven just up the road. *A cup of hot coffee would be really good about now*, the killer thought. He was sure the caffeine might help settle his nerves.

Like every murderer, the killer will always make some mistake, regardless of how well things are planned. This murder was no exception. The decision to stop would be one that he would live to regret. He had forgotten about the video cameras mounted on the 7 Eleven building. Of all people, he should have known better than to have made such a careless mistake.

M. HARMON HALL

CHAPTER 4

Marilyn and MacArthur had met by chance in December of 2004, when Marilyn came to the police department to file a restraining order against her ex-boyfriend, Sonny Barrett. MacArthur knew Sonny all too well, but he hadn't told Marilyn during their first meeting. Sonny had been picked up and booked a couple of times for suspected theft, but neither charge stuck. It was common knowledge on the streets that it was Sonny who had stolen the items reported missing by two separate families living in the Banks community. The stolen items were never recovered and there was not enough evidence to make the charges stick. The case was dropped.

Sonny Barrett had been manager of Gold's Gym on Main Street downtown Wilcox for the last three years. Before that, he had several jobs around town, but never managed to put down any roots. His pattern was the same, after a short period of time he would either quit or was asked to leave. He was quick to tell people it was not his fault, always someone else's. It had been over 12 years since his divorce. Folks around town said he went downhill after the divorce, others said he wasn't worth a damn before the divorce. Alcohol and drugs had taken center stage in his wasted life.

However, he had his moments. He still talked a good game and could even be charming when the occasion called for it.

Sonny had been the local football hero back in the glory days, but now he was just another graduate of Wilcox High School that never lived up to his potential. Liquor and too many bad decisions had taken their toll on Sonny Barrett.

Sonny walked on North Carolina State's football team, in the fall of 1979. He made the team, but not the traveling squad. He was placed on the scout team. When he would visit home during the holidays, Sonny told a different story. According to him, he was the 3rd string quarterback and it would only be a matter of time before he would get his chance. It was never going to happen. He wasn't even on scholarship and wouldn't be.

In December of 1979, following his first and only season on the football team, Sonny came home for the Christmas Holidays and did not return to school. True to form, he told friends that during the final week of practice, while preparing for the Harvest Bowl, he had sustained a career ending injury to his left knee.

Those who knew him best all agreed that this was Sonny's way of saving face. He had never been able to accept rejection. What he hadn't told anyone, including his parents, was that he had been dismissed from the team two weeks before coming home for Christmas.

He got a job with the local hardware store in Wilcox. He and his high school sweetheart, Wynette Goddard, were married in early March, 1985. After three years of marriage and two formal complaints of abuse by Wynette, Sonny Barrett quietly agreed not to contest the divorce.

Marilyn had been in Wilcox for three months when she decided to check out the gym. She was very health conscious and enjoyed working out. Before long, she would have her very own personal trainer, Sonny Barrett. He worked out every night after work. He often helped some of the guys with weight lifting techniques. He was in exceptional condition considering he was almost

44 years old. It was there he met Marilyn. Without asking for his advice, Sonny started helping her with her workouts.

Within weeks, Marilyn and Sonny were seen around town together. They both seemed to enjoy the same things. They went biking together, spent nights camping out at the nearby state park, and of course, loved working out in the gym. Marilyn wasn't looking for a long-term relationship, but for now, she enjoyed Sonny's company.

"He's kind and makes me laugh. He's considerate, and makes me feel like a young woman again," Marilyn told the girls at work. They wanted to warn her about Sonny, but decided not to interfere. Marilyn thought Sonny's sexual appetite was a bit insatiable, but it was nice to be desired again, she reconciled.

As the weeks turned into months, Marilyn began to notice a change in Sonny, or perhaps she was beginning to see the real Sonny Barrett. Especially, in the bedroom. His overly stimulated sexual appetite had progressed into wanting rough sex. This made Marilyn very uncomfortable.

Then, there was his jealousy and quick temper. Sonny had become very possessive, wanting to know where Marilyn was and who she was with. This type of behavior was getting too much for Marilyn. The voice inside her head, along with her friends, told her she needed to end this relationship. By now, Marilyn had become afraid of Sonny.

She decided to pick a public place to break the news that it was over.

O'Hara's Restaurant was filled to capacity when the hostess seated Marilyn and Sonny. After some small talk, Marilyn told Sonny she had something she needed to say.

"I'm sorry Sonny, it's just not working out, it's over."

As expected, Sonny didn't take the news very well. He was completely caught off guard. A minute passed before he said anything.

"Marilyn, you're upset right now, you just need a little time to think this through," Sonny said, in an unusually calm voice.

"I'm not upset, nor do I need any time to think about what I just said. Sonny, I like you," Marilyn lied. "I hope we can be friends, if not, I understand. I just don't see our relationship going anywhere," she continued.

Suddenly, Sonny pushed back his chair and stormed out of the restaurant leaving Marilyn with the check and no way of getting back to her apartment. The owner of the restaurant, Mickey, walked over to Marilyn's table and offered to call a cab. Embarrassed, she thanked him as she opened the back door of the yellow cab and calmly sat down. Within 15 minutes, Marilyn arrived at her apartment. As she looked in her purse for the keys to apartment #1A, she cursed herself for ever getting in this situation in the first place.

Slowly, she opened the door. When she turned the lights on, she was startled by a male figure standing in the middle of the living room.

"What the hell are you doing in my apartment?" Marilyn asked angrily.

"I wanted to tell you how sorry I am about losing my cool back at the restaurant," Sonny said with all of the humility he could muster. "I still think we can work this out if you're willing to give me another chance?"

"It's too late Sonny. It's over! It's not going to work! I'm sorry if I hurt you, I didn't mean to. The feelings I had for you are gone. There is nothing else I can say. I'd like for you to leave now," Marilyn said with conviction.

"Just like that? Did all of the good times we had mean anything to you? What about the nights we spent together? I thought we had something special?
"

"That's all they were Sonny, just good times, nothing more. There is nothing special between us now. Please, leave Sonny," Marilyn said, as her voice tightened.

Sonny walked past Marilyn, picked up the half-empty bottle of scotch, and slammed the door behind him.

Marilyn locked and bolted the door and decided to take a long bath. After pouring a glass of wine, she emerged in the warm water and finally began to relax.

How could I have been so wrong about this guy? What is it about me that falls for such losers?" Marilyn asked herself.

The next morning Marilyn showered, got dressed, and headed out the door. As she headed to her car, she stopped in her tracks. All four tires on her car had been slashed. *He's crazier than I thought,* she said to herself, while looking for the number of the cab company.

The rest of her day wouldn't get any better. Shirley and Tamara called in sick, her 9 o'clock and 10 o'clock canceled, the supplies she had requested were on back order, and her mother called to tell her that Aunt Laura had fallen and broken her hip. Closing time finally came. Michelle, the latest girl hired, offered Marilyn a ride home.

"No thanks, the guy at the Road Mart just called and they have my car ready. He should be here any time now. I'll see you tomorrow."

As she walked into her apartment, she checked her messages only to find there were over 20 from Sonny. Some were apologetic, some were begging, most were just plain pathetic. The last message caused her dark eyes to open wide. She knew Sonny was crazy, but this message scared her.

As she played the message a second time she knew right away whose voice it was. In a drunken stupor, Sonny shouted frantically, "Bitch, you played me. Nobody makes a fool out of Sonny Barrett. This ain't over!"

She called the police. The attending officer answered the call and Marilyn explained her reason for calling. The officer told her she would need to come down to the station and give a statement.

As Marilyn walked into the police station, she couldn't help but notice how quiet it was. On TV and in the movies police stations looked and sounded like a mad house. The officer at the information desk got her name and address and phone number. "Take a seat over there Ms. Hampton, somebody will be with you in just a few minutes," the young female officer said politely.

Marilyn took a seat on the hard bench thinking how much she would like a cup of coffee. The walls in the police station were decorated with authentic pictures of downtown Wilcox as early as 1910. Wagons loaded with cotton to be brought to market filled the streets of Wilcox. There were other pictures of the First Bank of Wilcox with the small staff smiling. Pictures of the stores lined up along Main Street were also on display. On the wall just behind Marilyn, was a glass case where a picture of a fallen comrade who lost his life in the line of duty proudly stood.

Detective MacArthur Nowlin, chief investigator of the homicide division, with more than 17 years of experience came out and introduced himself to her. Normally, he would not be handling such a frivolous complaint, but at the time there were no homicides to investigate, so Chief Aldridge had asked him to help out since the officers who normally handled these matters were out. Keeping it to himself, MacArthur felt as though this assignment was beneath him.

Marilyn's good looks and great body did not go unnoticed by him.

"How can I help you today Ms. Hampton?" MacArthur asked, while trying not to stare.

"I would like to get a restraining order against someone."

"Please, follow me to my office," MacArthur urged, using his best manners.

Marilyn was impressed with Detective Nowlin's professional demeanor as she methodically told her story. When she finished, MacArthur asked her to sign the complaint document. He assured her that this would be a top priority and she could expect to hear from him first thing in the morning.

"Meanwhile, Ms. Hampton…"

"Please, call me Marilyn."

"Marilyn, you should be aware of your surroundings and be sure your doors are locked. Does Mr. Barrett have a key to your apartment?" MacArthur asked.

"To my knowledge, he does not," Marilyn said with confidence.

I like confidence in a woman, especially if she looks this good. MacArthur thought.

"Is there a number where you can be reached?"

"Yes, 308-6758, that's my cell number." She stood up and started to walk out of MacArthur's office, but before she put her hand on the door handle, he stopped her.

"There is one other thing I would like to ask you. Ms.-uh-Marilyn, I hate to have to ask you such a personal question but, would any other males have access to your apartment?" MacArthur asked, pretending to be embarrassed.

"No, Detective Nowlin. Now, may I leave?" pretending to resent the question.

"Of course, I just want to make sure we are taking all precautions at this point."

As Marilyn walked out of his office, she could feel his eyes baring down on her. *I was wondering if he was ever going to notice me*, she thought.

The next day the judge signed a restraining order against Sonny Barrett. Marilyn was glad to get Sonny Barrett out of her life.

In the following days she and MacArthur's paths would cross again. MacArthur made sure if it.

Sonny hit rock bottom. He lost his job at the gym and began drinking almost every day. He supported his habit by hustling pool at City Corner beer joint in the afternoons and working part-time at Stan's gas station at night. His aunt, in neighboring Calhoun County, sent him money from time to time, believing his hard luck stories.

Sonny Barrett left Wilcox, but not for good.

CHAPTER 5

Detective MacArthur Nowlin was not the most popular "dick" in the unit. In fact, most of the other officers didn't particular care for him. He was arrogant, moody, distant, and never gave much attention to how he dressed or carried himself.

His 6 foot frame displayed evidence of time spent in the gym. His arms were muscular and his neck looked out of proportion to the size of his rapidly balding head. His eyes were set deep within his forehead. At first gaze, they appeared to be blue but a closer look would reveal a light shade of gray. His eyebrows were bushy and beginning to show signs of gray.

His dark complexion and square jaw were the most distinguishable characteristics of his physical appearance. Marilyn once jokingly described him to her mother as someone who looked like "a cross between Tom Selleck and Marlon Brando."

While MacArthur could never hold the title of "Mr. Congeniality" among his peers, he was the best detective in the homicide unit. There was no denying that. His 17 years of experience was unequalled among his colleagues. Once MacArthur Nowlin was on the case, he was relentless until he got an arrest and conviction. His style was unique, his manner sometimes offensive, but always effective. The same could not be said about his personal life, especially with women.

James Nowlin and Beulah Crenshaw were married in a quiet ceremony in Platts, North Carolina on the first day of August 1964. James Nowlin was a traveling Methodist minister who was gone from home for weeks at a time. When the Reverend Nowlin's young wife, Beulah, would beg her husband not to leave again he would remind her that he was doing God's work. That work included attending to his "flock." However, what MacArthur's mother Beulah did not know was that his "flock" consisted of lonely widows and young women who had "lost" their way. Three days before MacArthur's seventh birthday, Reverend Nowlin left for a one week revival over in Pearl County. It would be eleven years before he would see him again.

Abandoned by her husband, Beulah Nowlin was left with the responsibility of raising her son and two daughters alone. MacArthur's mother would never again trust anyone. She taught young MacArthur and his sisters to be leery of everyone they came in contact with. "Never put your faith in people, because they will always let you down," his mother would often say. Unfortunately, this lesson would stay with him throughout his entire life causing failed relationship after relationship. MacArthur couldn't handle any semblance of sustained happiness, for fear that abandonment would eventually come. Therefore, he chose not to commit to anyone, especially the women in his life. He built barriers around himself, refusing to let anyone get too close. This dysfunctional thinking would later cost him his marriage and sabotage other relationships as well. His most recent relationship with Marilyn would be no exception.

Growing up without a father proved to have negative consequences for young MacArthur. His mother could not provide the kind of discipline a young, angry boy needed. He resented the fact that his friends' dads came to school functions, baseball games in the summer, took them on vacations. *It is not fair that I don't have a dad like my friends*, MacArthur convinced himself. Like many fatherless boys, he acted out his anger and resentment by becoming rebellious in school. On several occasions his mother had to meet with the principal, to hear yet again, how he had resisted authority.

A turning point came as he entered the 9th grade, and his mother's prayers were finally answered. His mother met and fell in love with rookie police officer, Jonathan Garrett. After two years of dating Jonathan and Beulah were married. In the beginning, things did not go well for MacArthur and his "new dad." Jonathan tried his best to create a bond with his new stepson but MacArthur refused to accept him.

After several attempts, Jonathan finally convinced MacArthur to go to the shooting range with him one Saturday afternoon. Jonathan's expert marksmanship impressed a curious MacArthur and fueled a secret desire to learn how to use a gun. This link would pave the way for a budding relationship that would last for many years.

This fascination with guns and police work resonated with MacArthur, and would lead to a career in law enforcement. It was after Jonathan was promoted to the position of detective in the homicide division, that MacArthur became intrigued with murder. The question of how one person could actually kill someone else became the driving force behind him in becoming a homicide detective. Ironically, after years of investigating many homicides, he still didn't have an answer. MacArthur could attest to the fact that 90% of murders involve family members or someone that the victim knew.

MacArthur graduated from North Carolina State University with a degree in criminal justice in the spring of 1989. Following graduation the same year he and his new bride moved to Potts, North Carolina where he would begin his career in law enforcement as a police officer with the Potts Police Department. Potts was a small town located 35 miles north of Chapel Hill, North Carolina. In this town of 3,000, the crime rate was almost nonexistent. Saturday night drunken domestic calls were the "main event." Some of the more frequent calls involved assisting teenagers who had locked their keys in their car at the local Dairy Queen near the high school. But, Officer Nowlin was already learning to read people's faces. Over time, he soon developed a sixth sense when it came to determining if someone was being truthful or if they were lying. His ability for assessing a particular situation was evident early in his career. His attention to the smallest details would prove to be a useful asset as his career in law enforcement developed. This skill, along with his perseverance would play a huge role in his success as a homicide detective in the years to come.

MacArthur's love life was an altogether different matter. Before meeting Kelli, he had dated several girls in college, but it wasn't until the beginning of his senior year that he became interested beyond just a causal relationship.

Her name was Kelli Masters. A brunette with hazel green eyes, dimples, a quick smile, and an athletic figure captured his heart. He had seen her at a party at the beginning of the semester, but neither he, nor his friend Jake knew who she was. True to his investigative nature, MacArthur was determined to find out something about her. After several dead ends, he decided it just wasn't meant to be.

Three weeks after his futile attempt to find out who she was, he and his Jake decided to visit one of the local pubs for a night of celebration after passing the mid-term in Dr. Whitaker's criminology class. Dr. Carmine Whitaker was the kind of professor that took pride in having the highest percentage of students' failing his courses. MacArthur wasn't the most dedicated student when it came to studying and making good grades. His philosophy was very simple, a "C" was good enough. After all, who's going to remember 50 years from now who made "A's" or "C"s? MacArthur's goal was to get a diploma. His class ranking meant absolutely nothing to him.

"Jake, there she is."

"What are you talking about MacArthur?"

"The girl I told you about three weeks ago."

"Yeah, what about her?"

"Well, that's her sitting at the table with a guy that's in one of my classes."

"MacArthur, I don't think it's a good idea for you to try to impress her tonight, you're drunk,"

MacArthur ignored Jake's advice and glided over to where they were sitting. He pretended not to see them until he was within arm's length of their table. *What the hell is his name*? MacArthur asked himself. Not wanting to risk calling the guy by the wrong name, he decided to approach his study partner with just a hello. Anything to give him a reason to get her attention. As he approached the couple, his study partner recognized him.

"Macmillan, how's it going? Sit down and have a beer. I want to introduce you to a friend of mine. Her name is Kelli Masters. Kelli this is one of my study partners in our group project," Jimmy said, as he ordered another drink.

It was obvious that he was eager to "show off" his prize date in hopes that "Macmillan" would tell the other members of the group tomorrow in class. MacArthur didn't bother to correct his new found friend about the name thing.

MacArthur was about to try and say something cute, but before he could Jimmy, *oh yeah, that was his name*, asked him if he would mind sitting with his date until he could get back. He said he had to make a very important phone call.

"No problem," MacArthur said, as he stared at the most beautiful girl he had ever seen. He began to take his coat off, but because he was very close to being smashed he had trouble get. Needless to say, Kelli Masters was not impressed. Giving it his best effort to sound clever and sober, MacArthur asked her how long she and Jimmy had been dating.

"Oh, we've only gone out a few times. He's just a friend."

MacArthur was pleased to hear that. He made a quick decision to ask her if she would like to get a pizza tomorrow night. Kelli was thinking no way, but said "give me a call tomorrow." She was sure that this guy would not remember anyway. She would later say that she had no intentions of going out with MacArthur, who obviously had had too much to drink. *But, he was kind of cute and funny*, she thought, but was quick to remind herself he was not her type. Jimmy came back and MacArthur walked back over to where he and Jake had been standing hoping he hadn't made a complete ass of himself. He no longer saw Jake and figured his friend had called it a night.

The following morning, he couldn't wait to tell Jake of his date with, *what the hell was her name*? MacArthur had forgotten her name. He did remember that in their short conversation she said she worked part-time as a cashier at Walgreens in the afternoons and full-time in the summer. MacArthur had a plan. He would get Jake to go to Walgreens and think of some reason to ask the pretty cashier a question. In doing so, he would be able to see her name on her store badge. But, there was one small problem. His mystery date was assigned to the women's personal hygiene department.

"No way!" Jake argued. "What in the hell am I going to ask for in that department?"

"You don't actually have to speak to her, just mill around and get her name and leave," MacArthur explained. Jake relented, and in less than an hour, he was back at their apartment.

"Her name is Kelli," Jake reported.

MacArthur would make a brilliant decision, or just a plain lucky one. He decided rather than call her about tonight's dinner date, he would go down to her workplace and remind her in person and confirm what time he was to pick her up.

Neither one of them would ever date anyone else. As the weeks turned into months, Kelli and MacArthur became inseparable. They became engaged two months later. Their wedding date was set for July 23rd.

After they were married, Kelli used to joke with him that when he showed up that day at her Walgreens, she was so stunned she couldn't think of a good excuse for not keeping the date. She remembered that had MacArthur called, she certainly would have easily thought of some reason to cancel the date.

Eleven months later, MacArthur and Kelli were married in her home town of Summerton, North Carolina on July 23rd, 1989. Jake Rhymes was his best man. It was a simple wedding held at the First Baptist Church of Summerton with her pastor residing over the ceremony. A reception was held at the community center ballroom. The happy couple honeymooned at the Myrtle Beach Resort in South Carolina. Life was good!

Kelli had always made it very clear she wanted children. She thought MacArthur felt the same.

But, when the subject would come up, MacArthur always said the same thing, "it's not the right time now. Let's wait a few years until we get settled in and have more money."

The right time never came. Beginning the third year of their marriage, MacArthur and Kelli started drifting apart. MacArthur had become so obsessed with his work he had failed to realize he was no longer the loving, thoughtful, and caring husband Kelli had married only a few years ago.

Kelli had been hired as a first grade teacher with Potts Elementary School months after they were married. They attended the First Baptist Church of Potts and were members of the newly married couple's Sunday school class. MacArthur did not attend on a regular basis in spite of Kelli's pleading.

It wasn't that MacArthur didn't believe in God, his mother had always insisted that her children were in church every Sunday. He was faithful in his prayers and attentive in the Sunday school class every Sunday. He just never got the concept that God would actually answer his prayers. Besides, he mused, *if God was so loving and caring, why he would allow my father to leave me and mother and my sisters*?

Kelli ate most of her dinners alone, in fact she did most things alone. MacArthur worked long hours. She always waited up for him, regardless of how late it was. He was not sure if Kelli had noticed, but their conversations were very routine and something was missing. Even on rare occasions when they went out, Kelli and her friend and fellow teacher Janis, only talked about school matters. MacArthur tried to pretend to be interested, but he wasn't. When he tried to change the subject and talk about his day Kelli pretended to be interested, but MacArthur saw through her attempts to seem to care about his work.

In his view, Kelli was not interested in what he did and he didn't think she ever would be. Their nights out became fewer and fewer. Their social life became non-existent. Kelli missed being with her friends, but she never complained. She accepted MacArthur's role of a policeman and all of the baggage that went with it. She loved him and was determined to make the marriage work.

The intimacy in their relationship suffered as well. He was "too tired" most nights due to his tough day at work. Kelli had come to the conclusion that maybe he no longer found her attractive. She began to go to the gym three nights a week, bought new lingerie, and changed her hair style hoping to rekindle the passion they once shared.

Kelli confided in Janis that she was worried about their marriage. Kelli asked for the name of a good marriage counselor. MacArthur would have no part of this.

"There is nothing wrong with our marriage, and we sure as hell don't need to see a marriage counselor," MacArthur lied.

He knew in his heart their marriage was in trouble, and he knew it was because of him, not Kelli. He didn't know how to express his feelings, nor did he make any effort. He had never learned about unselfish love for another person. Sure, he loved Kelli, but it had to be on his terms.

The truth was, MacArthur's heart had become hardened without him realizing it. He was in denial. He had been most of his adult life. This selfish attitude would take its toll in the very near future.

Kelli kept her marriage problems from her mother and father. She would pretend everything was ok when her mother would ask. MacArthur and Kelli celebrated their fifth anniversary with a small cookout. While most of the guest were still there, MacArthur left. His excuse was that he was needed down at the station.

I can't take much more of this. I'm losing him. Has he changed or have I? Kelli thought, as she cried herself to sleep.

CHAPTER 6

Amanda Whittington was beginning her third year as secretary with the Potts Police Department. She was highly respected by the entire police force as someone who was very good at her job. Amanda and her husband, Christopher had been married for seven years with no children. She and Christopher were opposites in many ways. She liked outdoors he preferred to watch TV and listen to his music. Amanda was not into the religious scene as she described it. Christopher was very active in church activities. Things had gotten so strained at home that they were no longer sharing the same bedroom. Amanda told a friend that she wasn't so sure she had married the right man. Christopher adored Amanda and was broken hearted that things had gotten to this point. He was afraid he was losing her.

What began as just a friendship between colleagues, soon evolved into something more. Amanda began to find reasons for working late at the police station. She confided in MacArthur, she didn't want to go home many nights. All the ingredients of an affair were in place. Neither was happy at home. Both felt that they could talk to each other with the other understanding how they felt. MacArthur would share with Amanda that he loved Kelli, but felt they were growing apart. Amanda would talk of her doubts about Christopher.

MacArthur was the first to express his feelings for her, and that he thought about her "too much." Amanda would soon share the same message, but suggested they take things slowly.

Within two months, their talking sessions turned into something more physical. MacArthur confessed to Amanda he thought he might be falling in love with her. He even went so far as to tell her it was possible he was prepared to leave Kelli. Amanda was not so quick to go that far.

She did tell him that she thought she was falling in love as well. Their late night rendezvous' soon were followed by long lunches. This did not go unnoticed by the other police officers. It was no secret that something was going on between MacArthur and Amanda. Like most spouses who are victims of an illicit affair, Christopher and Kelli would be the last to know.

MacArthur told Amanda that Kelli couldn't understand why he had to put so much time into his job. Kelli said he was obsessed with it. He couldn't understand why she stayed on his back constantly, never letting up. Didn't she know that his job was very important?

As their marriage slowly unraveled, Kelli's friend, Janis reluctantly asked her if she thought MacArthur was seeing someone else. She confided in Janis that she suspected the secretary at the police station, but had no proof. Kelli said she thought her name was Amanda. Janis tried to get her to hire a private detective to see if MacArthur was cheating. She refused, perhaps because she didn't want to know the truth.

The day after the Labor Day holiday Kelli got home from school around 4:30 pm. She was surprised to find that from MacArthur was already home. When she walked in the house, he was sitting at the kitchen table with a strange look on his face. She immediately noticed how nervous he seemed. Suddenly, she had a very bad feeling.

"We need to talk," he said, almost apologetically. Kelli sat down after putting her purse and car keys on the counter.

"I have something to tell you, and it's going to hurt," MacArthur began. "You and I both know we have grown apart. Our marriage is no longer working. In fact, it hasn't for a long time. I'm not blaming you, it's just we want different things in life. You want children, I want a career. Kelli, what I'm trying to say is, I don't think I can ever be the husband and father you want me to be."

"MacArthur, I love you, and I believe we can still make this…"

"I've been seeing someone else. I don't know how it happened, it just did," MacArthur interrupted. "Kelli, you deserve someone better than me. You deserve someone that will give you children and a happy home. We both know I'm not that person."

Kelli stood up and slowly poured a glass of water, saying nothing. She knew their marriage was not what it could be. But, she never thought it was beyond repair. She still loved MacArthur.

"Do you love her? "

MacArthur didn't have the courage to look at her as he stared at the floor and answered, "I think so."

"So, you don't love me anymore? Maybe you never did."

"Yes, I do love you Kelli, but not in the same way. Sometimes two people can fall out of love."

Kelli regained her composure, stood up and threw the glass of water in his face.

"How could you do this to me, to us? Didn't the vows you took mean anything? Were they just lies too? I have tried so hard to make this marriage work, while you slither around and screw a married woman. I've suspected something for a long time, but I didn't want to let myself believe you could actually betray me."

Kelli flopped back down in her chair with her head in her hands, sobbing loudly. There was a long pause. Kelli slowly raised her head, wiped the tears from her face and looked straight at MacArthur.

"Do you expect me to forgive you and pretend nothing happened?" Kelli shouted through the tears.

"I'm not asking for your forgiveness. What I am asking is that you try to understand."

"Understand?" Kelli screamed. "You come into our home and tell me you don't love me anymore. You think you may love another woman and you expect me to understand? Understand this, I want you out of this house today. I never want to see you again. When I get back, I expect you to be gone." Kelli stormed out of the house, but stopped, and went back into the kitchen where MacArthur was still sitting and asked, "Is it the slut secretary, Amanda?"

She didn't give him a chance to answer. She turned around and walked out of the door. She got into her car and drove the streets of Potts. Kelli was washed with the reality of what had just happened. She felt as though she was suffocating, she couldn't breathe. What would she do now? How could she tell her parents? There was a numbness that flooded her entire body. Kelli pulled into Walmart's parking lot and wept uncontrollably.

MacArthur sat motionless. He got up and went into the bedroom and started packing his bags. The truth was finally out. He asked himself if Amanda was worth the cost of losing his wife. As gut wrenching as it was, his answer was yes. Kelli would find someone to love again, he rationalized.

Three hours later, Kelli opened the front door and sat down on the sofa. This was the worst day of her life. She pulled a blanket over her and tried to sleep. But there wouldn't be any sleeping tonight.

MacArthur called Amanda from the Holiday Inn to tell her that he had moved out. He was finally going to be free, and once she left Christopher, they could be together for the rest of their lives. He had expected her to be excited about the decision he had made. However, Amanda's response was subdued. Not the response he had expected or hoped for.

Maybe it was just because she was so excited about the good news that caused her less than jubilant response, MacArthur tried to convince himself. He suddenly had a bad feeling about the turn of events. Things had to work out, after all he had just burned his bridges. There was no turning back.

The divorce became final six weeks later. MacArthur gave Kelli the house and anything in it she wanted. He took only a few personal items. With the proper pages of legal documents read and signed by both parties, what was once a happy marriage, filled with love and great expectations had evaporated.

If he had any feeling of guilt or remorse for betraying Kelli it didn't show. The truth was, he didn't. MacArthur Nowlin's dark side had surfaced.

He and Amanda begin to see less of each other over the next few weeks. He sensed it was the beginning of the end of their unfaithful affair. Two months after his divorce, Amanda called and told him they needed to talk. Over coffee, she explained how she still loved her husband, Christopher. She told MacArthur he would always have a special place in her heart, but their relationship was not meant to be. She said she was going to try to save their marriage. She hoped he would understand. Those words were all too familiar. He had asked Kelli the same question.

MacArthur realized that the tiny town of Potts was not big enough for him and his ex-wife to carry on their lives as though nothing had happened. He knew that relocation was eminent. He could not work in the same office with Amanda either. It turned out that he wouldn't have had to, she resigned from her job two weeks after her break up with MacArthur.

In law enforcement, networking is crucial and very common. It is essential that police units from other districts and towns work together sharing information in attempts at solving crimes. With this type of communication, the announcement of job openings was a by-product. Most police chiefs who were worth their weight were always on the lookout for sharp dedicated policemen.

Three months after his divorce, MacArthur contacted police Chief Harold Johns about an opening he had been told about from a mutual friend. Chief Johns had only two more months before his retirement went into effect. MacArthur drove to Wilcox, interviewed and was offered the job the next day. After giving a two week notice to the Potts Police Department MacArthur, packed his personal items, rented a U-Haul truck, and began the next chapter in his life.

MacArthur couldn't help but look back as he passed the "Welcome to Potts" sign as he drove out town and out of Kelli's life. He was sorry he failed Kelli. He was sorry he was so screwed up, and most of all, he was sorry for himself.

His infatuation with Amanda had cost him his marriage. He blamed himself for being such a fool. MacArthur wondered how he could have thought Amanda would really leave her husband. Left holding nothing but regrets, he almost found it funny that he was now getting just what he deserved. His false sense of pride wouldn't let him pick up the phone and ask Kelli to forgive him and let him come home and be the husband she once knew. MacArthur would regret that decision for the rest of his life.

His greatest fear, had always been that he would be exposed as the imposter he was. If people only knew the real MacArthur Nowlin! Tears filled his eyes as the city lights grew dim behind him.

What the hell, I've been here before. I don't need a woman in my life anyway. I'll do what I have always done, depend only on myself, not anyone else. Mother was right.

M. HARMON HALL

CHAPTER 7

On Saturday morning, August 9th, the day after the Sprayberrys' murder, two bikers noticed something beside the trail that looked like a manikin. When they took a closer look they were shocked to find a nude female body partially covered in fresh leaves. There were multiple stab wounds to her face and chest. A pink silk blouse and a short grey skirt were folded neatly beside the body.

The call came into the station around 12:05 pm. Detective Waddell Wright was just getting back to the station when he was notified of a possible homicide out on Connell Road, near the county lake. Once on the scene, Detective Wright could see that it was a Caucasian female lying face up, hastily covered with small branches and leaves. Beside the body, he saw two pieces of clothing neatly folded near the head of the victim. There were no signs of a struggle. It looked as though she had been assaulted somewhere else and the body had been dumped at this location. It was obvious that the killer wanted her body found. Even with his limited experience, due to the severity of the assault this was most likely a crime of passion. Facts gathered later in the investigation would confirm this.

Uniformed officers searched the surrounding area for traces of evidence that might help to explain such a horrific murder. There was no id or any other personal items found. She would become "Jane Doe" until her identity could be verified.

MacArthur tried calling Marilyn several times to apologize about last night. There was no answer, so he left messages. He was beginning to get concerned. It was not like Marilyn not to answer her phone, even if she was angry with him.

He decided to drive over to her apartment on Lexington Avenue. When he arrived, he noticed that her red Nissan Altima was not in her designated parking space. He walked up to apartment #1A and knocked on the door. Although he didn't expect her to be there, since her car was not, he decided to go in and take a look around. He used the key Marilyn had given him to open the door and as he called her name, he noticed a half-empty wine glass, some chocolates, and unopened mail lying on the coffee table.

Marilyn was obsessed with the idea of leaving her apartment spotless before leaving for work. *This was not like her at all*, MacArthur thought. He walked into the bedroom and saw that her bed had not been slept in. Something was not right about this situation.

After going over the entire apartment, he turned to leave, but noticed a piece of paper wedged between the sofa cushions. He walked over and removed the note that appeared to be handwritten by Marilyn. It was a "to do list" that included picking up clothes from the cleaners, purchasing washing powder, calling city hall about her utility bill, and getting the locks changed to her apartment. Macarthur was confused by this last item on the list.

She hadn't mentioned anything to me about getting the locks to her apartment changed, MacArthur thought.

Leaving Marilyn's apartment, he decided to go back to the Sprayberrys' home to take a second look. Meanwhile, he would keep calling her number; *that's all he could do at this point*, he said to himself, with an uneasy feeling in the pit of his stomach. He went through the motions, distracted, looking for anything he might have missed last night at the crime scene. His thoughts kept coming back to Marilyn. He called the beauty salon where she worked. He was told she was not there since it was her day off. He didn't try to explain. He didn't want to jump to conclusions, just yet.

It was 11:00 am when he left the Sprayberrys' residence. He decided to drive out on Hwy # 87. He had seen a new antique shop last week. He knew Marilyn loved antiques, so trying to get in good graces again, he went in and found a couple of end tables he thought she might like. He was feeling very smug as he got into his car with the two tables, thinking Marilyn would be so happy with her gift, she would forgive him for their lost weekend.

Somewhere around noon, MacArthur headed back to the office, but he decided to stop off at Pete's Dinner and have lunch.

"It sure was bad about the Sprayberrys," Sally said, as she brought MacArthur's order of a cheeseburger and fries with sweet tea, no lemon.

MacArthur reluctantly responded that the deaths were tragic indeed.

Sally came over a second time and asked, "Sweetie, today's special is peach cobbler covered with vanilla ice-cream, how about it?"

MacArthur couldn't resist. He asked for a to-go cup for his sweet tea and tipped Sally two bucks and thanked Pete for lunch. There was no ticket. Pete always let the policemen eat free at lunch.

MacArthur took a right on to Jefferson Street and then made a left turn on to Lexington Avenue back to Marilyn's apartment. He was going to go by one more time just to see if her car was there.

Detective Waddell Wright had completed his investigation of the area where the body was found. He arrived back at the station around 1:50 pm. MacArthur had heard on the police radio dispatch of a female body found out on Connell Road.

What are the odds of two separate murders in small town Wilcox in a 24 hour period? He thought.

Detective Killingsworth arrived at the station around 2:00 pm. Detective Wright was sitting at his desk talking on the phone.

"I've never seen a more gruesome murder in the few years I've been here," Wright said to his caller.

When he hung up, Killingsworth asked him about the case. Wright gave him what few sketchy details they had on the homicide.

"Not much to go on right now, it looks like the only thing we have is a single tattoo of a butterfly on the left ankle, and a heart shaped ring on the pinky of her right hand. Right now, that doesn't mean a thing. One thing is for sure, this definitely looks like a crime of passion. I mean, it was major overkill."

Killingsworth sat straight up, trying not to change his facial expression or show any emotion. He asked Detective Wright to describe again what kind of tattoo was found on the body and where was it located. He asked the color of her hair and if she was wearing any jewelry.

"Black, and she did have a ring on the pinky of the right hand."

Wright asked Killingsworth why he was so interested in this case; after all, it had been assigned to him by the Chief. Killingsworth answered in a matter-of-fact tone, he was just curious. Wright said no problem, and went back to his paper work, never suspecting anything; Killingsworth hoped.

Killingsworth knew exactly who this was. He knew he couldn't ask too many questions at this point in the investigation. He was not about to incriminate himself by revealing information that only someone intimate with the deceased could know. He casually walked out of the office and down to the morgue where the body of Marilyn Elizabeth Hampton was lying.

Tim Killingsworth, showing no emotion, hovered over the female body lying on the coroner's table. Marilyn's once beautiful face was almost unrecognizable. She had a stab wound on her upper left cheek, as well as other stab wounds on her head and shoulders. Her chest had similar wounds as well.

When the official report of the coroner came out, it would state that the deceased had a total of 35 stab wounds to her face and chest. Killingsworth could see the huge gash made around her throat. Marilyn's hands were still wrapped with evidence bags so that DNA or any other substance found under her nails might provide a link to the killer or killers. She had defense wounds on both forearms, indicating she put up a fight.

As Killingsworth was staring at his lifeless lover, MacArthur was upstairs on his second cup of coffee. He knew that sooner or later he would have to confront MacArthur about his involvement with Marilyn. This was not the time or place.

MacArthur and Killingsworth were anything but friends. Killingsworth blamed MacArthur for him not being promoted to lead detective of the homicide division. He had accused him of spreading gossip throughout the station concerning his sordid past.

Killingsworth was told that it was MacArthur that leaked the facts of his dysfunctional family. Of course, it wasn't MacArthur, but he never denied either. He didn't like him at all. "And he didn't give a damn if Killingsworth liked him," he told Rachel. He thought he was never thorough enough during his investigations. MacArthur didn't like the way Killingsworth cut corners. He never really trusted him.

Often times, MacArthur would have to follow up on Killingsworth's investigation to make sure it was properly carried out. He didn't think Killingsworth was dedicated enough. He sized him up as a spoon fed rich boy that had been given a job because of who he was, not because of his abilities. He resented Killingsworth because he had worked hard to get to where he was. No one had given him a thing. He carried a chip on his shoulder and didn't care who knew it.

The feeling was mutual. Killingsworth disliked everything about MacArthur. He felt he was heartless, uncaring, and lacked sympathy for the victims. He thought he bullied his way around the station. The truth was, Killingsworth was jealous of him. It was true, MacArthur handled everything and everybody with a heavy hand. But, there was no disputing who the best detective in the division was.

Tim Killingsworth had made it his mission to get rid of MacArthur Nowlin. He just didn't know how yet. In some strange way, MacArthur reminded him of his father. A personality filled with the need for complete control with no regards of the feelings of those he came in contact with.

His assessment of the character of MacArthur was not shared by everyone, however. No, he was not warm and fuzzy, but he was well respected and considered to be trustworthy. No one questioned his integrity.

Marilyn Hampton had grown up in Thousand Oaks, California. Her father had abandoned her mother and two sisters when she was nine years old. She and her sisters had attended public schools, and in May of 1981 she graduated from high school. Her years in high school had been pretty normal. She was a majorette in the band her junior and senior year. She had been elected by her classmates as an alternate for homecoming queen her senior year. Her grades were above average. She dated some, but had not ever gotten serious with anyone.

She applied and was accepted at UCLA. She began her college career in September of 1981. After two semesters, she dropped out. She came home and enrolled in a local community college where she took cosmetology classes.

During her senior year Marilyn met Mitch Roberson, who was in flight school at the nearby air base. They began dating, and within weeks, each confessed their love for the other.

They were married in June of 1984 in her hometown of Thousand Oaks. With their first anniversary approaching, he received orders to report to Maxwell Air Base in Montgomery, Alabama. They were there for two years. His next assignment was an air base in Charleston, South Carolina.

Marilyn gave birth to a son in the third year of their marriage. Mitch was elated. He spent a great deal of time with their son and was very helpful when it came to taking care of him. Marilyn had found a job in a beauty salon only minutes from their home. It was about that time when she and Mitch began to grow apart. He spent more and more time with his buddies, hunting and fishing while she stayed home alone with their son. She tried to get him to see what was happening in their marriage, but he refused.

On the day before Thanksgiving, of 1992, Marilyn was cleaning house and doing the laundry as usual. As she was picking up one of Mitch's shirts off of the floor something fell out. It was a small piece of paper with a telephone number written on it. She asked him about it later, over dinner, and he said it was the number of a guy that had a shotgun for sale that he was interested in.

She kept the note, thinking Mitch would get it from her later. A week later she and Mitch and some of their friends were out for dinner. As usual, the men's conversation consisted of hunting tales or making plans to go hunting with the weekend approaching.

Mitch had gone to the restroom when one of his friends asked Marilyn what she was going to get him for his birthday next week. She said she was thinking of getting him a new shotgun. Mitch's friend suggested a bow since Mitch didn't hunt with a gun any more.

On the way home that evening, Marilyn could not get her mind off of what Mitch's friend had said, Mitch only hunted with a bow. That night she couldn't sleep. She got up and went to the kitchen and made coffee. As she drank her coffee, she got the note out of her purse and stared at it.

Why would Mitch be interested in buying a shotgun when he already had three and never used them? And, what about the friend's comment?

Later on that morning, she dialed the number. After three rings, a woman answered the phone. Her worst fear had been realized. When Marilyn asked who was speaking, the woman hung up.

Marilyn confronted Mitch that evening. He first denied knowing this person, but finally admitted his betrayal. He said she worked in the office on the base. They had been seeing each other for almost a month. Marilyn asked him if he was going to stop seeing her. His refusal to answer, told her what she didn't want to know.

Two weeks later, she filed for divorce. They had been married nine years. Three months later, February of 1993, their divorce was final.

Marilyn continued working at the beauty salon in Charleston raising their son alone. Mitch remarried and moved away. His contact with their son became less and less. The child support check stop coming as well.

Marilyn moved to Chapel Hill, North Carolina the following year. She worked in the same beauty salon for almost ten years. During that time she dated, but never was willing to make a commitment. She devoted her time to her son. Her trust in men had been shattered with the betrayal of Mitch.

In February of 2003, one of her co-workers and best friend had a friend that owned a beauty salon in Wilcox, North Carolina. She told Marilyn it was for sale. Her friend told her she thought it was a good business investment. Marilyn visited Wilcox and fell in love with the small town.

In April of 2003, Marilyn moved to Wilcox, North Carolina.

M. HARMON HALL

CHAPTER 8

On August 9th, the morning following the murders of Dr. and Ms. Sprayberry, MacArthur was knocking on Chief Aldridge's door. The Chief didn't usually come in on Saturday morning, but today he came to go over the notes again of the Sprayberry murder/suicide. Chief Aldridge knew why MacArthur was there.

He didn't waste time with small talk. He told the Chief that the Sprayberry case was not a murder/suicide, but rather a double homicide. Chief interrupted him by saying the official ruling declared it a murder/suicide, end of story.

The Chief knew MacArthur well enough to know that he would not take this lightly. True to form, MacArthur told Chief Aldridge he was making a huge mistake. He continued by saying he could come up with enough evidence proving this was a double homicide.

"MacArthur you're a good cop, but you are wrong on this one. The crime scene tells the whole story. You've got a suicide note and two shell casing from the same gun found in Dr. Sprayberry's hand. Besides, what motive would anyone have for killing the Sprayberrys?"

"Chief, with all due respect sir, did you go to the scene of the shootings? Have you read the suicide note?" MacArthur asked, treading on dangerous ground.

"No, I didn't. Yes, I did read the suicide note. Detective Killingsworth has submitted his report and I have gone over it thoroughly. The coroner also believes this was a classic case of murder/suicide."

"Sir, why would a perfectly happy man kill his wife of 33 years and then kill himself? It just doesn't add up."

MacArthur asked Chief Aldridge to hear him out. He assured the chief that he had at least four good reasons he believed this was a double homicide. One, none of the neighbors heard gun shots fired, secondly, why would Dr. Sprayberry kill his wife then himself, when they had planned a two week cruise with their close friends, the Dayton's? Thirdly, why would he shoot his wife while she was taking a bath? It would have been much easier to shoot her as she slept? Lastly, MacArthur brought up the suicide note. In his opinion, it did not appear to be authentic.

"Are the two children buying this idea of murder/suicide?" MacArthur asked.

The Chief replied that they had mixed emotions. While they found it difficult to accept that their father would do such a terrible thing, however they trusted the police and its early findings.

"Chief, just give me some time and I will get you the evidence that proves what I'm saying."

Chief Aldridge had heard enough. He told MacArthur he would give him 48 hours to come up with some concrete evidence that would prove his theory. He told MacArthur the only reason he was agreeing to this was because of his successful track record.

"Forty eight hours," Chief Aldridge repeated, with an authoritative voice. "If you don't produce some real evidence instead of theories, this case will be closed permanently. Do you understand?" he asked.

"Yes sir, and thank you Chief," MacArthur said with a genuine voice.

"You can thank me by getting your ass out of my office, I have work to do."

"Chief, there is one more thing. I would like permission to have Officer Peavey work with me on this case. I think she has good instincts and could be of help, since I have such a short time to come up with the evidence you need," MacArthur asked sheepishly.

"Did Officer Peavey put you up to this?" the Chief asked, suspiciously.

"No sir, Officer Peavey has no idea I'm making this request. Besides, I don't know if she is interested."

The news of the identity of the female body found up on Connell Road spread quickly through the police station. By now it was no secret who it was. "Did MacArthur know?" they all wondered.

It would be Rachel Peavey, the human resource officer, and closest thing to a friend MacArthur had on the force that would break the news of Marilyn's death.

Chief Aldridge called Rachel Peavey into his office. He told her he wanted her to tell MacArthur of his girlfriend's death. He "pulled rank" because, if the truth was known, he didn't have the stomach for it.

She accepted the directive from her boss and excused herself. As she walked toward MacArthur's office, Rachel decided not to mince words.

As she knocked on the closed door, he motioned her to come in. He was on the phone trying once again to reach Marilyn. Rachel quietly walked in and sat down. MacArthur asked Rachel how she was doing.

"I'm not doing so well, Detective Nowlin. I'm afraid I have some bad news."

"I don't mean to sound rude, but I'm very busy right now, Officer Peavey I have a lot to do," MacArthur interrupted.

"Detective Nowlin, I'll get straight to the point," Rachel said.

"It's Marilyn…"

"Have you heard from her?" MacArthur asked eagerly

"Marilyn has been killed, sir. It happened last night. Her body was found off of Connell Road by some bikers around 11:45 this morning. One of the girls at the beauty salon made the positive identification about an hour ago. I'm very sorry to have to tell you this Detective Nowlin."

MacArthur knew Officer Peavey well enough to know this was not some kind of sick joke. He took a deep breath and sat back in his chair trying to process this staggering information. With his mind racing, MacArthur couldn't think straight. There were so many questions.

Rachel quietly turned and walked out of MacArthur's office.

He sat in silence; stunned and empty. He studied Marilyn's picture on his desk. His eyes fixed on her face as if he expected her to say something.

MacArthur knew what he had to do next.

He got up from his chair and started the long walk downstairs to the medical examiner's lab. Along the way, people going about their usual work routines tried not to stare as MacArthur passed by. No one could remember ever seeing Detective Nowlin so drained of emotion nor had they seen such a blank stare coming from his sad eyes.

Dr. George Pickett was on call, and would be performing the autopsy later in the day. He recognized MacArthur as he approached the two huge glass

KEYS TO MURDER

doors that led into the lab. Dr. Pickett was a seasoned veteran, but this case was too close to home. He would find himself getting emotionally involved as he saw the pain in Detective Nowlin's face. Regardless of differences of individuals within the department, everyone watched each other's back. That is, with the exception of Tim Killingsworth. There was an unspoken bond that was shared by each man and woman that served in the Wilcox Police Department.

MacArthur asked Dr. Pickett if he could be alone as he slowly began to remove the white sheet that covered the body lying on the metal table. He saw the customary tag attached to one of her toes. He saw her swollen face with the many bruised blue welts. He saw the cut marks on her forearms as she had apparently tried to fight off her attacker. He saw the many puncture wounds to her chest. MacArthur slowly pulled the sheet back over the lifeless body of his beloved Marilyn. For the first time in his life, he felt guilty.

If I hadn't canceled our weekend trip she would still be alive. If I had just called her last night to check on her, she might still be alive. My whole life has been about keeping the sacred oath of an officer of the law, to protect and to serve. Yet, I couldn't protect the one woman I loved. MacArthur thought, as anger rose within him.

As he walked back to his office, co-workers expressed their sympathy. MacArthur was touched and confused by this outburst of compassion on their part. He realized he hadn't been much of a friend to any of them, so why would they care about his feelings? They were probably just trying to be nice, MacArthur thought.

The truth was, MacArthur had been wired in such a way he could never understand the meaning nor the display of empathy.

Chief Aldridge dropped by MacArthur's office to tell him how sorry he was, and that if he needed some time off it would not be a problem. He told MacArthur to take as much time as he needed. Not surprising to Chief Aldridge, MacArthur thanked him, but said he would rather be working. Besides, he now had two murder cases to deal with.

"I don't want you working on Marilyn's case for obvious reasons. I don't think you can be objective."

"But Chief…"

"I want your word that you will stay away from this case. I'm sorry, I know you want to find Marilyn's killer, and I promise you we will."

"I understand, you have my word, but I would like to be kept in the know until you find that son of a bitch that killed her,"

"Detective Killingsworth will be lead investigator on the case. I'll have him keep you in the loop."

"Thanks Chief."

Marilyn's mother was to arrive on Sunday to take her daughter home. Because of the ongoing investigation, Marilyn's mother was not allowed to take any personal items from her apartment for the time being. The funeral had been set for Wednesday, August 12th with services to be held at the Assembly of God Church in Thousand Oaks, California. Marilyn was survived by her son, who lived with her mother, two sisters, and several cousins.

MacArthur had never met Marilyn's mother. She had never told him that her father had abandoned her mother and sisters when she was nine years old. This wouldn't be the only secret she had kept from him.

He made the difficult decision not to attend the funeral. He knew Marilyn would understand. He couldn't take three days off, the time it would take to fly out to California and attend the funeral, when there were two other homicides to solve. On Sunday afternoon, hours before her body would be flown back to California, MacArthur went to see her one last time. The funeral home that handled the arrangements was located across town. When he arrived, he was escorted to a room near the back of the funeral home.

As he sat beside the coffin, MacArthur thought about the past nine months and how happy she had made him. Marilyn had a way of reading his emotions and seemed to know what he was feeling and what he was thinking when he was with her. Before Marilyn, only Kelli had been able to love him for who he was; not who she wanted him to be. And now, he had lost both.

MacArthur spoke softly, as he told her he was sorry for not protecting her and keeping her safe. He told her how happy she had made him. He told her he would miss her and that he would never forget her. In his final minutes with her; MacArthur was overcome with an emotion he wasn't familiar with - loneliness. *Strange, so this is what loneliness feels like?* He said to himself.

M. HARMON HALL

CHAPTER 9

MacArthur decided to go to his office instead of home. He knew he had to keep busy. He had to stay focused. He was torn between finding Marilyn's killer, and recovering enough evidence to convince Chief Aldridge to open the Sprayberry murders. He was glad the Chief had given him a chance to prove this was not a murder/suicide. He was also glad Rachel had been assigned to assist him in searching for evidence on the Sprayberry murders.

When MacArthur entered the police station Sunday afternoon around 3:30, he was surprised to see Rachel in her office.

"What are you doing here on a Sunday afternoon?" MacArthur asked.

"I was just going over some paperwork; checking out some background information on active application forms."

"What are you doing here? Shouldn't you be anywhere but here after all that's happened? Detective Nowlin, I'm sorry I'm the one that had to give you the terrible news." Rachel sighed.

"Thanks, but this is the one place that keeps me sane, believe it or not." Besides, I can't sit idly by while three people have been murdered under my watch."

"I understand Detective Nowlin."

"I'm glad I ran into you Peavey. I have a proposition for you. Chief Aldridge has given me until eight o'clock Tuesday morning to come up with enough evidence to convince him the Sprayberry murders were just that. Not a murder/suicide, as Killingsworth suggest."

"I don't understand Detective? Why would he do that?"

"Because it was not a murder/suicide. It was a double homicide, a professional hit I'm guessing." MacArthur said emphatically." My proposition is this, I want you to be my partner for next 48 hours. If we can come up with enough evidence the Chief will open this up as a homicide rather than murder/suicide. I have watched you these past months. You have the instincts of a good investigator. I could use your insight on this case."

"I'm flattered Detective, but I have no experience in homicides. What could I bring to the table in way of helping you?"

"You bring a second set of eyes, a fresh perspective on evidence waiting to be uncovered. If I didn't think you could do it, believe me, I wouldn't have asked Chief Aldridge to bring you aboard on this thing."

"You asked Chief Aldridge? Give me some time to think about this Detective," Rachel asked.

"How much time do you need? Look, I'm not going to beg you Peavey. Either you're in or out. Make up your mind. I really don't give a damn either way," MacArthur lied.

Rachel Peavey's insides were jumping with excitement, but she was not about to let him know. It has been her dream since graduating from college to become a homicide detective. She still couldn't understand why her? Did Detective Nowlin have some ulterior motive? He was more than capable of doing this alone. After all, that's the way he worked. *Are you crazy? This is my one chance, don't be a fool*, she said to herself.

"I'm in!"

"Good, now let's get to work."

"Detective, I'm grateful for this opportunity but I need to get this out on the table right up front. I want you to understand, I will be assisting you with the case only, nothing else, if you know what I mean? Am I clear on this?"

"Crystal! Peavey, I can assure you it's all about the investigation, nothing else."

"Sir, may I be honest?"

"What?"

"You know sir, I don't think you're the 'a-hole' that people here in the station say you are," Peavey said with a huge grin.

MacArthur almost smiled. *She's going to be alright*, he thought.

M. HARMON HALL

CHAPTER 10

Rachel Peavey was a very private person. She did not socialize with any co-workers at all. She had been the human resource officer for almost two years and had earned their respect. Her future looked bright with the Wilcox Police Department.

Rachel had met and married Charlie Peavey five years before coming to Wilcox. He was a fireman in the town of Clayton, North Carolina. She and Charlie were very happy.

One fateful day in June of 1992, the training exercise was no different than the many times the firemen had gone through before. But today would end with a terrible tragedy. Charlie was the last of his group to exit a fiery building exercise. As Charlie was making his decent from the building on to the ladder, for reasons no one would ever know, his feet got tangled up on the first rung of the 50 foot ladder. Everyone stood in disbelief as Charlie fell to the ground. Efforts to save him were unsuccessful. He had broken his neck. Rachel's world changed forever that day.

The loss of Charlie changed Rachel's outlook on life. She was no longer optimistic that good would always prevail over evil. She never could find a suitable answer to the question, "why do bad things happen to good people?"

There were those who said Rachel's entire personality had changed. She was no longer outgoing and friendly. She had become a loner. She preferred her own company. She was asked out a few times, but always declined.

Rachel poured herself into her job. That became her main purpose. Her goal was to become an FBI agent. Rachel remained in Clayton for two years before transferring to the Raleigh Police Department. She was assigned to the human resource division upon her arrival.

Almost two years went by before she starting dating again. She and a fellow policeman on the force started out as just friends, but he became more serious and eventually told her he had fallen in love with her. She tried to make herself love him, but it was just not there. When he tried to give her an engagement ring, Rachel said she could not marry him. She told him," she loved him, but she was not in love with him."

In the fall of 2001, she applied for and got a job as human resource officer with the Wilcox Police Department. Her brother had told her about the job opening. He lived in Wilcox and worked as an accountant with the firm of Edwards & James. She moved in with him. After six months, she found an apartment on Lexington Avenue.

At the beginning of Rachel's second year on the job, her brother was transferred to Charleston, South Carolina.

Rachel liked her job as human resource officer with the Wilcox Police Department. She was highly respected by her co-workers, just as she had been in Raleigh.

She befriended MacArthur while serving together on the police department's improvement committee. He thought she was distant and at times could be condescending, but he did respect her because of her work ethic. She came to work early and stayed late. Her dedication to her job impressed MacArthur.

He could see she had potential. *If she tried hard enough and was willing to learn, she just might make a homicide detective*, he thought.

Rachel found MacArthur's instincts were right most of the time. His perseverance and determination when carrying out his duties were very evident. It was too bad he was such a jerk. But, she was impressed with his track record in solving crimes.

He and Rachel never discussed anything other than police matters. He didn't care about her personal life, nor did he want to share his with her. MacArthur didn't realize it, but Rachel would not have shared any information about her personal life even if he had asked. It was none of his business what went on in her life outside the walls of the police station.

Although MacArthur was almost 14 years her senior. The two of them shared some of the same traits and ideologies. They both believed that police work was part training and part instincts. They both shared the idea that hard work and dedication weren't an option when it came to police work.

They both had a dark side, but then everybody does, MacArthur would say. He and Rachel were very adept at disguising this element of their personalities. There were secrets neither was willing to share with the other. They had experienced tragedy in their lives. Both had lost loved ones. They felt they had been dealt a bad hand.

M. HARMON HALL

CHAPTER 11

Detective Killingsworth was not sure he was up to taking the lead in Marilyn's murder investigation. Chief Aldridge had assigned young Detective Wright to assist him. Detective Killingsworth was determined not to let MacArthur have anything to do with the investigation of Marilyn's death. He also knew that sooner or later he would have to tell MacArthur of his and Marilyn's affair; but now was not the time he reasoned.

Monday morning, August 11th, Killingsworth called Detective Wright to his office. Killingsworth informed him he would be working on this case with him. He also told him that due to the sensitive nature of this murder investigation, he was not to share any information with Detective Nowlin. Killingsworth continued briefing Detective Wright with the reason Detective Nowlin shouldn't be involved. "It's just that the Chief and I believe Detective Nowlin could not be objective in this situation and this might jeopardize the entire investigation. It's such a tragedy, Detective Nowlin losing his girlfriend that way," Killingsworth said, with a straight face.

"Yes sir, it certainly was. You can count on me sir to do as you have asked. Detective Nowlin will not get any information from me."

"At some point, Nowlin is going to pressure you into sharing with him any evidence you may have turned up, but remember, we are doing this for his own good," Killingsworth lied.

Wright walked out of Detective Killingworth's office thinking, *how arrogant Killingsworth was to think that I bought that bullshit about wanting to spare Detective Nowlin's feeling by withholding evidence in Marilyn's murder case. Killingsworth is up to something and I am going to find out what it is.*

What Killingsworth didn't know, was that MacArthur had already had a conversation predicting Killingsworth's next move. Detective Wright had already assured MacArthur he had his back.

No one, including Chief Aldridge, knew that Waddell Wright was actually the nephew of MacArthur Nowlin. His mother and MacArthur were brother and sister. He had recommended him for the job of investigator in the homicide unit. He agreed to help his nephew get the job only if he did not disclose the fact that they were related. This meant falsifying information on the application when asked, "Are you related to any one on the staff?" It was against the hiring policy of the Wilcox Police Department. But that was not the real reason.

MacArthur felt that having a secret ally on the force might pay dividends one day. His feelings of not trusting anyone had not changed, in fact they had intensified. But, he would have to go out on a limb and trust Waddell. MacArthur couldn't have known he was about to put that trust to the test. MacArthur had no way of knowing that he would be implicated in the death of Marilyn.

Killingsworth was convinced that MacArthur was some way involved in the death of Marilyn. He couldn't prove it yet, but his gut told him MacArthur was guilty. He believed that somehow MacArthur had found out about the affair, and in a jealous rage killed Marilyn. Now was not the time to publically accuse MacArthur. He needed some real evidence that would link him to Marilyn's brutal death.

If the investigation went as he hoped it would, MacArthur Nowlin was about to go down for murder of Marilyn Hampton. Killingsworth was on a mission.

M. HARMON HALL

CHAPTER 12

Waddell Wright was an only child. Both of his parents doted on him as expected. Young Waddell learned at an early age that not telling all you know could go a long way in making friends and keeping friends.

When Waddell was 13, he and three of his friends, under the cover of darkness stole some pears from the widow that lived up the street from his house. They put them in the baskets on their bikes and hid underneath the small pine trees some 30 yards from the highway. The rules were very simple, you didn't throw at the windshield, but at the trailer only. The sound of a "thump" indicated the pear had met its mark. Uncontrollable laughter followed.

Waddell's father got a call from the small town police department. They wanted to ask his son some questions. His father asked what this was about. The officer told him that it had been reported on two separate nights that some kids were throwing something at eighteen wheelers passing by on Highway 231, just across from the Caldwell ponds. He and his father made the short drive to the police station downtown.

Waddell was not going to rat on his buddies. When asked if he was involved, or if he knew who might have done this, he calmly said he was not and didn't know anything about any pears being thrown at eighteen wheelers. He hated the idea of lying, but he couldn't give his friends up.

With only suspicions and no proof, the Chief Morton dismissed him. As he was leaving with his father, the chief told him if he did happen to hear anything about this incident, please notify him. Waddell assured him would do just that.

M. HARMON HALL

Mysteriously enough, there were no more reports of pears being thrown at passing eighteen wheelers.

Waddell was the unspoken leader of his small group of buddies. He made average grades throughout school and was not a trouble maker. He was friendly enough, played baseball and football up to the 10th grade. He lost interest in sports at that level. He always liked to play these two sports, but in high school they took the game too seriously. All those long hours of practice, lifting weights, and running in the summers was not his idea of fun.

Waddell's first inkling of his desire to be in law enforcement came when he was a freshman at the nearby community college. He had bought a used car, at the displeasure of his mother, and commuted the 30 mile round trip to classes. To pay for his car, he worked nights as a dispatcher at the small police station in his home town.

Even though there was limited action in such a small town, Waddell loved the atmosphere around the small police station. He was really interested in investigations of burglaries and break-ins. The attention to minute details in trying to solve these types of crimes was fascinating to him. His career choice was never in doubt, he wanted to be a police detective.

He continued to work as a dispatcher throughout his college years. He commuted for all four years. He would often tell friends he preferred the action around the police station to that of partying in college. He would finish college in three years due, to taking classes each summer.

Waddell's strongest trait was loyalty. If you were a friend, you could count on him to have your back. This trait would serve him well as he grew into adulthood.

After graduating with a major in criminal justice, Waddell applied for several jobs in and around the area, but had no luck. Receiving a tip from a buddy of his over in Peach County, some 35 miles from his home, he applied for a patrolman's position with the Shiloh Police Department. When he received the call from Chief Kelley offering him the job, he could hardly contain his excitement.

Within a month, Waddell had found a small house to rent. He started on the third shift with the police department. The nights were brutally long and boring; but he was doing what he had always wanted to do.

The department employed a total of eight police officers. The small town of Shiloh was buffered from the crimes that one would see in large cities. An occasional domestic violence call, speeding violations, and working the basketball and football games at the local high school would be the bulk of his duties in Shiloh.

Waddell worked with the Shiloh police department for two and a half years. He was offered a patrolman's position with Moss Creek police department located just 45 miles north of Pleasant, North Caroina. On March 1st Waddell joined the force. Within two years he applied for and got the entry position of investigator with the homicide division.

With the title of investigator, he could not have been happier. He was highly respected by his fellow officers. They always knew he had their back. He never complained and often came in during his off days to help out.

His first murder investigation occurred just one month after he had joined the homicide division. Until then, Waddell had never seen a dead body, much less, lead a murder investigation. He and his partner had just finished their shift when the call came in. He had left the station and was headed home when he heard the call over his radio. Shots fired at Sammy's Lounge on Windham Road; possible victim down. He signaled in and told the dispatcher he was in route.

He was surprised to find that he was the first police officer on the scene. Detective Wright noticed several people standing on the curb in front of the lounge. As he approached the group, one woman was visibly upset, crying, and screaming, "Oh Jesus, he killed Antwon."

Detective Wright was glad to see backup arrive. He tried to get the woman away from the group so he could find out what happened. A man standing next to her said he was her brother, and he saw what happened.

Detective Wright and his partner entered the lounge and found a black male lying on the floor near the restrooms. It appeared he had been shot multiple times in his stomach and chest. The paramedics arrived moments after the first responders. Efforts to resuscitate the male was not successful. An hour later, he was pronounced dead by the coroner on the scene. By now several police units had arrived, and were establishing crowd control as a large crowd gathered.

He took statements from several of the alleged eyewitnesses. However, he would find several different accounts of the shooting. He finally got the "girlfriend" to calm down so he could ask her some questions.

She told him her name was Cynthia Townsend, and her boyfriend's name was Antwon Shipman. Wright asked her if she could come to the station to give a detailed account of the shooting. She said she would come in the morning. He insisted she come in tonight and give a written statement.

Even though this was his first homicide investigation, he knew that overnight stories could be conjured up, certain information forgotten, facts distorted, or potential witnesses disappearing for a number of reasons. Ms. Townsend agreed to meet him at 8:30 pm at the station. It was now 7:20 pm.

Later at the station, Cynthia Townsend sat nervously in the first interrogation room on the right down the hallway. When Detective Wright walked into the room he asked her if she would like some water, or a soda, or coffee. She asked for a diet coke. He tried to make her as comfortable as he could. When the coke was delivered he asked her to tell him exactly what went down.

Cynthia Townsend began to tell a version that sounded like a well-rehearsed story. She said that she and Antwon were sitting at a table near the entrance to the restrooms, suddenly a man with dreadlocks came out of the restroom pulled a pistol out and began shooting in their direction. She said she got under the table while Antwon rushed the man. She said she heard shots and when she looked up Antwon was lying in a pool of blood. The man with the dreadlocks ran out the back door. Everyone was screaming and running for the door. She said she couldn't see the shooter's face.

Wright had problems with her version of the shooting.

"Ms. Townsend, you say a complete stranger with dreadlocks came out of the restroom and starting shooting toward the table you and Antwon were sitting.

"Yes, that's right Detective." She began to cry, but there were no tears.

"Ms. Townsend, I'm not sure I understand. Why would a complete stranger start shooting at you and Antwon?" Could he have been shooting at someone else behind you and your boyfriend?" he asked, already knowing the answer.

"Oh no, he was shooting at us," she said, between sobs.

"Ms. Townsend, I've got to be honest with you. I don't think the shooting went down as you have described it. I think you shot Antwon out of jealousy. You were both drinking and he went to the restroom and when he came out you started shooting."

The bartender had told Detective Wright before he left the scene that the two of them had been arguing and Cynthia was known to carry a pistol in her purse. Detective Wright was betting on the fact that the bartender was correct, although he said he did not actually see her shoot him.

"Is it true, Ms. Townsend, that you and Antwon had been arguing and that you accused him of being unfaithful?"

"So we argued, but that don't mean I shot him."

Detective Wright was trying to get a confession out of her by telling her that when they check for gun residue, it still could be detected, even if someone had washed their hands and face. He was certain she had washed her hands before she came to the station.

He waited a couple of minutes, letting what he had just told her sink in. He began to see a change in her demeanor. She began to rock back and forth, unaware of her involuntary movement.

"Cynthia, may I call you Cynthia? You're not a bad person. You lost control tonight and made a mistake. I'm sure you would take back everything that happened tonight if you could, but the fact of the matter is we can't," he said, with an empathic tone.

"Why don't you do the right thing and tell me what really happened tonight?"

Cynthia Townsend lowered her head into her hands and began to cry real tears. Detective Wright sat quietly giving her plenty of time to respond.

"I begged Antwon to leave her alone. That bitch didn't care about him, she just wanted his money. He said he loved me and that he wanted to be with our child and me. Why did he lie to me? I should have shot her ass!"

An hour later a written statement was taken and signed by Cynthia Townsend confessing to the murder of Antwon Shipman.

Over the course of the next three years, Wright played an instrumental role in the arrest and conviction of 3 homicides in Moss Creek, South Carolina.

In 2003, he got a call from Uncle MacArthur in Wilcox, South Carolina.

"Waddell, how are you doing? Remember, I told you a couple of years ago if there was an opening up here in homicide I would give you a call? Well, there is."

"What do you think the chances are that I can get that job?

"I wouldn't be calling you and getting your hopes up if I didn't think you had a good shot at it. Besides, I've already told the Chief about you and your success with the homicide division there at Moss Creek. If you are interested, give me a call before the end of the week. Chief Aldridge is setting up interviews for next week."

"I am very interested, Uncle MacArthur."

"Good, I'll see the Chief this afternoon and Officer Peavey, the human resource officer, will give you a call to give the details of the time and place for the interview. Remember Waddell, you can't let anyone know you are my nephew during the interview or if you come to work here. Chief Aldridge instated that rule after he hired his own nephew. "

"Uncle MacArthur, I can't thank you enough. If I should get the job, I promise I won't let you down. If there is anything I can ever do for you, don't hesitate to ask," Waddell promised.

"Oh, by the way, mother says hello. She wonders how her baby brother is from time to time. She and Aunt Emma are always talking about you three getting together for a visit."

"Well, tell her I said hello, and I might just surprise them and come visit soon," MacArthur said knowing it wasn't going to happen. Too much water under the bridge to think that brother and sisters could ever be close again. *Hell no, there won't be a reunion between the three of them now, or ever, as far as he was concerned.*

MacArthur had refused to acknowledge his father many years ago and he sure as hell wasn't going to open his arms now. No, not to a father that abandoned him and his mother and sisters despite his sisters' urging. As far as he was concerned the only father he had died 10 years ago when his step dad passed away.

MacArthur had always pretended that he didn't care if his sisters disowned him. The truth was he was deeply hurt by this. Of course, he would never admit it to anyone.

CHAPTER 13

Thomas and Gladys Killingsworth announced the birth of their son, Timothy Richard Killingsworth on November 18[th,] 1978. His maternal grandparents had amassed a fortune in the shipping industry in Savannah, Georgia, in the mid 50's. Tim's father, Thomas Killingsworth had inherited a very large sum of money. Thomas Killingsworth never held a job, nor did he spend any quality time with his family, especially his son Tim.

Tim Killingworth's up bringing was just the opposite of MacArthur's. Tim wanted for nothing. He went to the best schools. He was exposed to the arts and theater at an early age. He and his family vacationed abroad in the summers and owned a second home in the Hamptons. Tim grew up accustomed to the finest things money could buy.

But, Thomas and Gladys Killingworth had a dark secret that remained hidden behind the lush walls of their high rise mansion. The Killingsworth family gave the outward appearance of a well-adjusted, loving family. But, within these walls, lurked abuse of the worst kind.

Thomas Killingworth, Tim's father, was bipolar and suffered from mental illness. His condition would require brief periods of hospitalization in the psychiatric ward. During these visits in the hospital, his absence was explained as out of town business trips to the West Coast.

Just after he turned eight years old, his father paid late night visits to his room. Young Tim was confused as his father told him that if he loved him and wanted him to get well, he should try and please his father. He knew that what was happening wasn't normal, but he didn't want his father's failing health and possible death on his conscious. Tim's father exploited his love for him in a sick and deranged manner.

Tim grew up thinking that he was never as important as his father and protecting his father always came first. The only time he felt safe was when his father was away on "business." He once tried to tell his mother of his father's visits to his room, but she accused him of lying and said that if he ever mentioned it again, he would be sent off to boarding school. Sadly, Mrs. Killingsworth knew the truth, but did nothing. She would regret this for the rest of her life.

In the summer of 1992, an incident involving his best friend, Frankie Briscoe, would have a profound impact in the life of Tim Killingsworth. On a typical hot July afternoon, Tim, Frankie, and a few other friends were enjoying the swimming pool at the Killingsworth home. A popular game the boys played, for the sole purpose of impressing the girls, was to dive down to the bottom of the deep end and touch the drain.

This fateful afternoon, Frankie took his turn and successfully touched the drain, and the other boys, including Tim took their turns. After a few dives, one of the other boys suggested that instead of just touching the drain, the new rule was to retrieve what the other swimmer had put there in the previous dive. When it came Frankie's time, he dove in and was making his decent towards the drain. As Frankie reached the drain, his hand became lodged in the openings of the drain. He tried to get free but couldn't. As Tim stood looking down waiting for Frankie to make his way back up, he realized it was taking too long.

"Something is wrong!" Tim shouted. He dove in, and when he got to Frankie, he could see that his hand was stuck in the drain. Acting quickly, he managed to pull Frankie's hand free. With only seconds of air left, he and Frankie swam to the top.

Tim had saved Frankie's life. Frankie's father was called, and as he and his son were leaving he turned around and told Tim how grateful he was for saving his son's life. He told him that if he ever needed his help in any way, regardless what it was, all he had to do was ask. This act of bravery would be repaid much sooner than Tim could have ever imagined.

Tim never had sleepovers at his house. He always spent the night at his buddies' houses. Finally, after almost two years of being abused by his father, Tim confided in Frankie. On the phone, he told him how his father came to his room late at nights. He asked Tim why he didn't tell someone. Tim said he had wanted to for so long, but he was afraid what might happen to his family.

As Frankie was hanging up the phone he turned around to see his father standing behind him.

"Frankie, tell me what's going on?"

Reluctantly, he told his father the entire story of Tim's father's abuse and how Tim suspected that his father was abusing his younger brother as well. He explained to his father that Tim was afraid to go to the police. Frankie then made his father promise he would not go to the police.

"Son, you have my word, I will not go to the police."

Frankie's father, Carmine Briscoe had business "associates" that were rumored to be involved in racketeering, money laundering, and bookmaking. Frankie would not know until he was almost 21 years old that his father was a "made" man.

Frankie's grandfather had come from Sicily after World War II and settled down in River Heights, New Jersey. Carmine Briscoe and his wife

Victoria inherited his father's dry cleaning business when his father died. Victoria Briscoe would give birth to a son and named him Frank Delano Briscoe. Frank had one brother and one sister to come along within the next four years.

The Briscoe family appeared to be just like any other middle class family living in the small town of River Heights. The family's dry cleaning business was very successful. Some thought it was a little strange that the Briscoe's drove the nicest cars, had a cabin on the lake some 25 miles north of Trenton, and belonged to the exclusive country club, all on the profits of one dry cleaning business.

They were a close-knit family in every way. They were well respected by the citizens of the town. They attended charity events, worshipped at the local Catholic Church, and was involved in other civic activities on a regular basis. They attended their children's school events regularly. Carmine was asked to run for commissioner in his district but declined saying he was not a politician.

The following morning of Frankie's phone conversation with Tim, Carmine Briscoe made a phone call.

Two weeks later, two men dressed in black suits walked into the "Gentlemen's Club," where Thomas Killingsworth spent two or three nights a week drinking and playing gin rummy.

One of the men asked to speak with Thomas Killingsworth. He was told that because he was not a member, he and his friend wouldn't be allowed to stay without being the guest of a member. The man in the black suit apologized. Both men walked out the same door they came in. They walked to their car, but didn't leave.

They waited patiently until Thomas Killingsworth, the child molester, came staggering out the front door, heading for his car. He did not see the two men walking towards him. Just as he reached for the door handle of his car, one of the men hit him on the back of his head with a sawed off baseball bat.

When Killingsworth finally regained consciousness, he looked around trying to figure out what happened. The last thing he remembered was reaching for his car door. Now his head felt as though it was in a vice. As he began to regain his senses, he realized his hands were tied behind his back and a rope was tied around his neck. The other end of the rope was tied to the bumper of the car that belonged to the two men in black suits.

"I'm only going to ask you one time. Did "yous" sick bastard mess with your own son?" the short stocky guy asked with a heavy Brooklyn accent.

Killingsworth's entire body was shaking uncontrollably, beads of sweat running down his face and his mouth so dry that his lips almost stuck together.

"I don't know what you're talking about."

His interrogator suddenly landed a blow to his stomach, causing all of the air to rush out of his lungs. He was not able to get his breath for what seemed like a full minute.

"I told you I was only going to ask you one time, Moose, start the car."

"Wait, alright, I did what you said, but I was screwed up on drugs and didn't know what I was doing. I'm so sorry. I plan to make it up to my son, I swear I'll never touch him again. I have money, lots of it. I'll give you guys whatever you want, just let me go," Thomas Killingsworth pleaded.

"You're right sick - o. You won't ever touch him again." The short stocky guy got in the car and gave the driver orders to take off.

The mutilated body of Thomas Killingsworth was never found.

Carmine Briscoe had repaid the debt he owed to young Tim for saving his son's life.

The family's explanation for the disappearance of Thomas Killingsworth was that he lost his life while sailing off the coast of Massachusetts. There were three people who knew the real story. Frankie's father would share with his son, some 15 years later, that he had taken care of the "problem" many years back. Frankie didn't need to ask questions.

The scars of such a tragic childhood would always be with Tim. As he grew into manhood, it was very difficult for him to blend in with those around him. He had spent so much of his life pretending abnormal was actually normal. He would spend his adult life trying to unravel the oddities of his misguided childhood. Tim was never able to forgive his mother for not intervening and putting an end to the hell he endured those two years. *She had to have known, why didn't she stopped him*? Tim would ask that question throughout his life.

Tim Killingsworth dropped out of Boston University after his first year. He bounced around for almost two years with no direction in his life. He blamed himself for what happened to him as a boy. It would be years of intense therapy before he started to see life with some normalcy. He was determined to find his own way in life. The problem was, he didn't know where he belonged in a society that could let something as sinister as what he experienced go unnoticed.

At the age of 27, Tim decided to go back to college. He enrolled in a small university south of Boston. For no particular reason, he later explained, he started taking courses in criminal justice. He found the forensic science curriculum very interesting.

In four years, Tim Killingsworth earned a B.S. degree in forensic science, with a minor in criminal justice. His first job, with the help of his well-connected uncle, was working for Liberty Police Department in Liberty, Massachusetts. The department was very small, with only three employees in the forensic department. Over the next two years, Tim made a name for himself with his excellent skill set and hard work. He stayed in Liberty for three years before accepting the position of head of the forensic department in nearby Salem, Massachusetts.

Tim met a beautiful girl, Dorothy Daniels his second year in Salem. They dated two years before getting married on June 15, 1995. One year later, a daughter was born. Two years after the birth of their daughter, a son was born.

In spite of his wonderful family and his success at his job, Tim could never escape his past. He never discussed this with his wife, nor did he share it with his closest friend at work.

To escape from the demons that haunted him, he turned to alcohol. In the beginning it was just a few beers after work. Within a few months, he was stopping by Mickey's Lounge two or three nights a week. His wife, Dorothy began to notice and begged him to slow down. She tried to get him to talk to her and tell her what was bothering him. His answer was always the same, the stress of his job was the cause of his situation. He kept promising her he would be alright, it would work out; not to worry.

It didn't work out. His boss began to notice a change in his appearance as well as his work performance. Tim had always taken great pride in his work and was a perfectionist when it came to completing a project.

Dorothy tried to get him to see a counselor but Tim refused. His drinking had gotten to the stage where he was putting vodka in his coffee thermos, thinking no one could tell he was drinking on the job.

His boss, Jack, called him in and told him that he was concerned about him and that he was getting several complaints from co-workers concerning his numerous absences, getting to work late, and leaving work early. Jack had been his friend for years, but he told Tim he could not keep covering for him much longer. He told Tim to take a week off and get himself together.

The end came two weeks later. Dorothy had kicked him out of the house after he showed up drunk at their son's baseball game. After the game he caused a scene with the coach over his son's not getting to play enough innings. When he got home, after stopping off for a few beers with the boys, he started an argument with Dorothy and accused her of being unfaithful. There was no basis for his accusation, only his drunken imagination. Dorothy told him to leave and not come back until he could sober up.

Tim reached rock bottom the next day. When he walked into his office, he reeked of alcohol. His boss, Jack, walked into his office and asked for his keys to his office. He had gone too far, he was fired.

Tim had lost his wife and family and now his job.

He had no place to go but back to his mother's house. Swallowing his pride, he agreed to check into a 28 day rehab center. After several threats to leave, Tim stayed and completed the treatment with success. He would stay sober for almost six months before relapsing. He attended the rehab center for a second time. This time the treatment seemed to help him a great deal.

His mother told him now that he was sober and clean, it was time he started to get his life back in order. He had hopes of returning to his family one day, if Dorothy could forgive him. But, too much had happened to save their marriage. She filed for a divorce one week after he completed his second stint at rehab. Their marriage was over.

On July 31, 1997, the divorce became final. Tim was granted joint custody with the provision that Dorothy had the final say as to the times he would be allowed to see his children. She warned him not to expect to see them until he could get his life straight and stay sober.

The next two years, Tim Killingsworth traveled abroad. His mother thought a change of scenery might be what he needed to get himself straightened out. He traveled to Spain and stayed there for six months. He then made his way to London where he stayed for almost a year. From there he would complete his time in Europe in Rome.

He remained alcohol free the entire time he was in Europe. Then, on a Sunday morning, he got a call from his brother telling him that their mother was gravely ill. Tim arrived back in the states in time to see her before she lapsed into a coma. She passed away four days later. During his last visit, Tim's mother told him how sorry she was for allowing his father to abuse him. She asked for his forgiveness. With her last words, she told him how much she loved him and how she wished she go back and change things.

He never responded. He could not lie and tell her he forgave her. Tim would carry the scars of abuse the rest of his life. He would always blame his mother as much as his dad for the abuse he endured as an adolescent. Why she stood by and let it happen he would never understand.

Two months after he returned from Europe he was hired by the Wilcox Police Department in South Carolina. His uncle, Allen Aldridge, Chief of Police gave him a job as a detective in the homicide division. It was rumored among family members that Tim's mother gave her brother a sizable amount of money to show her appreciation. Tim was given a chance to start his life over.

Since there was no forensic department in the Wilcox Police Department Tim, was assigned a homicide detective position. His extensive background in police forensics combined with his degree in criminal justice qualified him for the detective position, his uncle explained to the mayor. Only his uncle, Chief Aldridge, would know of his past problems with alcohol.

Veteran Detective MacArthur Nowlin, questioned the hire. He had recommended someone else for the job that had several years' experience in homicide. But, Chief Aldridge hired Tim Killingsworth instead.

CHAPTER 14

On Sunday night, August 10th, just two days following the murders, MacArthur and Rachel were working late at the station.

"Peavey, I think the first thing we need to do is develop a time line. Let's go over what we know. The medical examiner concludes that the time of death of the Sprayberrys was somewhere between 6:00 pm and 9:00 pm."

Peavey responded, "According to witnesses, no one heard shots fired. If it was a professional hit, do you suppose the shooter used a silencer?"

"Good point, Peavey. Has anyone checked for marks on the barrel of the weapon found at the scene? If there a silencer was used, it should've left markings on the end of the barrel."

"Peavey, I want you to check out the Sprayberrys' financial situation. Find out if they were in debt. Check their bank account. Talk to the people he worked with. Try to find out what kind of guy was he? Talk with the principal of the high school where Mrs. Sprayberry worked. Ask him if she had any issues at home or at work. I want to know where Dr. Sprayberry spent his spare time. Did he have any hobbies? Get me as much as you can on both of them ASAP." MacArthur said, while he stared at his note.

"I'm on it Detective."

"Also, check the college where he was dean to see if there had been any complaints by female students. See if there has been any formal grievances filed against him in the last year or so. We've got to find out why someone wanted Dr. Sprayberry and his wife dead. There's something else Peavey, what motive would Dr. Sprayberry have to kill his wife of 33 years and then himself? Why kill her in the bathtub instead of waiting until she was asleep?

The stats don't lie, over 95% of murder/suicide involves the male shooting his wife or girlfriend while she was asleep in bed, then turning the gun on himself. I've got a problem with the suicide note as well. Wouldn't you think that Dr. Sprayberry would have hand written the note making it more personal in nature? Also, with his background having published two novels, it is very unlikely that he would have made the mistake of using "you're" when it should be "your" at the close of his "suicide note".

Something else to consider, the best friends of the Sprayberrys told me the couple seemed very happy and the two couples were only two weeks away from going on a cruise together. That doesn't sound like someone who is about to commit suicide." And take a look at these pictures taken in the bedroom where he supposedly shot himself. Do you see anything strange about any of them? Take a close look at the pillow on his side of the bed. See any blood splatter?" MacArthur asked, as he kept firing questions at Rachel before she could answer the first one.

"If he shot himself in the manner in which most suicide shooters do, there would be gun residue found on his hand and face, and a mark on his temple where the barrel made contact with the skin. There was none. Another thing Peavey, the gun found in Dr. Sprayberry's hand is not consistent with a suicide shooting. That is, when the firearm is discharged, the recoil of the gun makes it very unlikely that it would have remained in his hand. Rarely does it happen that way. Only in the movies. I'm going to see what the tech department found about the note. I bet you lunch, Peavey that note didn't come from the Sprayberrys' home computer."

Rachel was impressed with MacArthur's knowledge of a crime scene. His attention to detail was just as good as other detectives said it was. It's was obvious to her, he knew what he was doing.

"Detective Nowlin, why is it that no one else has bothered to question these inconsistencies? They had to see what you've seen, didn't they?"

"They saw what they wanted to see. I'm not suggesting that they are intentionally overlooking evidence. It's just that in some cases detectives experience "tunnel vision." When something appears to be obvious, it is easy not to look any further."

"Sir, why don't you go home and get some rest? I'm going to be here a little while longer."

MacArthur told Rachel that tomorrow was going to be a busy day and an important one.

"I'll think I will go and try to get some sleep," he said, as he was taking the pictures of the crime scene and pinning them to the chart board.

As he was walking out of the door he suddenly turned around and came back in.

"I almost forgot, we are going to the funeral service tomorrow morning. I want you to observe the immediate family members of the Sprayberrys during the service. See who the son and daughter talk to. We also need to try and identify any strangers that seems to look out of place. It is not uncommon for the killer to show up at the funeral of their victims."

Twenty minutes later MacArthur was getting in his car. As he had done before when stressed out, he was took the long way home. He believed he did his best thinking while driving. In less than an hour, he was back at his apartment.

When he turned the lamp off, sitting on the night stand beside his bed, he noticed it was 10:45 pm. He couldn't sleep. His mind was racing with questions about Marilyn's murder, as well as the Sprayberry murders. He knew he had to give his undivided attention to the Sprayberry case, because of the short window that Chief Aldridge had given him.

His instincts told him that Marilyn's killer was probably someone that lived in the area. Someone that walked the streets of Wilcox. Someone that was known to everyone in the community. Someone Marilyn knew.

What MacArthur didn't know was that the evidence being gathered by Detective Killingworth's investigation would eventually cast a net of suspicion over him.

MacArthur hardly slept, and when he did manage to get to sleep he had this strange dream where he kept seeing Marilyn's face and heard her cries of desperation. What made this dream even more unbearable was because in this dream MacArthur would arrive just in time to save her. He made a mental note to go by the pharmacy tomorrow to pick up more Ambien.

MacArthur noticed the small clock beside his bed, it was 2:45 am. He felt as though he hadn't been to sleep yet. As he was feeling for the bathroom door, he cursed himself for not leaving a light on so when he did get up at night he could see where he was going. His hands slid across the wall of his bedroom until he felt the handle of the bathroom door.

He turned off the bathroom light and made his way into the kitchen. As he opened the refrigerator to get a drink of orange juice, MacArthur began to internalize for the first time the magnitude of Marilyn's death. He sat down at the kitchen table and was overcome with pent-up emotions that he had ignored until now.

On the table, were two tickets for their flight that would have taken them to Destin, Florida. Located in the panhandle with its beautiful beaches and great restaurants Destin was their favorite get-away. There were small cafes where they would eat lunch at the docks and watch the scrimp boats come in late in the afternoons. MacArthur remembered the walks on the beach late at night. He remembered the peacefulness and the closeness he felt as he and Marilyn held on to each other as they touched their toes in the warm waters of the Gulf of Mexico.

He even laughed aloud as he remembered the time they rented mopeds and rode up and down the strip. He remembered how cute she looked in her red safety helmet. Suddenly, without any warning tear drops ran down his face.

Only Marilyn could get MacArthur to sun bath on the beach in the middle of the day's heat. He remembered how she would make fun of him because he was the only guy on the beach that still had his shirt on even though he was sitting under a rented umbrella.

MacArthur realized at that moment how much he needed her. He could have never guessed that losing her would leave such a void in his life. He was experiencing feelings that were all too similar to that of losing Kelli. The only difference was Kelli was still alive.

I already miss her. I just can't believe she's gone, MacArthur thought with a sadness he wasn't familiar with.

He finished his orange juice and threw the tickets in the trash.

The hard ass, Detective MacArthur Nowlin, the man who had appeared to lack compassion for anyone, the man who went through life lacking empathy for anyone, made his way back to bed, turned the lights off, pulled the bed spread over him, and sobbed.

M. HARMON HALL

CHAPTER 15

MacArthur and Rachel sat in the back of the United Methodist Church located across from the city park. Relatives of the Sprayberry family gathered together in a room designated for the family only. There was a table with coffee and cookies available for the grieving family members.

The sanctuary was almost filled to capacity. The pastor said all the things you would expect at such an occasion. He spoke of the Sprayberrys many contributions to the community over the 30 years they had lived in Wilcox.

Two songs were sung by the choir, there were two testimonials given by close friends of the deceased, and then Sean Sprayberry was last to address the podium. He spoke of his wonderful mother and father, and how they had raised him and his sister to become good citizens. He thanked them for their unconditional love, and for their support. Many of the people in attendance noted how composed Sean was, and how they admired him for being able to speak while grieving at a time like this.

But, there were two people in the service that couldn't help but think that Sean Sprayberry was too calm and collected to have just lost a mother and father two days ago. While his remarks were touching, and there was hardly a dry eye in the sanctuary, MacArthur and Rachel sat studying his face. They both witnessed that during the graveside service Sean Sprayberry never once broke down. Rachel said she could not imagine anyone getting through that speech without a tremendous display of emotion. MacArthur answered Rachel by telling her that some people mourn the loss of loved ones differently.

Outside at the graveside, MacArthur and Rachel separated to observe the on lookers as the service came to a close. Nothing stood out of the ordinary, as family members and friends of the family hugged and kissed each other goodbye.

Rachel noticed a young man with long hair that did not appear to be a member of the family. She watched him as he stood near the tent where the immediate family members sat during the pastor's final prayer. When the service ended, he did not stay and talk to anyone. He got into his BMW and left.

She told MacArthur about the young guy with long hair; they both she dismissed it as probably a friend of a friend of one of the family members. She told MacArthur that she wrote down the tag number of the car he was driving, just in case they might ever want to find out who he was.

"Damn good work, Peavey. You can never have too much information in a case, and you never know if the smallest detail might break open a case. That kind of thinking was the reason I wanted you on this case."

"Thank you sir, that means a lot to me to hear you say that."

"Don't let it go to your head. Until we solve this case there won't be any awards given out. I want to have a little chat with the son, Sean." MacArthur said, as he started to walk towards the grieving son.

"I'm very sorry for your loss Mr. Sprayberry. I'm Detective Nowlin from the Wilcox PD. I would like to ask…"

"I know who you are, Detective. Thank you for coming. I assume you came out of respect for my parents and not just doing your job," Sean Sprayberry said with a touch of sarcasm.

"Absolutely Mr. Sprayberry…"

"Detective, now is not a good time for me. If you would like to give me a call in a few days, I'll be glad to meet with you and answer any questions you may have. I just want the killer caught, and brought to justice."

"I certainly understand Mr. Sprayberry. I will give you a call later this week. Again, I am very sorry for your loss," MacArthur said, with as much compassion as he could render.

"He's hiding something Peavey. When we get back to the office I want you to do a complete background check on our grieving Mr. Sprayberry and his sister."

Rachel Peavey was beginning to feel a bit overwhelmed. She wasn't sure she could get the information Detective Nowlin was asking for in the time he was expecting it. But, she reminded herself, such was the life of a homicide detective. Leave nothing to chance. Working under pressure came with the territory. With less than 48 hours under her belt investigating a murder, she knew this was what she wanted to do, the rest of her life.

The funeral service was over around 12:30. MacArthur and Rachel got into his car and started back to the office. He asked her if she wanted to stop at the City Café and get some lunch. She said lunch sounded really good. As they pulled into the parking lot, Rachel saw Sean Sprayberry and his family going into the restaurant. Then she saw the guy with long hair from the funeral service pull up beside her and MacArthur.

"Detective Nowlin, don't get out yet," she said with a sense of urgency. "That's the same guy I saw at the service. You know, the one with long hair."

"That's very interesting Peavey, but this is a public restaurant, and anyone can stop here if they like," MacArthur said teasingly. "I don't think he has broken any laws yet."

MacArthur agreed to wait and see what the guy was going to do.

"He's on his phone, sir." In less than a minute, he put the phone back into his pocket.

"Peavey, I thought you said you were hungry."

"I am sir, but just give me 60 more seconds to see what this guy does."

"Time's up Peavey, I'm going in," MacArthur said, as he put his hand on the door handle.

As he started to get out of his car, Sean Sprayberry came out of the restaurant without his family. MacArthur sat back down as they watched him walk over to the car where the young guy with long hair was sitting. The two had a conversation that lasted less than two minutes. Sean Sprayberry got out of the car and went back into the restaurant.

The guy had never turned his engine off. He then put his car in reverse, backed out, and slowly drove away.

"What do you make of that Detective?"

"There is obviously some kind of connection with Sprayberry and your mystery guy. Run a check on the BMW's plates, and let's find out who this guy is," MacArthur said, as he got out of the car. They had been seated about five minutes when Sean Sprayberry walked over to their table.

"Detective, I apologize if I came across as being rude back in the cemetery."

"No apology necessary Mr. Sprayberry. If anyone should apologize, it should be me. It was not the right time to approach you with the details of your parents' murder."

"I understand you're just doing your job. Give me a call later this week and I'll be glad to answer any questions you may have. Believe me, I'm as anxious as you to find the person that killed my parents."

"Thank you, Mr. Sprayberry, I'll be in touch," MacArthur said.

"Wow, that was unexpected," Rachel said.

"Yeah, a real friendly guy," MacArthur said with sarcasm.

They got back to the station around 1:15. After checking his messages, he saw that a John Smith had called him with some information about the Sprayberry killings. MacArthur noted that the caller had referred to the Sprayberry case as the killings, not the murder/suicide terminology the media had used earlier.

He called the number, but no one answered. He tried three more times the same afternoon, but never got an answer.

"Do you think the son could be involved in the murder of his parents?" Rachel asked.

"You can never rule out that possibility in this stage of the investigation. I do think before we start digging in that direction, we've got to present the evidence in a systematic way that will convince Chief Aldridge to open this case as a homicide. We have until tomorrow afternoon to complete our report and submit it to the Chief." He said, as he pulled his folder out and started to go over the evidence again.

Rachel returned to her office and contacted the person responsible for running ID's on plates. The officer assured her he would have it on her desk no later than tomorrow morning. She said that wasn't good enough. She wanted on her desk this afternoon, no excuses.

Sean Sprayberry, or his sister had any priors, not even parking tickets. Sean Sprayberry worked for the Boeing Company, located 20 miles from Silver Creek. He was a project engineer in the quality control division. He had been employed there for 12 years. His wife was a physical therapist with the Silver Creek Baptist Hospital located in town. Their two children attended the only private school in Silver Creek. They were in grades two and five.

The daughter, Susan S. Login was married to Mark Login. They had been living in Fisher, South Carolina for five years. They did not have any children. Mark Login was a pharmacist with a chain drug store in the small town of Fisher. His wife, Susan was an LPN working at Dr. Rodger's clinic, also in Fisher.

Co-workers of both couples told Rachel that they were well liked and well thought of in the community. Sean, his wife, and the children spent some weekends at their cabin on Lake Gunter, once or twice a month during the summer months. Susan and her husband were very active in community service, as well as The Presbyterian Church.

Rachel reported to MacArthur late that afternoon that she had not turned up anything significant in either of the two sibling's background that might look suspicious. There was one thing however, Sean and Susan were the contingent beneficiaries of two life insurance policies Dr. Sprayberry had taken out several years back. The total amount of both policies was $800,000. This was to be split equally among the two surviving children, should he and his wife die. The executor of the will was Sean Sprayberry.

When Rachel told MacArthur about the large sum of money the children would inherit, he became more curious.

"Peavey, when trying to solve murder cases, one of the first questions the investigator should ask is, who would benefit the most from the death of the deceased? What would the benefits be? Would it create instant wealth? It is very clear that the son and daughter of the Sprayberrys would certainly benefit from mom and dad's death," MacArthur explained.

"Do you actually think either one or both could have had something to do with the murders?"

"It sure wouldn't be the first time grown children have killed their parents for an early inheritance," MacArthur responded.

Rachel left and went back to her office and began searching for the information they had just discussed.

It was getting close to 4:00 pm as MacArthur was finalizing his report to be submitted to Chief Aldridge. Rachel returned to his office and knocked on his office door. He motioned her in as she sat at the work table where MacArthur had notes spread out.

"Sir, I got an ID on the plates. The car is registered to a Michael C. Benjamin. The address is 344 Rose Circle, Silver Creek, North Carolina. I called the number given on the registration plates, but it was no longer in service."

"Is that where Sean Sprayberry lives now?" MacArthur asked.

"Yes sir, it is. I'm running a trace on the guy now to see if he shows up in the system."

"Peavey, I want you in on the meeting with the Chief tomorrow morning. Don't be late. Let me do all the talking, understand?"

"Yes sir. Sir, I almost forgot to tell you that when I ran a check on the finances of Sean Sprayberry and his wife, guess what I found?"

"Peavey, I don't have time for games, what did you find?"

"Sean Sprayberry and his wife filed for bankruptcy one month ago. It was not made public until last Friday, the day of his parents' murders."

"That's interesting. Of course, it could be just a coincidence. Dig a little deeper Peavey. Good work. Remember, 8:00 am, Chief Aldridge's office."

MacArthur continued to study his notes for another hour. He decided he would not stay too late tonight. He needed to be well rested and sharp when he pleaded his case for opening a homicide investigation on the deaths of the Sprayberrys. At six o'clock, he locked up and made his way to the parking lot.

Cheeseburger, fries, and sweet tea would be his dinner tonight. He joked that if he should ever end up on death row, he would request this menu for his last meal.

But, that could never happen, could it?

CHAPTER 16

MacArthur tossed and turned most of the night. He kept going over in his head the report he was going to present to Chief Aldridge. He didn't want to make the mistake of not being totally prepared to show how this case was not a murder/suicide. The victims deserved justice. He arrived at the station at 7:00 am.

MacArthur knocked on Chief Aldridge's office door with his report in hand exactly at 8:00 am. He could see that the Chief was on the phone, so he waited outside. While he waited, the chief's secretary politely told MacArthur how sorry she was to hear about the death of Marilyn. He thanked her and returned to his notes while he continued to wait.

Where in the hell is Peavey? MacArthur could feel his face getting red. *I told her to be on time."*

Just as Chief Aldridge was motioning MacArthur to come into his office; Rachel walked up.

"You just did make it. You better have a real good excuse being late," MacArthur snapped.

"I do sir."

"We'll talk about it later," MacArthur said, with a hushed voice.

"Have a seat MacArthur and Officer Peavey," the Chief said politely.

"Officer Peavey, how's it been working with Detective Nowlin?" He ain't likely to win Mr. Congeniality here in the department, but he is damn good at what he does, wouldn't you agree?"

"Yes sir, well, I mean yes about the part of being a very good detective," Rachel replied.

"Just kidding, MacArthur," Chief Aldridge said laughing. "What have you got for me?"

"Well sir, as I told you yesterday, there are several inconsistencies in this case. I won't read the whole report to you sir, you can read for yourself. I would like to bring to your attention five facts in this case that I believe will call for a full investigation for the murders of Dr. and Mrs. Sprayberry. The first item is that there was no gun residue on the alleged shooter's hands or face. It would have been impossible for Dr. Sprayberry to have shot himself and no residue found anywhere. I realize that gun residue can be wiped clean, but obviously if it were suicide there would be traces.

Secondly, we know the windows were opened in the bedroom where the shooting took place. If Dr. Sprayberry had shot his wife and then himself, the sound of gun fire could easily have been heard.

The third thing I present to you sir, and the data will back me up on this, in 95% of all murder/suicides, the first victim is shot while he or she is asleep in bed. As you know, Mrs. Sprayberry was shot while in her bath tub.

Chief, these three facts are things I mentioned to you in our last conversation. There is more, however.

They've been happily married for 33 years. It just doesn't make sense that Dr. Sprayberry would kill his wife and then shoot himself. They were scheduled to go on a cruise with their friends two weeks after the day they died.

Sir, the fourth reason I believe they were killed, and I think this might be the most compelling piece of evidence, is the suicide note. Dr. Sprayberry's background as a teacher, author, and Dean of the English Department, suggests he did not write the note. As a published author, he would have never made the mistake of using the word "you're" as was written in the note. The correct usage should have been "your." Along with that, the suicide note found at the crime scene did not come from Dr. Sprayberrys' computer at home or the computer in his office.

Lastly sir, statistics prove that in a shooting involving someone taking their own life, the angle or path of the bullet is almost always slightly upward. According to the autopsy report that was not the case in this shooting."

"Well, MacArthur, I have to say, you present a compelling case. I'm going to look over your written report and talk with the D.A. to get his opinion. I will have an answer for you tomorrow morning," Chief Aldridge said, as he rose from his chair.

"Thank you Chief."

"What do think?" Rachel asked, as they walked back to his office.

"It's hard to read him sometimes. We'll just have to wait until tomorrow."

MacArthur asked Rachel to see if she could find out who this Michael Benjamin is. "I think I am going to have that talk with Sean Sprayberry sooner, rather than later."

The meeting with Chief Aldridge had lasted over an hour. It was now 9:15 am. Rachel went back to her office and started the process of trying to locate Michael Benjamin, if that was his real name.

MacArthur sat at his desk wondering if he had convinced the Chief. He thought if the case was not opened at least he had tried. Besides, if the Chief didn't agree to open the case this would give him more time to find Marilyn's killer. He walked to the coffee room and poured himself a fresh cup of coffee. As he entered his office, his phone was ringing. He thought about not answering it, but did.

"Is this Detective MacArthur Nowlin?" the voice on the other end of the line asked.

"Yes it is, how can I help you?"

"Detective Nowlin, this is Sonny Barrett. Do you remember me?" Sonny asked with a slur in his voice.

"Yes I do, what do you want? I'm very busy and I'm not in the mood to talk to a drunk tonight."

"Well, you know me and Marilyn split on not so good terms. I heard about the killing and I wanted to know if you have found the bastard that killed her. She didn't deserve to die like she did. I mean, for somebody to stab her to death, cut her throat, and then just leave her naked in the woods like some dead animal, well, that just ain't right." Sonny's knowledge of how Marilyn was murdered didn't go unnoticed by MacArthur. Not all of the details about the murder had been made public.

"Sonny, you mean, why would someone shoot her?" MacArthur replied, testing to see if Barrett would stand by his theory as to how she was killed.

"Well, I heard she was stabbed, but I could have heard wrong," Sonny said.

MacArthur decided not to press Sonny on the phone. He didn't want Sonny thinking he might be looked at as a possible suspect. At least, not now.

"Sonny, can you come by the station in the morning and we can talk about it? "

"I don't know Detective, I'm pretty busy these days," Sonny lied.

MacArthur told him it hadn't been announced yet, but there would be a substantial reward offered to the person who had information that would lead to the arrest and conviction of Marilyn's murderer. Of course, there had not been any discussion of a reward.

"Well I might be able to come by in the morning. What time?" Sonny asked.

"How about 10:00 o'clock?"

"Alright Detective, I'll be there," Sonny said, as he hung up.

Sonny did not show, apparently he had skipped town.

MacArthur asked himself, *Was Sonny calling to see if the murderer had been caught because he still loved her and he wanted justice? Was it because he was getting nervous because he might be involved. Was it just because he was drunk? But why would he call me and agree to come to the station only to skip town the next day? It just didn't make sense.*

The rest of the day was uneventful. Two more calls came in, one caller said that he thought he knew who killed the lady that was found at the park. After a few minutes, it was clear both calls were bogus. Later on in the afternoon, MacArthur called the friends of the Sprayberrys that were going on the cruise. He asked if Dr. Sprayberry had shown any signs of depression. He also inquired about the relationship between the Sprayberrys. The friend said they never argued. There was no sign of trouble in the marriage. When he asked if they believed Dr. Sprayberry would kill his wife then himself, their response was absolutely not.

MacArthur was still going over all of the information he had collected when his phone rang. "Detective, I knew you would probably still be there this late. I have some information I want to go over with you. Are you going to be there a while?"

"Rachel, it's late. There is no need for you to come down here at this hour. I'm…"

"Detective, I've got nothing else to do, besides I am anxious to tell you what I found today. Be there in 20 minutes."

MacArthur was glad she was coming, but he couldn't help but think she must not have much of a life after work.

Fifteen minutes later, Rachel was knocking on his office door. MacArthur told her of the conversation with Sonny and how he seemed to know too much about the details of the murder. He told her he was meeting with Sonny in the morning and was going to find out how Sonny had gotten his information.

They both agreed, either Sonny was involved, or someone had told him about the murder. MacArthur was determined to get answers.

Rachel pulled out a file from her tote bag and begin to read the report she had prepared for him. "Michael Charles Benjamin is a 22 year old graduate student at Liberty College in Pelham, or was. His major was in European Literature. Guess who he was doing his internship with? You got it! Dr. Samuel Sprayberry," Rachel reported.

"It seems that Benjamin was the leading candidate for a full grant at a very prominent university in England, however he was found guilty of plagiarism in the thesis he submitted to the Dean and not only was he dropped as a candidate, but was expelled from Liberty College. And you're not going to believe who was responsible for his dismissal. None other than Dr. Samuel Sprayberry."

Rachel continued by telling MacArthur that Dr. Sprayberry's secretary told her in a telephone interview earlier today that she overheard the two of them arguing in his office. Benjamin was accusing Sprayberry of setting him up. Sprayberry told him to get out of his office; as he stormed out he made threats."

"What is the connection between Sean Sprayberry and Benjamin?" MacArthur asked.

"I don't know for now, but I'm going to find out," she said with determination.

"Well, let's not get ahead of ourselves here, Peavey. Unless the Chief opens this case, we are just chasing rabbits." Hell, it's almost 10:00 o'clock. We've got a busy day tomorrow Peavey. Why don't you go home? There's nothing we can do for now until we get the word from Aldridge," he said, as he poured out the cold coffee.

"How about some pancakes at the Waffle House?" Rachel asked. "I'm starved!"

"You're always starved," MacArthur said smiling. *I could use some company, I don't really want to go to that empty apartment just yet*, he thought. "Sure, why not. I'll meet you there in about 15 minutes."

Rachel was already gone when MacArthur walked to his car. He suddenly had the feeling he was being watched. He checked his rear view mirror and saw nothing. *I must be getting paranoid in my old age*, he told himself.

MacArthur had always possessed keen instincts. This night his instincts were correct again.

Detective Killingsworth had stayed out of sight as he waited for MacArthur to leave. He watched as MacArthur and Rachel drank their coffee and with their pancakes. Later, Killingsworth watched as MacArthur entered his apartment alone. He sat in his unmarked car across the street from the apartment complex munching on a left over donut from earlier that morning. He decided to stake out the place for a couple hours before heading home. He wasn't sure what he expected to see. He dozed off to sleep. He was awakened with the cold barrel of a pistol resting against his cheek.

"What the hell are you doing staking out my apartment? And why have you been following me all night?" MacArthur said angrily, as he continued to point his nine millimeter pistol at Killingsworth.

After catching his breath, he calmly told MacArthur to put the gun away.

"Answer my question," MacArthur instructed.

"MacArthur, you know that everyone close to the victim is a suspect until we can prove otherwise."

"So you're saying that I'm being looked at as a possible suspect of Marilyn's murder?"

"Look, I'm just doing my job MacArthur. The Chief assigned me to this case, I didn't ask for it."

"I don't like being tailed, and I damn sure don't like the idea of you casing my apartment. Unless you plan on arresting me tonight, get the hell out of here."

"I get it you're upset, MacArthur, but the sooner I can prove your innocence, the sooner I can move on with my investigation," Killingsworth lied.

He agreed with MacArthur that he should have chosen a better time and place to let him know he was being looked at as a possible person of interest. What he didn't tell MacArthur was that he was the leading suspect at this time. While Killingsworth danced around the truth, MacArthur seemed to calm down some, and put his gun back in its holster. He wasn't buying his explanation of why he was following him and why he was staking out his apartment.

"Why would I want to kill Marilyn? What motive would I have for doing such a thing?" MacArthur asked truly agitated.

Killingsworth asked MacArthur if he could come into his apartment and get the interview over with tonight. He agreed, much to Killingsworth's surprise.

"You got 30 minutes," MacArthur said, as he turned to walk back to his apartment.

As Killingsworth entered MacArthur's apartment he was surprised to find it very clean and neatly arranged. *Marilyn probably did the arranging for him,* Killingsworth thought.

MacArthur was in no mood for small talk. He told Killingsworth to ask his questions and go.

"What time did you get back to the station after leaving the Sprayberry's residence on the night Marilyn was killed?"

"I don't know, probably somewhere around 9:00 pm. I really don't remember. You were the last person I saw before I left."

"Did anybody see you when you returned to the station?" Killingsworth continued.

"Probably not, I went into the break room and got a cup of coffee and then went straight to my office. What has that got to do with Marilyn's murder?" MacArthur, felt himself getting angry.

"I'm just trying to establish some kind of time line. Marilyn was believed to have died sometime between 8:30 and 10:30 pm. Did you go straight to the station when you left the Sprayberrys'?

"No, I went and had a pedicure. Of course, I went straight to the station," MacArthur said sarcastically.

"But you said that no one saw you at the station during that time?" Killingsworth asked.

"No, I didn't say that, you dumb ass. I said, no one saw me enter the station, but I met with Officer Peavey the same night. We went over the notes I had taken at the Sprayberrys and discussed some of the reasons I felt that this was not a murder/suicide."

MacArthur didn't realize it at the time, but actually it was the following night he and Rachel met and went over the notes of the murder scene. An honest mistake. This small, but very important oversight would prove to be the catalyst that would launch a full scale investigation with MacArthur Nowlin being named a prime suspect for the murder of Marilyn Hampton on the night of August 8th, 2005.

Detective Killingsworth picked up the pace in his questioning technique. He then asked MacArthur if he and Marilyn had ever had violent arguments. He responded by saying yes they had arguments, just like most all other couples, but he it never got physical.

"Are we done here?"

"I have one more question, had Marilyn told you it was over between you two?"

"Hell no, why would you ask that?"

"Just asking," Killingsworth replied, while he stood up to leave. As Killingsworth turned to go to the door, he noticed a spent cigar in the ash tray.

I didn't know MacArthur smoked cigars, Killingsworth thought.

"Sorry for all the questions MacArthur just doing ...."

"I know, just doing your job, now get the hell out of my apartment."

M. HARMON HALL

CHAPTER 17

The next morning Killingsworth dropped in on Rachel. He asked her if she and MacArthur had met in his office the night of the murders. She asked why the question. He brushed if off as following up on a minor detail. She told him she remembered they had gotten together the night after the murders to discuss the case.

Why would MacArthur lie about working with Peavey unless he had something to hide? Killingsworth thought.

The case against MacArthur was gaining momentum. Not only was a motive established, but Killingsworth now had evidence that MacArthur had the opportunity as well. From the time he left the Sprayberry residence, MacArthur could have driven out to the cabin and committed the murder and then driven back to the station. There was no one to substantiate his claim that he was in his office from sometime around 9:25 until midnight. He now had to prove that MacArthur had knowledge of Marilyn's rendezvous at the cabin on the night she was killed. This was not going to be easy. Only he and Marilyn knew of their secret meeting that was to take place. Or at least he thought so.

Is it possible that Marilyn called MacArthur after she and I planned our meeting? Killingsworth wondered. He knew the only way to find out was to locate Marilyn's phone. At this point in the investigation, her phone was nowhere to be found. Only the killer would have such information.

In spite of not liking MacArthur, Detective Killingsworth found it hard to believe that he could have actually killed Marilyn, but the evidence was mounting. He felt he had Marilyn's killer in his sights. It's never easy for one cop to turn in another, but in this case the facts could not be ignored. Besides,

Killingsworth would never admit it, but he was going to enjoy putting MacArthur away.

Had Chief Aldridge known about his personal involvement, he would have never put Killingsworth in charge of this investigation. Unfortunately, MacArthur was about to become the sacrificial lamb in the murder investigation of Marilyn Hampton.

CHAPTER 18

On Tuesday morning, four days after Marilyn's murder, Detective Killingsworth's first order of business was to find the exact location where she was murdered. It was obvious that she had been killed somewhere else due to the fact that there was no blood found near her body.

Killingsworth decided to drive out to the cabin where they were to have met. He wondered if she ever made it out there. He decided to go by her apartment and take a look around.

He went to the manager of the apartment complex and got him to open Marilyn's apartment even though he had a key. He did not want anyone to know. As he walked, in he noticed nothing out of the ordinary. The rooms were orderly and clean with no signs of a struggle. He saw the empty wine glass sitting on the coffee table. He inspected her bedroom and then went in to her walk -in- closet. Nothing out of the ordinary stood out. He made his way into the bathroom where he saw her make-up kit on the vanity. Everything appeared to look as it should. After an extensive walk through of her apartment it was obvious that she was not killed there.

Killingsworth left Marilyn's apartment with the same questions, but still no answers. He drove back by the station and picked up Detective Wright. They drove out to the cabin where he was to have met her on the night she was killed. He lied to Detective Wright about getting a tip that would take them to the cabin. He told Wright that it was probably just another phone call that would lead to nowhere, but all of the leads had to be checked out. He hoped that Wright bought his story.

Killingsworth noticed as he turned on to the dirt road that led to the cabin there were no tracks due the heavy rains from the past two nights. He casually told Detective Wright that he had been here before. He explained that he and some of his hunting buddies had stayed in the cabin while hunting for deer. He said it had been two years, no maybe three, since they had camped out here. Satisfied that he had given plenty of information as to how he knew of this place, he asked Wright to go around to the back door as he entered the front door. As he approached the front door he saw that it was not locked.

As he opened the front door leading into the cabin it was very obvious that a struggle of some sort had taken place. The lamp was knocked over, as well as the coffee table. On the kitchen counter was the key to the front door. Killingsworth looked to see if Detective Wright had seen it. Satisfied he had not, he put the key in his pocket.

He saw two wine glasses. Both appeared to have been wiped clean. Detective Wright was going through one of the two tiny bedrooms off the kitchen. The bed was untouched, with the bedspread neatly folded, and the pillow cases in place.

Both men made their way into the other bedroom finding the same situation with the bed undisturbed. When they walked back into the living room, Detective Wright noticed something that looked like wine spots on the floor. Killingsworth took a closer look and he told him that this could be blood. After taking a closer look, a large amount of blood stains were found on the sofa cushions that had been turned over.

Killingsworth remembered there had been a huge rug that covered a great deal of the living room area. His experience told him that this crime could have taken place on the sofa, and the killer most likely rolled Marilyn's body up in the rug. This would explain why there was almost no blood on the floor.

He told Wright that he thought the forensic squad should be summoned. Wright made the call into the station giving reasons why they believed the murder might have taken place in the cabin.

Within an hour the cabin was crawling with men and women going over every inch of the cabin. It would be determined later, that the "wine spots" were indeed blood. Days later, forensic determined that the blood found in the cabin matched Marilyn's.

It was a foregone conclusion, she most likely died in that small cabin on that fateful Friday night. Her killer then dumped her body at the site where she was discovered.

Detective Killingsworth interviewed her co-workers at the beauty salon where she worked and found that most of them were all too eager to report that she and Detective Nowlin had been arguing a great deal in the last few weeks.

He asked if Marilyn had ever mentioned Detective Nowlin had ever gotten physical in any of their arguments. No one could recall her ever mentioning that. He asked them to contact him if they should remember anything that might be important in finding out who killed Marilyn.

Before he left, he assured Marilyn's co-workers that he was not implying Detective Nowlin might have killed her. He told them that these were just routine questions when investigating a homicide. The truth was, he had done exactly what he intended to do, plant the seed that MacArthur could somehow be involved.

His next stop was down the street at the ladies dress shop where Marilyn often bought her clothes. Liz Thornton had worked there for almost 12 years.

She and Marilyn had become friends over the past year. When she shopped there, it was always Liz who waited on her. Killingsworth said he wanted to ask some questions about the investigation of Marilyn's murder. Liz asked if he had found the killer yet. He told her he had not, but there were some promising leads. He added that there were a couple of people of interest that he wanted to talk to. Of course, this was a lie. Liz answered the same questions he had asked the women in the beauty salon. Her answers were much like the women at the salon. However, she volunteered information that he wasn't prepared to hear.

"I think Marilyn was getting ready to break up with Detective Nowlin."

"What makes you think that?" Killingsworth asked.

"Well, she didn't just come out and say it, but I think she was seeing someone else. Marilyn told me she had met someone she liked, but they were only friends. I didn't believe her. I asked her if this mystery person would have anything to do with her breaking up with MacArthur. She just laughed and said I had been watching too many juicy soaps on TV."

"Did she tell you his name?" Killingsworth asked nervously.

"No, she didn't say."

"Thanks Liz, if you think of anything else, just give me a call at the station."

If there were any doubts that MacArthur could have been responsible for Marilyn's murder before, they had certainly disappeared now, Killingsworth said to himself. *Marilyn had probably told him it was over between them and she was moving on with her life.* He guessed that MacArthur couldn't handle this rejection and most likely went off the deep end and decided that if he couldn't have her nobody else would either. It was one of the oldest motivations for murder in the book, jealousy.

When he returned to his office, he saw the toxicology report from the results of the autopsy. There was evidence of alcohol in her blood system, but not at an extensive level. Nothing else was found. The report concluded that cause of death was a severed artery in the upper left portion of her chest located just above the left breast. The coroner suggested that the numerous other knife wounds were administered after she was already dead. That would be the same assumption with the severe slashing of her throat. There was evidence of rape as well. There were no traces of semen found on the clothing. Forensics concluded the attacker must have used a condom. What they would never know was that Marilyn had been raped a final time after she was dead. Only, the killer would know this.

Killingsworth decided to walk down to Rachel's office. He had seen her and Marilyn together over the past couple of months. The two had become friends after Marilyn began dating MacArthur. He knocked on her open door. She told him to come in.

"Officer Peavey, of course you know I'm in charge of the investigation of Marilyn's murder. I wanted to ask you a couple of questions if you don't mind."

"Sure, but I don't how I could be of any assistance. We had been friends for only a couple of months."

"I understand, I was just curious if she ever mentioned her relationship with MacArthur?"

"In what way Detective?"

"You know, if they were having any problems. If their relationship was going any further? A possible break up? Things like that."

"No, she never did. There was one time she told me they seemed to be arguing more lately."

"Did she say MacArthur was ever physical during these arguments?"

"No. Do you think Detective Nowlin had something to do with Marilyn's murder?" Rachel asked as she rose from her chair.

"Of course not, I'm just trying to rule him out as a person of interest. You know, we cops have to watch each other's back. That's all I'm doing." Killingsworth thanked Rachel for her cooperation and left.

Rachel saw through his attempt to pretend to clear MacArthur's name. She went straight to his office.

"Watch your back, sir. Killingsworth is snooping around asking questions about your and Marilyn's relationship. He just left my office. What a piece of work."

MacArthur made a few more calls before leaving for his apartment. He felt as though today had been a wasted day. No new evidence, too many loose ends, and his investigation was bogging down. He knew the next few days were critical if he was going to find the killer of the Sprayberrys. Like any good cop, he knew the longer the investigation went on, the chance of finding the killer diminished.

He drove by Marilyn's apartment for one last time on his way home. He thought how the next occupants would never know the beautiful woman that had once lived there. They would never know her fate.

CHAPTER 19

As was his pattern the past few nights, MacArthur slept very little. He showered, shaved, and left for his office at 7:00 am on Wednesday morning, the 13th of August. He and Rachel had an 8:00 am meeting.

Rachel walked into her office around 7:30 am. She went into the workroom where there was always a fresh pot of coffee. As she was pouring her first cup, MacArthur walked in to get his second cup.

"Good morning Peavey, today's a big day," MacArthur said in a friendly manner.

"Yes, it is. Sir, I was looking over some of my notes last night when I got a call from Michael Benjamin. He wanted to know why I had been asking people questions about him at Liberty College."

"What did you tell him?"

"I told him I was just asking routine questions about anyone who had any contact with Dr. Sprayberry at the College."

"What was his response?"

"He said he wanted to meet with me and discuss the death of his ex-professor. He said he knew he was probably a suspect because of the conflict between him and Dr. Sprayberry. He then said he had nothing to do with the death of Dr. Sprayberry. I told him I would call him back this morning. I wanted to talk with you first. Besides, if the Chief doesn't give us the green light, a conversation with Benjamin would be a waste of time."

"Yeah, definitely have another talk with him."

Detective Killingsworth knocked on MacArthur's office door around 10:30 later the same morning.

"MacArthur, we need to talk," Killingsworth said, as he stuck his head in the door.

"We talked last night and you got your interview. Unless you've come to arrest me we have nothing else to talk about."

"This is personal. There's something you should know about Marilyn." Killingsworth said very deliberately. "You see, she and I have been seeing each other for the last few weeks," he confessed.

"What do you mean, seeing each other?" MacArthur asked.

"We've been together. We've been meeting at the Inn on the outskirts of town. For what it's worth, she felt really bad about betraying you. She..."

"I don't believe you."

"It's true. She was going to tell you last weekend when you two were going on your getaway. She told me that it was over between you two, and that she thought she was falling in love with me."

MacArthur sat motionless. His first thought was to pull out his gun and shoot Killingsworth right between the eyes. Common sense said otherwise. His thoughts was jumping all over the place. In a matter of seconds, his range of emotions went from feeling betrayed, to blind anger, and revenge. *How could Marilyn think of dropping me for a loser like Killingsworth?* He wondered.

"MacArthur, I never intended for this to happen. Marilyn called me here at the station one night crying after one of your arguments. I met her for coffee as I listened to her vent. In spite of what you think, I didn't initiate this thing."

"You sure as hell didn't do anything to stop it. So, when were you going to tell me that you were sleeping with my Marilyn? This is all beginning to make sense. So you think she told me about you two, and I killed her? That's why all the questions last night. You bastard, you are going to try to pin Marilyn's murder on me. Just for the record Killingsworth, if I were going to kill anyone, it would have been you and not Marilyn," MacArthur said, as he stood up.

"Look MacArthur, you only have yourself to blame for Marilyn wanting to break up with you. You took her for granted. She never knew if you really cared about her, or if you were just having your fun. MacArthur, I have worked with you for a long time. You're a damn good cop, but you treat women like you own them. She would have never reached out to me if you had treated her with the respect she deserved."

"Killingsworth, you'd better stop there. Who the hell are you to tell me how to treat women? You were cheating on your wife with Marilyn and you stand here giving me a lecture on how to respect women. For the record asshole, it's none of your business how I treat women or anybody else. All this time, you and her have been playing me like a chump. Let me get this straight. You think that after I left the Sprayberry murder scene the night Marilyn was killed, I went looking for her? If that was the case, where would I have supposedly killed her? The place of her attack and murder hasn't even been determined yet."

"Actually it has. She was killed in the old hunting cabin off of Connell Road. The killer dumped her body at the park. Forensics confirmed that last night. I think she called you to tell you that it was over and she had found someone else. Then she told you she was meeting me at the cabin. That's when you followed her. I think you went ballistic, and in a fit of jealous rage, things must have gotten out of hand and you killed her."

"Do you really believe that story, Killingsworth? Why would I choose a place we had been before only to kill her there? That would have been stupid. Why am I even having this conversation with you?"

"MacArthur, you had the motive and opportunity to commit this crime. It will go easier on you if you do the right thing, and just confess what you did," Killingsworth said to MacArthur, as if he were some kind of common criminal.

"You're serious aren't you? You really think I did this. Let me tell you one thing, you damn well better be able to prove what you are suggesting. You and I both know I didn't do this. You're making the biggest mistake of your life if you go through with this nonsense. The consequences will be something you won't be able to handle."

"Are you threatening me, MacArthur?"

"You can call it whatever you want. I'm telling you here and now, you will regret going through with this," he said, as his eyes narrowed.

Tim Killingsworth turned and walked out of MacArthur's office. He decided it was time to fill Chief Aldridge in. It was important for the Chief to back him on this. He would show the facts of the case and let him decide for himself.

Around 11:30 am Rachel knocked on MacArthur's door. He motioned for her to come in.

"Sir, have you heard anything from the Chief?"

"No, not yet Peavey. I can't explain it all to you right now, but I'm the number one suspect in Marilyn's murder. I'll fill you in on the details after our meeting with the Chief. Just remember this. What's about to go down is nothing but bullshit."

MacArthur's phone rang, "Hello, yeah this is Nowlin. Be there in five minutes. The Chief is ready to see us."

Rachel and MacArthur walked down the hall that led to Chief Aldridge's office. As they passed by Detective Killingsworth's office, MacArthur resisted the urge to go in and beat the hell out of him.

"The Chief will see you now," his secretary said politely.

"Have a seat, Detective Nowlin and Officer Peavey," Chief Aldridge requested.

"I asked the assistant D.A. to sit in on our little meeting this morning. I hope you don't have a problem with that," he asked, not really caring if they did or not.

"No sir, not at all," MacArthur replied.

Chief Aldridge began, "The past two days I have reviewed your report and I've met with the medical examiner as well as the coroner. They originally felt that the Sprayberry case was a murder/suicide, as did Detective Killingsworth. However, based on the facts you have presented, this case will now be classified as a double homicide."

Chief Aldridge continued, "I want to remind you that our resources are limited. You will have only Officer Peavey assisting you due to the lack of manpower because of the other ongoing investigation. The Mayor has called expressing his wishes that we wrap this matter up as soon as possible. We don't want the citizens of Wilcox to panic."

MacArthur assured him that he would not stop until the killer or killers were apprehended. He thanked the Chief for allowing him to find the people responsible for the murders of Dr. Sprayberry and his wife. He and Rachel excused themselves and went back to his office.

"Let's get to work. Call Benjamin and have him come down to the station today if possible. I'm going to meet with Sean Sprayberry this afternoon if I can get him to come in. But, before we jump off into this case, you need to know something. Killingsworth is convinced I killed Marilyn. The two of them had been seeing each other for almost a month. He thinks I found out about it and killed her out of jealousy. You can walk out of here right now and I will understand. For what it is worth, I didn't kill her and I intend on finding out who did. However, any efforts on my part will have to be kept under wraps. I don't trust Killingsworth."

"Sir, I appreciate you sharing that with me, but it does not change my opinion of you. I don't believe for one second that you had anything to do with her death. I don't understand how anyone could believe that you would actually kill Marilyn. Does he have an axe to grind with you or something?"

"I honestly don't know Peavey, but I am not going to let him railroad me into a conviction. The real killer is out there somewhere, and I intend to find out who that is. Thank you for your vote of confidence. I think we are going to make a good team."

"However, I still want to make sure that we keep everything on a professional level, if you know what I mean?"

"Rachel, I get it! That's the way I want it too," MacArthur said earnestly.

It was less than an hour before the paper called to ask about the now double murder investigation. MacArthur gave the usual vague answers when asked about any potential suspects. He later told reporter Jo Kessler that there were some people of interest he wanted to talk with.

Jo Kessler had been with the *Wilcox Herald* for over six years. She was married and had two children in primary school. Her husband was the manager at the Goodrich Tire Store in Wilcox. Jo had a reputation as an honest reporter and one that would not give up her sources at any cost. She had worked with MacArthur on other cases, and had a great deal of respect for him. She knew what kind of investigator he was. He had always been straight with her.

MacArthur trusted Jo and respected her for her honest approach, as well as her integrity. He would give her interviews and keep her informed with certain information while refusing others. He was experienced enough to know that in some circumstances, a piece from the local newspaper might help an investigation.

Two years earlier, Jo had investigated a prominent citizen of Wilcox suspected of using his office for personal gain. In spite of threats, she was relentless in her approach to getting the facts. It was because of her perseverance that the grand jury indicted the individual. He was later convicted of bribery.

"Rachel, I want to go over a list of questions I'd like for you to ask Benjamin. Be sure he understands that we know about his connection with Sean Sprayberry. Of course, we really don't know anything other than what we saw at the restaurant. Make him think we know more than we do. Also, ask him about the alleged heated conversation in Sprayberry's office that his secretary told you about. Let's give him a chance to lie about it, and if he does then we may be on the right trail. See if he mentions his dismissal from the college and why he was dismissed. If he does talk about that ask him who turned him in. Of course, we already know that, but he doesn't know we do. Try and get a read on his attitude towards Dr. Sprayberry."

"Sir, I also want to ask him if he knows Sean Sprayberry, and if he does, what is his relationship with him?"

"That's an excellent question Rachel."

She left MacArthur's office and stopped by the restroom before going to pick up some lunch. The pain was worse today. She thought that she should get it checked out, but didn't have time now. She planned to see a doctor when this case was over.

MacArthur had a feeling that the key he found in the exterior door of the Sprayberrys home held some hidden meaning. Just what, he wasn't sure of. He could feel his adrenaline starting to flow. He looked forward to sitting down and talking to Sean Sprayberry. He was convinced that he knew more than he was letting on.

"MacArthur, I ran down to the sandwich shop and picked up some chicken salad and a grilled cheese. Which do you prefer?" Rachel asked.

"Thanks, I'll have the grilled cheese," MacArthur answered.

"By the way Rachel, don't forget to ask Benjamin if he has ever been to Dr. Sprayberry's home."

It was almost 12:45 when Michael Benjamin walked into the station. He was early. He asked to see Officer Peavey. Five minutes later she stepped out of the office to greet him. Benjamin noticed how professional she looked. He imagined how she might look without the uniform on, maybe in some tight jeans. *Maybe a "7"*, he thought to himself.

"Thank you for coming in today Mr. Benjamin."

"Call me Michael, please."

"Sure. Michael, I know you are probably very busy, so I won't take much of your time. If you will just follow me. Would you like something to drink? A soda, coffee, or water?" Peavey asked politely.

"Yes, I'd like some water please."

Benjamin noticed how neat her desk was it as he entered her office. She asked him to have a seat.

As they exchanged pleasantries, Rachel noticed how his demeanor was gradually changing. He looked to be more on edge than when they met out in the lobby. She also noticed a change in his body language. His shoulders began to drop slightly, his face was drawn, and he was constantly tapping his fingers on her desk.

"Michael, you don't have to answer any of my questions if you don't want to. You can leave anytime during our discussion. As we spoke on the phone yesterday, you indicated that you had a relationship with Dr. Sprayberry while you were enrolled at Liberty College. Is that correct?"

"Yes, that's right."

"How would you describe your relationship with Dr. Sprayberry?"

"Well, he was the Dean of the English department, and I was his intern while I was in graduate school. I was a candidate for a grant to study in Europe in the fall, but, I'm sure you already know, I was accused of plagiarism. This not only cost me the grant, but I was also expelled from school."

"Yes, I did know about that. It was Dr. Sprayberry that turned you in, was it not?"

"Yes, ma'am. It was. I tried to explain to him what happened, but he wouldn't listen. I tried to tell him that the thesis I submitted was only a draft and not the completed work. I went to see him in his office. We had words and he told me to get out. I admit I made some kind of a threat. I don't even remember what it was. His secretary must have heard me as I walked out of his office. I know this looks bad, Officer Peavey, but I swear I didn't mean what I said, and I certainly didn't kill Dr. Sprayberry or his wife."

"Michael, where were you on the night they were killed?"

"I was alone in my apartment. My girlfriend was coming over, but she called and said she wasn't feeling well and would have to take a rain check. That would have been on a Friday, I believe."

"Did anyone see you at all on that Friday night?

"No, I called in a pizza around 9:30 pm, but they screwed up my order I guess because no one ever delivered it. I watched a movie, and when it was over I went to bed. That would have been around 11:30 I'm guessing."

"Michael, do you know Sean Sprayberry?

He hesitated, then told Rachel he didn't. He said he knew Dr. Sprayberry had a son, but he didn't know his name. He said Dr. Sprayberry had spoken of him often, as well as his daughter. "I believe her name was Susan."

Rachel had caught Michael Benjamin in his first lie. She changed the direction of the questioning and asked, "Were you and Dr. Sprayberry friends before he turned you in for cheating?"

"I guess you could say we were. He nominated me as a candidate for the European study."

"Do you have any idea who might want to harm the Sprayberrys?"

"I really don't. I mean, everybody liked Dean Sprayberry."

"Michael, thank you for cooperating with me today. I do have one more question. Have you ever been to Dr. Sprayberrys' home?"

"No, I've never been in Wilcox before today."

Rachel noted, his second lie. She decided it was it was enough questions for now. "Thank you again for coming in. If you should think of anything that might help us find the killer, please give me a call." Peavey handed him one of her cards as he stood up to leave.

He assured her that he would get in touch if he had any information. As he left her office and walked through the main lobby, Michael Benjamin was proud of himself for the way he had responded to her questions. He convinced himself he definitely had the upper hand during the interview.

Rachel's delivery during the interview went well. She asked all of the right questions. She didn't confront Benjamin on the two obvious lies he told her. She conducted the interview as though she had been doing this for years. If she was the least bit nervous or anxious, it certainly didn't show. MacArthur would have been impressed.

The person who had been waiting anxiously, quickly answered the phone. "It was a piece of cake. I told you not to worry, didn't I? That lady cop was eating out of my hand by the time I left. Hell, man she was even coming on to me."

"You are so full of yourself. One day that cocky attitude is going to get you in trouble."

"How can you be so sure she was satisfied with your answers?" the voice on the other end of the phone asked.

"Look, I'm very sure, you keep your mouth shut and don't panic. You just let me work the plan. I've got everything under control."

"Did my name ever come up?" the voice asked, but never got an answer as Benjamin hung up.

MacArthur was wondering how the interview was going with Rachel and Benjamin when his desk phone rang, "Mr. Sprayberry is here to see you Detective Nowlin."

"Thank you Betty, let him wait a little while. In fifteen minutes send him in."

This was a trick MacArthur had used before when questioning a suspect or person of interest. He felt that this period of isolation was effective in the questioning process.

Rachel sat quietly at her desk going over the interview in her mind. She hoped she had asked the right questions. She took two pages of notes, not only recording what Benjamin said, but also her thoughts and reactions to his answers. MacArthur had taught her that a good detective keeps precise notes. He told her that during an interview not only were the facts important, but so was the attitude, demeanor, physical appearance, and level of cooperation of the person being questioned. Sometimes, what the person didn't say during an interview was equally important.

CHAPTER 20

"I'm sorry for the wait Mr. Sprayberry," MacArthur said, as he reached out to shake his hand.

"No problem, please, call me Sean."

"Sean, thank you for coming in. I know this must be a difficult time for you and your family. As you know, this case has now been ruled a double homicide. I can assure you and your sister that we are doing everything we can to find the person responsible for your parents' murder."

"Thank you Detective Nowlin, how can I help you today?"

"Do you or your sister have any idea why someone would want your mother and father dead?"

"My sister and I have discussed this these past few days and we can't think of anyone who might have wanted to hurt them," Sean Sprayberry said, as he pulled nervously at his collar.

"When was the last time you spoke with your parents?"

"I believe it was sometime after lunch on the day they were killed. My father had called me to remind me that he was going to be leaving town on Saturday morning instead of that Friday because his flight had been canceled. He told me he would be back on the following Wednesday. I think he said he was speaking at a writer's conference in Richmond.

"Was your mom going with him?" MacArthur asked.

"No, she was preparing to administer the annual standardized testing that her high school gives to the junior and senior students."

"Did she normally go with your father on these conferences?"

"Yes, she almost always goes," Sean replied.

"I'm sorry Detective, but what does that have to do with the murder of my parents?"

"Probably nothing, Mr. Sprayberry. I'm just trying to get as much information as I can regarding their daily routines. Sometimes this kind of information can turn out to be helpful."

"Were you and your sister aware that you and she stood to inherit $800,000 dollars upon your parent's death?"

"Yes, exactly what are you implying Detective?" Sprayberry asked, as if offended.

"I am not implying anything Mr. Sprayberry, just asking a question.

"According to our records, you and your wife filed for bankruptcy some weeks back, did you not?" MacArthur asked, turning up the heat.

"That's correct, but what does that have to do with this case?"

"Mr. Sprayberry, Sean, I'll be honest with you. I must say, the timing of this is quite a coincidence, wouldn't you agree?"

"No, I wouldn't. I don't like the implications being made here Detective. If you have something to say, then say it. Why don't you go ahead and ask me if I had anything to do with the deaths of my parents. The answer is no! I agreed to come in and answer your questions today, but I did not come in here to be insulted. Let me understand, you think because my wife and I are having financial problems, I would be involved in the death of my parents to get the insurance money?"

"Well, you have to admit Mr. Sprayberry, the question does come to one's mind when you are in the business I'm in sir. I certainly didn't mean to offend or insult you Mr. Sprayberry."

"Our meeting is over Detective. If you have any other questions, you can contact my lawyer."

"I understand Mr. Sprayberry, just one more question. Do you know someone by the name of Michael Benjamin?"

Sean Sprayberry chose not to answer and quickly stood up and walked out of MacArthur's office. MacArthur leaned back in his chair pondering the responses of Sean Sprayberry. He couldn't help but smile when he saw just how pissed Sprayberry had gotten. This was good, most people have a tendency to let their guard down when they become too emotional. The fact that he refused to answer the question about Michael Benjamin indicated to him that Sprayberry was holding back, but why? He rewrote his notes from the meeting. This was a practice he learned while just starting out as an investigator. After an hour he called Rachel and asked if she could come to his office so they could discuss their interviews.

Rachel gathered the ever growing file with her notes and headed toward MacArthur's office.

"Well, how did it go?" MacArthur asked.

"Benjamin was very sure of himself. He kept telling me that he realized how it looked due to the fact that he and Dr. Sprayberry had words, and that it was Sprayberry who had caused his dismissal from school. But, he assured me, he had nothing to do with the murders."

"Did you buy what he was saying?"

"Not all of it. He admitted that he threatened Sprayberry in his office and that the secretary had overheard it. When I asked if they had ever been friends he said they had. He said, in fact it was Dr. Sprayberry who had nominated him for the overseas grant and Dr. Sprayberry had invited him to intern within his department."

"Did he say he knew Sean Sprayberry?"

"He said he didn't, and when I asked him if he had ever been in Wilcox, he said no."

"Anything else?"

"Yeah, Benjamin said he was home alone on the night of the murders. His girlfriend was coming over, but she got sick and didn't make it. He seemed to have an answer for everything I asked. It was as if he had anticipated my questions."

"He's a smart guy, he probably did. Good work, Rachel."

"I didn't really get anything out of Sprayberry. He was very defensive from the beginning. When I mentioned the life insurance, he shut down. He seemed a little surprised when I asked about the bankruptcy filing. He started talking about getting "lawyered up" and stopped answering any other questions, especially the one about if he knew who Michael Benjamin was."

"How about checking out Dr. Sprayberry and his wife? See if there is something going on with them. You know, their personal lives. Was he involved with any of his students? Does she have any secrets? Were they happily married?"

"Detective, you know there are some marriages that do work. Not all husbands and wives cheat on each other. Without being too personal, I know about your failed marriage. I just think you see the world in a negative way."

"Are you through, Ann Landers? My personal life and how I view things has nothing to do with a murder investigation. Unfortunately, in this line of work we have to expect the worst in people. That is, underneath the façade of

143

a happily married couple you find lies, deceit, envy, and greed. The loving son or daughter doesn't want to wait for nature to take its course, so what do they do? They speed up the process. It happens all the time, Rachel. How else could we explain why people kill the ones they love?"

"I guess I just try to see the glass as half full, that's all sir."

"That's all well and good, but that attitude won't help you track down people who kill. You see, that's what this job does to you Rachel, you become cynical, develop a thick skin, and stop looking for the good in people. After a while it takes a toll on you. You wonder why I'm such a hard ass, now you know. I said before and I'll say it again, in many situations sometimes things aren't what they seem to be. You can't take things at face value if you are trying to solve a murder."

MacArthur knew he shouldn't have been so forthcoming with Rachel, but he felt as though now was as good a time as any to enlighten her on the realities of being a homicide detective. If she was going to pursue this line of work, she had better get used to the notion that there are bad people in this world. Many times people are not who you think they are. This was another example of his philosophy, everyone has a dark side.

Perhaps, she was beginning to understand what forces drive him to live a life of distrust in everyone he comes in contact with. She wondered if he trusted her.

If she could have read his mind, she would have seen that with the deceit and death of Marilyn, he was certain his spirit would never again be anything but cold. With the sleepless nights that followed Marilyn's death, he vowed that he would never again place his happiness and hopes in someone else. It was just too painful.

He couldn't remember who wrote the words, "No man is an island unto himself," but he was convinced that was bullshit. He would forever be an island unto himself, from now on.

"I'm sorry Rachel, I didn't mean to snap at you. Get back with me as soon as you find something. Meanwhile, I'm going to give Sean Sprayberry's sister, Susan a call."

After several tries, Susan Login finally returned his call. "Thank you for returning my call Ms. Login."

"Please, call me Susan. How can I help you Detective Nowlin? She asked timidly.

"Well, I'm sure by now you know we are investigating the death of your mother and father as a double homicide."

"Yes, my brother Sean and I had doubts all along. Our parents seemed so happy. I'm sorry Detective, you have questions for me? I don't have very long."

"Of course, I have to ask you what you were doing on the night of your parent's murder."

"My husband and I had dinner with some friends. We returned home somewhere around 10:00 pm. I bathed and went to bed, and my husband stayed up watching a movie. I don't remember what the name of it was."

"You have quite a memory Ms. Login. I can barely remember what I had for breakfast this morning," MacArthur replied, trying to make a joke.

"Because it was the night my parents were murdered, it's easy to remember what I was doing at the time. By the way Detective, you can check with the friends we went out with, if you don't believe me," she said sharply.

"Ms. Login, do you know of anybody that would want to harm your parents?" Did either of them ever bring up the subject?"

"Detective Nowlin, my parents were well respected and loved by everyone who knew them. I just find it hard to imagine why anyone would want to hurt them."

"I understand Ms. Login, but was there anyone at their workplace who was angry with either of them, or was there some kind of incident?"

"No, I don't know of any such things happening. I think I would have known because my mother and I talked almost daily," Susan Login volunteered.

"What was your brother's relationship with your parents?" Did your brother, Sean ever have any arguments with your parents?"

"I'm not sure I like where you are going with this Detective. If you think my brother could have had something to do with our parents' murder, you are very wrong. In fact, he and my father were exceptionally close. My brother idolized my father."

"I'm sure he did. One last question Ms. Login, did you know that you and your brother stood to inherit $800,000 at the death of your parents?"

"Detective Nowlin, are you suggesting that my brother or I killed our parents for money?"

"No I'm not, I'm just asking this and other questions in order to get to the truth. Actually, regardless of what you may think of me, I am trying to prove that neither one of you had anything to do with your parents' murder. I'm sorry if I offended you, but did you know?" MacArthur asked, knowing he was pushing the limit with her.

"Yes, I knew about the money. My father had shared with my brother and me their entire financial situation. Now, if you're finished insulting me Detective Nowlin, I really must go."

"That's all the questions for now. Thank you for your cooperation Ms. Login. I want to assure you that we are working around the clock to find the killer responsible for the death of your parents," MacArthur said sincerely.

Nothing in their conversation made him think she might be involved in some way in the murders of her parents. But, he wasn't ready to remove her from the list of possible suspects just yet.

He looked at his Timex and saw that it was almost 3:00 pm. He hadn't had any lunch. He decided to go over to the diner only three blocks away. Their blue plate special was a favorite of his.

As he entered the small restaurant, MacArthur looked for a table near the back. He always looked for a table near the back. The sign at the entrance read "suit yourself- seat yourself." MacArthur found a table and sat down. He was immediately approached by a familiar waitress bringing water.

"How's it going Detective? I haven't seen in you in a while," the friendly waitress sounded off.

"It's has been a while Sandy. How are you and the girls doing?"

"They're fine, you know, the twins are going into the second grade this year. It don't seem like they're are old enough, does it?

"No, but they grow up in a hurry, "MacArthur replied, already bored with this small talk.

He order the blue plate special with sweet tea and water. *I don't know why I order water, I never drink it?* MacArthur thought.

MacArthur saw Killingsworth and Chief Aldridge sitting together across the café. He pretended not to see them. He quickly finished his lunch and in minutes was in route back to the station.

He decided to take a detour and go by the cabin where Marilyn was supposedly murdered. As he drove slowly down the dirt road, he couldn't help but think that Marilyn didn't know it at the time, but this would be her last trip to the cabin. He pulled up to the cabin and got out of his car. He thought how terrible it must have been for her the last few hours of her life. He wandered around back and started walking nowhere in particular. He had been walking for about 15 minutes when he suddenly felt the presence of someone behind him. He slowly put his hand on his revolver and swung around prepared to defend himself.

"Damn, Peavey, that's a good way to get your head blown off." MacArthur fumed.

"I'm sorry sir, I thought you heard me walking up."

"What are you doing here?"

"I had a hunch you would be here. I can leave if you want to be alone; I understand."

"No, that's' fine. How did you find this place?"

Rachel told him that she'd overheard Detective Killingsworth talking to Detective Wright in the coffee room yesterday, about where Marilyn was believed to have been murdered.

"You were right MacArthur, Killingsworth does believe you killed Marilyn. He met with the Chief this morning. Chief's secretary and I are close.

She told me she heard Killingsworth mentioning your name in connection with Marilyn's death. She also told me that the Chief wanted to keep this quiet until there was enough evidence to bring an indictment against you.

"You mean the Chief thinks I could have done this?"

"According to her, the Chief didn't actually say if he agreed or not with Killingsworth's accusations," Rachel continued.

"So, they are sitting on their assess dialing in on me while the real killer is still out there," MacArthur said angrily. "The hell with them, did you find out any more about Michael Benjamin?"

"Still checking on his background. I should have all of the information no later than tomorrow," Rachel replied.

MacArthur suggested they head back to the cabin. He was still angry with her for sneaking up on him. He was thinking how easy it would have been to shoot her by accident, thinking she was a stalker.

Once they got back to the cabin, he decided to go inside and look around. He didn't see anything out of place, except that the bear rug was gone. The two of them talked for a while, exchanging ideas as to how this might have happened. MacArthur remembered that a few years back he and some of his hunting buddies used to shoot ducks on the small pond located about a mile behind the cabin. He suggested to Rachel they check it out.

Rachel was very comfortable in the outdoors having grown up with brothers and living on a farm. She actually loved the outdoors and kept reminding herself that she should get out more. After a long walk they reached the pond. MacArthur began to walk around the perimeter of the small pond not sure what he was looking for. When he reached the dam, he saw it.

M. HARMON HALL

CHAPTER 21

It had been five days since the Sprayberry murders and MacArthur and Peavey were not getting any closer to finding the killer. He was beginning to feel the pressure. He was still having trouble sleeping at night. If not for the Ambien, he wouldn't have gotten any sleep.

There had been a few calls into the station, but after following these bogus leads nothing was happening. Rachel was continuing to check out Benjamin. MacArthur decided it was time to lean on him. She made the call and he agreed to come in for a second interview.

Sean Sprayberrys' attorney had called to warn him that unless he had any real evidence against his client, he was to back off. He had no intentions of backing off. He was convinced that Sprayberry was not telling all he knew. As for as Susan, his sister, she was no longer a person of interest, as far as he was concerned.

MacArthur called Sean Sprayberrys' attorney, Maurice Penn, and requested that he and his client come in for some additional questioning. He knew he didn't have any legal grounds to force him to come in. He was counting on Sprayberry's arrogance and feeling of superiority that would tempt him to play a game of cat and mouse. It turned out his hunch was correct.

On the afternoon of August 14th, Sean Sprayberry and his attorney entered the police station agreeing to meet with MacArthur. The mood in the conference room was rather intense. Maurice Penn, Sprayberrys' attorney, was dressed in an expensive suit. With his hair graying around the temples, Penn gave the appearance of quiet the professional. His glasses were wire-rimmed and his cuff - links had his initials on them. MacArthur was sure that Mr.

Penn's services were not cheap. He wondered to himself, *if Sprayberry was in such financial difficulties, how could he afford to pay a high powered attorney like Penn?*

MacArthur spoke first. "Thank you, Mr. Sprayberry for agreeing see me again. There are a few questions I would like to ask. I know you are as anxious as I am to get this behind us."

"Detective Nowlin, I want to help anyway I can in this investigation. I am just as eager as you are to find my parent's killer or killers. Maurice has advised me, however, I don't have to answer any questions, just so we understand each other. I want to make it very clear, I am trying to cooperate."

MacArthur was taken aback by the sudden change in Sprayberry's attitude.

"Let's get straight to the point, Mr. Sprayberry. The ballistics report indicates a silencer was most likely used in the shooting. The gun found at the scene was the same gun that fired the bullets that killed your parents. Furthermore, this same gun belonged to your father, according to your testimony."

"Excuse me Detective, where are you going with this?"

"You see, I'm trying to understand why wouldn't the shooter bring and use his own gun. I don't think he would just decide the last minute to use the victims' gun, even if it was laying out in the open."

"Detective, it just might be possible that the shooter already knew where Dr. Sprayberry kept his gun," Penn added.

"That's exactly my point Counselor. That could only mean that someone told him where to find the gun or someone gave him the gun before he arrived that night. Either way, the shooter intended all along to use Dr. Sprayberry's gun that night. How else could he make it look like a murder/suicide unless he used Dr. Sprayberry's own gun?"

"Are you suggesting me or my sister could have had something to do with my father's gun and the shooter?" Sean asked quickly.

"I'm not suggesting anything Mr. Sprayberry. What I really want is for you to tell the truth. In our last meeting, I ask you if you knew Michael Benjamin. You never answered the question. Well, I'm asking again, do you know him or have you had any contact with Mr. Benjamin?"

Sean Sprayberry glanced at his attorney and started to speak, but before he could, MacArthur pounded his fist on his desk and said in a loud voice, "Why don't you stop playing games Sean and start telling the truth."

After a moment of silence, Sean Sprayberry said, "alright Detective, just hear me out, before you accuse me of stalling or lying to you."

"Sean you don't have to answer if you don't want to," Maurice interrupted.

"It's ok Maurice, I want to clear this up. I met Benjamin once while I was visiting dad at his office. He was doing some filing, I believe. A couple of weeks later Dad told me that he had discovered a problem with Benjamin's thesis. He didn't go into details, and I didn't ask any questions, because I hardly knew the guy. I guess it was about a week later, I get a call from Benjamin asking me if I could meet him at Toby's Bar and Grill for a drink. He said he wanted to discuss Dad's decision to review his case. Of course, this was a lie, but at the time I didn't have any reason to doubt what he was saying was true. I wasn't sure why he wanted to talk to me about the situation, but I agreed to meet him. I think it was on a Thursday afternoon."

"Sean, do you think you really need to go there?" Penn interjected.

"Yes I do, let me finish Maurice," Sean said quietly.

"After I sat down, he ordered a pitcher of beer. I excused myself and went to the restroom. Anyway, the last thing I remembered was sitting at the table with Benjamin and ordering another pitcher of beer. I have never been much of a drinker, but a few beers never affected me that way before. When I woke up the next morning, I was in Benjamin's bed. He was in the kitchen making coffee or something, I think. I got up and put my clothes on and walked into the kitchen where he was. I asked him how in the hell did I end up here in his apartment. He laughed and said it was my suggestion that we come back to his apartment. I told him I didn't believe that, and that he must have put something in my drink. He stopped smiling and told me maybe I would like to see the video he made last night, then I might believe him. I told him he would regret pulling this stunt. I walked out. A few days later, he called me on my private number and demanded $500 or he would send a copy of the video to my wife. I had no choice but to do as he asked.

"Detective Nowlin, I swear I have never done anything like that before. You see, he was setting me up from the start. But, until I have proof that such a video does not exist, I have no choice but to pay him."

MacArthur continued to look at Sprayberry without any expression on his face.

"He told my father a couple of weeks later, thinking that he could threatened to go public with this video and my father would dismiss the charges of plagiarism and would allow him to be re-admitted at Liberty University. My father was very angry. He threatened Benjamin and told him he didn't believe him and that he would not be threatened nor intimidated. My father called his bluff."

"Did your father believe you?" MacArthur asked.

"Yes, he did. He told me he didn't think for one second anything happened. He was convinced it was all a ruse to get him to change his mind about Benjamin's dismissal."

"Sean, I think that's enough for one day," Sean's attorney stated.

"No Maurice, I want to get this over with today. I want Detective Nowlin to know I did not have anything to do with my parents' death."

"Yes, I lied about knowing Benjamin. I know I shouldn't have. I was afraid that what I just told you would become public."

"Let me see if I've got this right, so you believe Benjamin killed your mother and father so that he could continue to blackmail you? Is that what you are saying?"

"Yes, that is exactly what I'm suggesting Detective," Sean answered quickly.

MacArthur asked, "what about the brief meeting you had with Benjamin last week at the restaurant. You know, when you got into his car while your family was inside. What was that all about?"

"That is when he told me if I paid him $10,000 in cash, he would give me the one copy of the video, and all of this would go away."

"And you believed him?" MacArthur asked jokingly.

"Detective, we're done here. I think it is very clear that my client made a mistake, but it did not involve murder," Maurice Penn said, as he got up from his chair. "I trust you will honor my client's request for discretion in this matter, for obvious reasons."

"Mr. Penn, I will do all that I can to keep this under wraps, but I'm not going to make you a promise that I might not be able to keep.

"Detective, I'm not trying to tell you how to run a murder investigation but..."

"Then don't Counselor," MacArthur countered.

"Sean, I do have one more question before you go. Do you have a key to your parents' home?"

Sean Sprayberry looked at his attorney as if to ask if it would be ok to answer. Penn nodded and gave his approval, after all it was a harmless question.

"Yes, Detective I do. Actually, I did, but it seems I misplaced the key a few weeks ago. I have been meaning to replace it, but I just haven't gotten around to it. Why do you ask?"

MacArthur responded nonchalantly "No particular reason. Do you know if anyone else might have a key?"

"My sister has one, and my parents' neighbors, the Daytons, have one, I believe."

"Thank you again, gentlemen for your cooperation. If you should think of anything else, please give me a call," MacArthur concluded.

As Sean Sprayberry and his attorney Maurice Penn walked out of his office, Rachel spoke for the first time.

"Wow, what a story, do you buy all of that?"

Before he answered, he stood up and poured himself a fresh cup of coffee, loosened his tie, and pulled off his shoes.

"Just for the sake of argument Rachel, let's suppose this bigger than life story is true. That might give Benjamin a motive for killing Dr. Sprayberry."

"I'm not sure I follow you MacArthur."

"Benjamin knew that daddy Sprayberry would expose him for the blackmailer he was, so he decided to get rid of him and his wife. He could have known his pigeon, Sean, would come into a lot of money with the death of his parents. That would ensure him of getting his money from Sean, give him the blank video, which probably never existed anyway, and disappear. He knew Sean would never go to the authorities, because it would be too scandalous."

"I suppose it's possible it could have gone down like that, but it does seem to be one hell of a stretch. Then, there's the problem with the lost key. He said he had forgotten to replace it. Who forgets that? "

"I agree, Rachel. That might explain how the "extra" key was found in the lock at the back door. He could have given it to the killer, and when the killer left, he forgot to take the key with him."

Rachel didn't know about the key being found in the door on the night of the murders, in fact no one did except MacArthur. She looked at her watch and said, "I'm going to run to my office to check for messages. I'll be back in a few minutes."

MacArthur nodded as he dove back into his notes.

Sean Sprayberry unlocked his car and sat down in the driver's seat. He and his attorney sat for a while without any words being spoken. Sean backed out of the parking lot and turned on to highway # 14. He finally broke the silence. "What do you think's going to happen now Maurice?"

"Well, I'm not sure he believed your story of blackmail. You have to admit Sean, most people might find that hard to believe. We're going to have to get Benjamin to come clean to the Detective, otherwise Nowlin's going to continue to be on your heels.

It's clear he has no other real suspect; he's reaching at this point in the investigation. Once he finds your story to be true, I think we will be in the clear."

Sean suddenly pulled off of the road and came to a quick stop, "Maurice, do you think I had something to do with this? You've known me for a long time, do you think I'm capable of doing such a terrible thing?"

"No, I don't Sean, if I did, I wouldn't be here now," Maurice responded.

"What should I do next, Maurice? Where do we go from here?"

"Nothing, let's see what Nowlin does first. It's my guess, he'll be contacting Benjamin before we can get back to Silver Springs. Of course, Benjamin will deny the whole thing unless you can provide Nowlin with some proof of Benjamin's blackmail. Right now, it's his word against yours." Penn assured him that it would all work out.

Satisfied, Sean put the car in gear and pulled back on the highway. There was very little conversation between the two on the trip back to Silver Creek.

Rachel returned to MacArthur's office some twenty minutes later. He continued to go over possible scenarios involving the "lost" key. She agreed that since there was no sign of forced entry, having a key to the back entrance would be a likely choice to enter the home undetected.

Rachel asked MacArthur, "Could Sean Sprayberry have hired someone to kill his parents? With his financial problems, perhaps he was desperate enough to kill his parents for the insurance money he and his sister would receive."

"It's very possible Rachel, but we've got to be careful that we overlook anything."

MacArthur continued with his theory on how the killings could have taken place. He told Rachel that the killer most likely used a key to let himself in. Then he quietly went upstairs and found Dr. Sprayberry asleep and probably heard Mrs. Sprayberry in the bathroom. He then could have shot Dr. Sprayberry while he slept using a silencer and then went in the bathroom and found Mrs. Sprayberry in the bathtub and shot her. He could have gone back into the bedroom and moved Dr. Sprayberrys' body on the bed to make it look as though he shot himself. MacArthur continued his theory by explaining that the shooter could have placed the suicide note on the night stand to make it look like a murder/suicide.

Rachel added that the killer had to have known the nighttime habits of the Sprayberrys. But, how could he know unless he was close to the family or if someone had told him, when the best time to enter the house would be.

As they exchanged different scenarios, MacArthur and Rachel kept coming back to Sean Sprayberry. In the days to come, Rachel would discover that Sean Sprayberry had a gambling problem. He owed several thousand dollars from placing bets on sporting events with a well-known bookie. His wife had no idea. He had been gambling away mortgage payments as well as two car loans at the bank. They were behind on their child's tuition fee at the private school where she attended. Their lake house was in foreclosure, and their home was about to be within the next few months, unless he got caught up in making the payments. Why hadn't he bothered to tell MacArthur about the foreclosure of his lake house? His financial records would show he was deeply in debt and behind on his car loans at the bank as well as his house mortgage. It was just a matter of time before Sean Sprayberry would lose everything unless he could get his hands on a large sum of money. He was a desperate man, but was he desperate enough to have his parents killed?

For now, he was definitely MacArthur's number one suspect, but Benjamin couldn't be ruled out either. MacArthur knew he needed a break in this case that was rapidly becoming cold. He knew he needed more than just speculation to arrest Sean Sprayberry for the murder of his parents. He needed proof. The next morning a much needed break would come.

Basil Cutler asked to speak with the person in charge of the Sprayberry murders. He told MacArthur he lived in the same neighborhood as the Sprayberrys. Cutler said that he didn't really think much about it at the time the officers were asking questions in the neighborhood, but he now remembered seeing a late model car cruising along the street as he was taking his dog for a walk. He said the car looked out of place for the neighborhood.

MacArthur asked him to come in and give a statement. He agreed to do so. Cutler said he didn't know what kind of car it was, but he noticed the license plate because it was not local. He said at the time he had no reason to get the tag number. When MacArthur asked the color of the car and if there was anything unusual about the car, the caller said he thought it was black or maybe dark blue. He said there was one thing that did catch his attention, the car had one taillight out.

A few days later another caller had reported he noticed a dark colored car earlier that day cruising through the neighborhood.

It wasn't much to go on, but it was something. With no license plates, or make of the car it was like finding a needle in a hay stack, MacArthur thought.

After the incredible story Sean Sprayberry just told, MacArthur decided that the next order of business was to get Benjamin back in the office ASAP. He would call Benjamin himself.

MacArthur was surprised when Michael Benjamin agreed to come in for a second interview.

The investigation was now on its seventh day since the Sprayberry murders when Michael Benjamin walked into the Wilcox Police Department. He appeared to be very calm and self-assured as he had been during his first visit with Rachel.

MacArthur didn't waste any time.

"Mr. Benjamin, when you met with officer Peavey a few days ago, you told her you didn't know Sean Sprayberry personally. Is that true?"

"Yes, that is true. But, of course you wouldn't be talking to me now if you didn't already know I had lied to her, now would you Detective?"

"You let me ask the questions, Benjamin," MacArthur snorted.

Why would you lie about knowing him? Did you two have any kind of relationship?

"I'm not sure I know what you mean when you say relationship? I met him in his dad's office one day and we started talking about biking. I told him I really enjoyed the sport. He said he and a few friends went biking on Saturdays and he asked if I would like to go. I did join them on a couple of Saturdays, but Detective that is the only contact I ever had with Sean Sprayberry. I lied to the lady officer because I was afraid that my name might be mixed up in the murders of Dr. Sprayberry and his wife."

"That's not good enough Benjamin. Why don't you tell me the real reason you lied about not knowing Sean Sprayberry."

"Detective, I swear that's the truth. I was scared. Everybody knew what happened at school and that it was Dr. Sprayberry that turned me in. When he and his wife were murdered, I was afraid I would be blamed," Michael Benjamin said, as he appeared to be on the verge of tears.

MacArthur watched Benjamin's mannerisms closely. He appeared to be truly frightened and upset.

"So Michael, are you still milking money from Sean Sprayberry for that one night out on the town?"

"I don't know what you are talking about Detective."

"I think you do Michael. Did you and Sean meet for drinks and end up back at your apartment for a slow dance?"

"No way Detective…"

"And you don't know anything about a video or blackmail?" MacArthur pressed forward, trying to get a response from Benjamin.

"Look Detective, I don't' know what it is you are trying to suggest, but I have never met Sean Sprayberry for drinks and he has never been to my apartment. If you don't believe me, I'll be glad to take a polygraph to prove I'm telling the truth." Benjamin's swagger and confident look had vanished.

"Who told you all of this bullshit? Was it Sean Sprayberry? You know what he's doing, don't you? He's trying to make it look like I killed his parents. Well, I had nothing to do with their murders. It's him you had better be looking at. I just told you why I lied about knowing Sean Sprayberry. What is it you want me to say? You want me to confess to killing the Sprayberry's? Well, I'm not, because I didn't have anything to do with their murders."

"Michael, I met with Sean and his lawyer and he tells me quite a different story. He says you slipped something into his drink and went back to your apartment and he woke up the next morning in your bed. He said there was a video, and you were threatening to expose his indiscretion, unless he paid you $500 a week."

"That's ridiculous Detective. Can't you see what he's doing? You've got to believe me, he's lying about everything."

"I'm not sure what the hell I believe right now," MacArthur said, looking confused. "I do know one thing, somebody is lying. And you can bet your ass I'm going to find out who. What about the meeting you two had at the restaurant on the outskirts of Wilcox?"

"I called him to ask for the money I had loaned him. He told me to meet him at the restaurant and he would settle up with me. But, when he got into my car, he gave me some lame excuse and promised to pay me within the week. He still hasn't paid me. Sean Sprayberry runs with some shady characters. I know this because one afternoon all of us were riding our bikes just outside of Silver Creek and a black Cadillac pulled along beside us. Sean motioned for us to take a break. While we were standing beside the road, I could hear Sean and some man in a black suit having a conversation. I couldn't hear everything that was being said. The man was very animated and appeared to be angry. I heard him tell Sean he wanted his money."

"That's interesting Benjamin, but it has nothing to do with what we are talking about here today," MacArthur replied.

"Do I need an attorney?" Michael asked, looking nervously at his watch.

"I don't know, do you? That's enough for now Benjamin, but don't leave the area," MacArthur warned.

Benjamin stood up to leave and said, "Detective, regardless of what you may think of me, I didn't kill the Sprayberrys." After making that declaration for a second time, Michal Benjamin walked out.

MacArthur remembered one of the neighbors saying they saw a dark colored car in the neighborhood hours before the killings. He decided to walk to the window and watched as Benjamin unlocked his car. It was a dark green Ford sedan. As he drove out of the parking lot, he could see that one of the taillights was out.

MacArthur picked up the phone to find reporter Jo Kessler from the *Wilcox Tribune* on the other end.

"How's it going Detective Nowlin? Got any info for me yet?" Kessler asked.

"How are you Kessler?" MacArthur asked, but not giving her enough time to answer. "I need a favor, off the record of course. I need you to do some checking on Sean Sprayberry and a young guy named Michael Benjamin. I'm not sure what I'm looking for, but there could be a connection," MacArthur lied.

"What's in it for me Detective?"

"How about information? That is, I'll give the exclusive when the time is right. You know this case is beginning to stir up a media storm. I think an exclusive story would certainly add to your resume, don't you?"

"I'll see what I can do," Kessler replied with a hint of enthusiasm.

"Of course, this is just between you and me."

"Of course."

MacArthur hung up and immediately dialed Detective Wright.

"Waddell, what's going with Killingsworth's investigation?"

"Hi Uncle MacArthur, how are you holding up? Got any good leads on the Sprayberry murders?"

"I'm fine, the investigation is coming along pretty well."

"Killingsworth told me this afternoon he's going to try and get a search warrant for your apartment."

"Waddell, make sure you are with him if he gets that warrant. What's he looking for? I don't want him planting something. You understand?"

"Yes sir."

"Thanks Waddell, let me know ASAP about the search warrant or any physical evidence he claims to have."

"Will do."

As MacArthur hung up the phone, he couldn't help but think that Killingsworth might go so far as to actually plant some evidence that would strengthen the case against him.

It was getting late and he was getting hungry. He called Rachel and asked her if she had eaten. She said no, and suggested they get together and share notes. MacArthur agreed, he suggested he pick up a pizza and meet at his apartment. Rachel did not answer right away, not so sure this was a good idea. After some seconds, she told him she would meet him in 30 minutes.

This was the first time Rachel had been in MacArthur's apartment and she felt a bit uneasy at first, became more comfortable as they began to share information and pizza.

"What do you make of the two stories that Sean and Michael are telling? It's obvious one of them is lying about the so-called affair."

"I don't know, but something tells me Michael Benjamin is telling the truth."

"What is it that makes you so sure Benjamin is telling the truth and Sprayberry is lying?"

"I don't know, just call it a woman's intuition."

"Well, I sure as hell don't know a thing about a woman's intuition or much less what they are thinking most of the time."

"MacArthur, think about it for a moment. Why would Michael lie knowing there was concrete evidence of the affair? Wouldn't it be easier to prove he did not, rather than prove he did have a one-nighter with Sprayberry?"

"Makes sense Rachel, but look what Sprayberry has to lose if he is telling the truth. It just doesn't make sense that he would lie about something that could ruin his reputation and possibly his marriage. What if Sprayberry is trying to provide a motive for Benjamin to murder of his parents? What if he is lying to divert suspicion away from himself?" MacArthur asked, as he finished the last piece of pizza and washed it down with a Mountain Dew.

"True," Rachel said.

He excused himself as he disappeared toward the back of his apartment. Rachel studied his apartment and found it to be almost what she imagined. That is, it was certainly MacArthur's style, simple with no fancy trimmings, a few cheap paintings with dull furniture that didn't match the color of the room, and a coffee table made of wood. There were very few books on the shelves, a few magazines- *True Detective, Sports Illustrated, and Guns.*

When he came back into the room, Rachel asked where the bathroom was. He gave directions as she left the room.

MacArthur was glad to have some company. He was tired of eating all of his meals alone.

As she returned, she noticed that the sink was filled with dirty dishes and old pizza boxes were stacked up on the counter. From the looks of the kitchen, she guessed that there probably hadn't been a cooked meal for quite a while.

They continued to go back and forth on possible scenarios for almost an hour. One thing they did agree on was the murders were done by a professional. The lack of any trace evidence found at the murder scene certainly suggested someone knew what they were doing and that it had been planned very carefully.

At this point in the investigation, the only real suspects were Michael Benjamin and Sean Sprayberry. Were they guilty of having tunnel vision? MacArthur wondered. These two were the only ones that might have a motive to hire someone to kill the Sprayberrys.

He surmised that Benjamin could have hired someone to kill Dr. Sprayberry out of revenge. After all, it was Dr. Sprayberry that was responsible for his dismissal from school. On the other hand, Sean could have had his parents murdered for the insurance money. Both agreed, that at this time these two theories were all they had to go on.

It was almost 11:00 pm when Rachel told MacArthur it was time for her to get home and check on her cat, Chester. He offered to walk her to her car, but she said it wasn't necessary and thanked him anyway.

He studied the notes a little while longer, perhaps to try and come to some real conclusion on this case, or was it because he dreaded the idea of going to bed knowing he would probably not get very much sleep?

MacArthur reached over and switched off the light that was on the table beside his bed. As he slipped off to sleep, his last thought was about that damn key.

The next morning MacArthur rode out to the cabin where Marilyn was murdered and walked down the dirt road behind the cabin that led to the small secluded pond. When he reached the pond he walked straight to the dam. There he saw what looked like an area where the grass leading to the edge of the pond had been disturbed. It was clear an automobile had likely gone into the pond. He decided not to tell anyone about this until he could investigate without Killingsworth knowing, or anyone else for that matter. He was very confident the car submerged under the water would be Marilyn's. He wanted to search the car for evidence himself, not trusting the findings of Killingsworth or any other officers. But, this would have to wait for now. One thing was for sure, the killer or killers had to be local. Who else would have known about the small secluded pond a mile behind the cabin? MacArthur made the long walk back to the cabin. He got into his car and drove down the dirt road that led back to the highway. Before, going back to the office he stopped and got a cup of coffee and donuts.

As he drove towards the station, he noticed the "Welcome to Wilcox "sign. It proudly stated that Wilcox was the friendliest city in the South. He couldn't help but smile, as he thought how he could use a friend about now.

When he entered the station he noticed the sights and sounds that were normal for most any morning with the activities being rather routine. To a visitor, this was anything but routine.

MacArthur recognized the man sitting on the bench waiting to be booked for public drunkenness. He heard another man explaining how his wife had keyed his new car. As he walked past the information desk he heard the receptionist speaking to someone on the phone. She was trying to explain that they would have to come in and give a statement as to how their neighbor's dog was keeping them up at night due to his constant barking.

How easy to resolve these kinds of problems in comparison to finding out who killed someone and why, thought MacArthur.

As he began to look at the messages on his desk, he remembered what Sean Sprayberry had told him the first time they met. Sprayberry mentioned he and his father were very close. But, when talking to some neighbors and some of the relatives, that was not the case. One of Sean's aunts reported that at a reunion two years back, Sean and his father had gotten into a heated argument in the presence of everyone there. The aunt couldn't remember what it was about.

Around 10:00 that morning, MacArthur received a very strange and interesting call. The caller suggested that the police might want to talk to the principal at the school where Mrs. Sprayberry worked. There were rumors of grades being changed for athletic eligibility purposes.

What does that have to do with the murder of Mrs. Sprayberry and her husband? MacArthur asked himself, sure this was just another crank call. After hanging up, he made a note to check this out. This was probably a waste of time, just as so many other leads had been, but he knew every lead had to be checked out, regardless how trivial it may seem.

MacArthur was going over his notes again, when Rachel called to tell him that Michael Benjamin had called her about ten minutes ago, and said he was moving back to his parent's home in Charlotte. He said he no longer had a future in Silver Creek, and that he was going to try and straighten out his life.

She told him that she had asked Michael if he had been in the Sprayberry's neighborhood on the day of their murders. He said he had been there. He told her he was going to Dr. Sprayberry's home to apologize and try to make peace with him.

"But, he said he never got the courage to actually stop, so he turned around and went back to Silver Creek without ever talking to or seeing Dr. Sprayberry."

"It would explain the sighting of his car on the same street earlier that evening," Rachel answered. "He didn't know he had been spotted in the neighborhood. Why would he volunteer that information that could possibly incriminate him? MacArthur, I don't think he's our man," Rachel said with confidence.

"If he's not involved, then that only leaves Sean Sprayberry," MacArthur replied, in the form of a question.

"It would seem so, unless we are overlooking others who might have a reason to kill the Sprayberrys. How do we get Sean Sprayberry to crack? He's too smart to let down his guard. If he did have his parents killed, we need to find who he hired to carry it out. That's not going to be easy, without some major stroke of luck."

"You're right Rachel, but there is no such thing as a perfect murder. There is always a mistake. We just have to dig deep enough to find the mistake made by our gun-for-hire, or his employer. I think we should turn our attention to possible connections of undesirables that Sean may have known. Somebody knows who made the connection between the shooter, and the one that hired him."

MacArthur sat quietly then said to Rachel, "Let's explore every possible link between Sean Sprayberry and his associates. Go all the way back to his childhood and see if a connection shows up. I know it's a long shot, but right now it's all we have."

CHAPTER 22

Detective Tim Killingsworth wasted very little time as he began to try and fit the pieces of the puzzle together. He was still convinced MacArthur had hired someone to kill Marilyn, besides who else would want her dead? She had no known enemies in Wilcox, nor did her past suggest she was running from something or someone.

There was that incident with Sonny Barrett a year ago. But the idea that he killed Marilyn just didn't seem to fly. Barrett was a loser no doubt, but was he a killer? Killingsworth did not think so. However, he would like to talk to him and clear his name once. The problem was that Sonny was nowhere to be found. Since his last phone call made to MacArthur, no one had seen him in Wilcox, or anywhere else for that matter.

There were a stream of anonymous phone calls coming in to the station. This was not unusual in a murder investigation. Most were made by people who had nothing better to do than try and get involved in a murder investigation. But, as Detective Killingsworth would soon find out, there is always that chance that information given could lead detectives on the right trial of the killer.

"This is Detective Tim Killingsworth, how may I help you?"

The caller on the other end of the line spoke with a muffled voice. He couldn't tell if the caller was male or female. "I know who killed that pretty woman found in the park two weeks ago. I also know that her phone was not found with the body. Is there a reward in this case?"

"Right now there is not," Killingsworth replied.

"Well, I was told the phone belonging to the woman who was killed can be found in Detective Nowlin's apartment. His cleaning lady told my friend she saw a phone in a drawer the last time she cleaned his apartment."

"How do you know all of this? Who is this?" Killingsworth asked, clearly interested now.

"That's all I got to say." The caller hung up.

There was not enough time to put a trace on the call to determine where the call was coming from. He decided to follow up on this tip. He needed to find MacArthur's cleaning lady and hear what she had to say. After making a few calls, he got the name and phone number of Gladys Horn. She had been cleaning other tenants in the apartment complex where MacArthur lived. She agreed to come in and answer some questions. Killingsworth told her not to mention her visit to the station to anyone, especially MacArthur.

The next day, Gladys Horn walked into the Wilcox Police station and asked for Detective Tim Killingsworth.

"Good morning, Ms. Horn thank you for coming in today." Killingsworth asked her to have a seat and asked if she would like something to drink. Gladys Horn was too nervous to drink anything right now. *She would love to have a cigarette about now*, she thought.

"What is this all about Detective?" Is my son in trouble again?"

"No ma'am, Ms. Horn this isn't about your son. Do you work for Detective MacArthur Nowlin in the Main Street Apartment Complex?"

"Yes, I do. Well, I do for now, but if he don't give me a raise, I won't be working for him much longer. He is such a cheap ass man. I never seem to do good enough for him. He is always leaving me notes to clean this, clean that, and I don't, cause it ain't my job. If he paid me more, I might do more."

Trying to sound sympathetic, Killingsworth said he certainly could understand where she was coming from. He asked her how long she had been cleaning his apartment. She told him over two years now.

"Do you remember seeing a pretty woman there from time to time?"

"Hell yes, that pretty woman was Ms. Marilyn, I heard she was "kilt" a couple of weeks ago. She was a very nice lady. Sometimes, she would be there when I came in to clean early in the morning. She was always very friendly. I always wondered why she put up with that Detective Nowlin."

"Did Detective Nowlin ever mention her death to you?"

"Naw, we didn't never talked to one another. I just did my job and got the hell of there. To tell you the truth Detective, I really don't like him."

"I can tell. Do you know who might have had anything against Ms. Hampton?" Killingsworth continued.

"I don't know why anyone would want to hurt her, like I said, she was a very nice lady."

"Since her murder, have you noticed anything unusual in the apartment? You know, anything missing or something there that was not there before she was killed?"

"Somebody else asked me the same question a few days back. Can't remember their name."

Killingsworth thought it was strange that someone else had inquired about what she may have or have not seen since Ms. Hampton's murder. He decided it wasn't important, so he dismissed it. He was hoping she would collaborate the caller's claim that she had seen a phone in a drawer in his apartment.

Ms. Horn told Detective Killingsworth she had not cleaned Detective Nowlin's apartment since Ms. Marilyn died.

"When was the last time you saw Marilyn Hampton?" Killingsworth felt as though she was lying, but he couldn't be sure.

"Let's see, it would have been on the Tuesday before she got "kilt"? I cleaned his apartment every other Tuesday. You don't think Detective Nowlin had anything to do with Ms. Marilyn's murder do you? Like I said, I don't like him, but I can't see why he would do something like that. But, it's like they say, you just don't never know about people."

"That's for sure. Well, I'm just trying to prove that he didn't have anything to do with it," Killingsworth lied.

Gladys Horn looked at the card he had given her with his name and phone number on it. She opened her huge purple purse and stuck it in a side pocket.

As Detective Killingsworth stood, he said to Ms. Horn, "Oh, there is one more thing Ms. Horn, please be sure you do not mention this to anyone."

Ms. Horn assured him she would not, and then got up from her chair, said goodbye, and walked slowly down the stairs that emptied into the main lobby of the police station.

He was disappointed she had not mentioned the phone. He decided to check it out anyway.

CHAPTER 23

MacArthur was beginning to feel the pressure detectives feel when a case is beginning to slip away. He knew with every day that passed, the likelihood of solving this murder would become more difficult. Soon it could end up as a cold case that would be put back on some shelf.

Something was not right, the case against Sean Sprayberry was too neat, too obvious. MacArthur was not as confident as Rachel that Sean Sprayberry had his parents' killed. He couldn't say why, he just had that old familiar gut feeling.

Up until now, the two people to benefit the most from the death of Dr. Sprayberry and his wife were the son and daughter. But, his experience taught him that cut and dried cases aren't always what they seem.

MacArthur decided to go back to the very beginning of the investigation. Perhaps, he had overlooked something. After spending several hours at his desk, he decided to take a break and get some lunch, even though it was almost 3:00 in the afternoon. He settled on MacDonald's and ordered a Big-Mac with fries and a Doctor Pepper. He sure as hell didn't want any company. After getting his order, he drove across the street and parked in the parking lot of the Wilcox Methodist Church. Somewhere midway through his lunch, he suddenly remembered a particular phone call about possible grading violations at the local high school. *What would that have to do with the Sprayberry murders?* He said to himself. Without finishing his sandwich, MacArthur hurried back to his office. He was not sure he had made any notes concerning this tip. Like so many others, it seemed a waste of time. He finally found the note with a number of the caller. He dialed the number. He was about to hang up, when someone answered.

"Hello, this is Detective MacArthur Nowlin of the Wilcox Police Department. I was looking through some of my files and I noticed where someone had called from this number into the station concerning possible grading violations at the high school. Who am I talking to?"

There was silence on the other end of the line. Finally, after several seconds a lady spoke.

"Detective Nowlin, it probably has nothing to do with the murder of Ida Sprayberry and her husband. On the day she and her husband were killed, we had lunch together. I teach at Wilcox High, where she worked. We had been co-workers and friends for several years." The caller continued, "On the day they were killed she seemed very nervous and distraught. I asked her what was wrong, she said there was something going on with some of the students' grades that was not right. I asked her what she meant, but she wouldn't say. She did say she may have stumbled on something that she was not supposed to see."

MacArthur asked the caller's name, but the person refused to give him her name.

"Detective, you may want to speak to the other two counselors at the high school. I have to go now." The caller hung up without saying anything else.

MacArthur buzzed Rachel, but got no answer. The officer on duty at the desk said she had stepped out about 30 minutes ago.

Just as she was walking into her office the phone rang.

"Rachel, do you have the names of the two counselors that worked with Ms. Sprayberry at Wilcox High School?"

"I don't think so, but I will get them for you. When do you want this information?"

"I'd really like to talk to them as soon as possible. I'm not sure if they can tell me anything that we don't already know, but it's worth a shot. Oh, and Rachel, be sure to asked them if it would be alright if I came out to the school and ask a few questions."

"Will do, Detective."

In less than 15 minutes Rachel returned with the names.

"That was fast, thanks Rachel."

"They said they have lunch from 11:45 to 12:20 and that would probably be the best time to catch them at school," Rachel informed MacArthur. He decided since it was almost 11:25 now, he would run over to the school and meet with both of them. Rachel asked if he wanted her to go along. He said it wasn't necessary, but would asked her to do some further checking on the background of the Sprayberrys. He asked her to check on things like, where they spent their time and money? Were they very social, and if yes, what activities did they participate in? Did they attend a local church? Who were their close friends?

MacArthur took the 10 minute drive to Wilcox High School and as he drove into the visitor parking lot, memories of his high school days flooded his mind. There were a couple of incidents that immediately came to mind.

During his senior year he had been assigned "office duty." Students were selected to work in the main office for one class period running errands for either the school secretary or one of the administrators. It was an assignment every senior wanted, but only a few were chosen.

MacArthur was certain he was chosen so that the administration could keep close tabs on him. He was not exactly a model student.

At homecoming, someone had taken down the opposing team's flag, located on their campus in front of the principal's office and replaced it with his school's flag. No one ever admitted to taking part in the incident, but it was common knowledge that most likely, MacArthur Nowlin had a part in it. The same was true when the trees along the entrance to the main building was rolled.

He would never forget the time he was called to the office during his junior year. When he entered the office, the school secretary told him he was wanted in the assistant principal's office. Of course, this was not his first trip to the office, so MacArthur was comfortable. In those days the paddle was still used. He had become acquainted with the "board of education". He knocked on the door and the assistant principal told him to come in. When he walked in, he could not believe his eyes. In a chair, located directly across from the assistant principal's desk, sat his father. He hadn't seen his him since he was in the 5th grade. The assistant principal excused himself and left MacArthur and the one man he hated the most on this earth in the tiny room together.

"How are you son?"

MacArthur stared at him and said nothing.

"I know you didn't expect to see me here, of all people. I don't blame you for being angry at me and I don't blame you for not wanting to see me. I deserve it. I'm sorry to surprise you like this, but I knew if I told you I was coming, you wouldn't have seen me. There is no use in saying how sorry I am for walking out of your life, too much has passed. I only hope someday you can forgive me."

Finally, MacArthur spoke, "I don't know who you are. You're damn sure not my father. You're the son-of-bitch that walked out on me and my mother and sisters. You never called me on my birthdays, and you never sent me or my sisters presents at Christmas. You come walking in here today and expect me to tell you how glad I am to see you? You think that by coming here and saying how sorry you are for what you did will make everything alright? Well, it won't. As far as I'm concerned, I don't have a father. He died several years ago."

Without waiting for a reply from his father, MacArthur turned and walked out. He would never see his father again. Six months later, James Nowlin checked into a cheap, run down motel on the steamy side of New Orleans, and calmly put the barrel of a 38 Smith & Wesson pistol in his mouth and pulled the trigger.

MacArthur walked into the school secretary's office and asked to see the two counselors. He told the secretary they were expecting him. She instructed one of the office aids to take him to their office.

"You must be Detective Nowlin? Please, come in. I'm Ruth Holman and this is Teresa Ross."

"It's nice to meet you ladies. Thank you for seeing me on such a short notice."

"What can we do for you today, Detective?"

MacArthur began by saying how sorry he was for the loss of their colleague.

"I'm here to ask a few questions concerning Mrs. Ida Sprayberry's recent death. I realize you two worked very closely with Mrs. Sprayberry and I apologize for having to bring this terrible tragedy up again. We are doing everything we can to find the killer or killers of Dr. Sprayberry and his wife," MacArthur continued.

Ruth Holman spoke first, "Detective Nowlin, I appreciate what you are doing. We both want to help in any way we can."

"Yes, we thought so much of Ida," Teresa Ross added.

"Can you think of anyone who might have wanted to harm the Sprayberrys, especially Mrs. Sprayberry? Did she have any known enemies here at school? Maybe a former student or co-worker?"

Ruth Holman quickly responded by saying she didn't know of anyone that didn't like Ida Sprayberry. She told MacArthur how helpful she was with the students she worked with and how she was respected among the staff and administration.

Teresa Ross sat without saying anything. MacArthur thought, she seemed uncomfortable.

He was not surprised by this, since he knew that some people react differently than others when being questioned by the police. Still, he felt that she might have more to say in private. He had the feeling Ms. Ross had something to say, but not in her friend's presence.

MacArthur spent the next 15 minutes asking the usual questions and at the same time trying to read the faces of both ladies. It was obvious that Ruth Holman enjoyed sharing information, as she dominated the conversation. On the other hand, Teresa Ross seemed more and more reluctant to speak up, as the conversation progressed.

He thanked the ladies for their time and reassured them for the second time that he was going to find the killer or killers sooner or later.

On the way back to the main office, he met a man dressed in a coat and tie. He assumed correctly that he was the principal. George Howell introduced himself to MacArthur and told him that if he, or anyone of his staff could be of any further assistance, please don't hesitate to give him a call.

As Howell handed him his card, he asked MacArthur where he was in regards to solving the case. Before he could answer, Howell said he had heard that the son was a leading suspect. MacArthur quickly assured the principal that everyone was a suspect until proven otherwise.

"I didn't mean to imply that Sean Sprayberry actually killed his parents, it's just that I had heard that on the streets," George Howell said apologetically."

"Well, I'm sure that in the business you are in rumors are all too common," MacArthur responded jokingly.

"You know Detective, people kill people for little or no cause at all these days. Some are even suggesting that Sean killed his parents for the $800,000 insurance policy. But of course, like you said, you can hear anything in a small town like Wilcox. People love to talk."

MacArthur agreed politely, shook George Howell's hand, and thanked him again for his cooperation.

On the drive back to the station, he had the feeling that this visit was probably a waste of his time. He did find it interesting how George Howell knew so much about the case and how eager he was to assist in any way.

MacArthur decided to stop and get gas. He had just started pumping the gas when he remembered the principal saying something about the $800,000 the two children would get with the death of their parents. This information had not been made public. Only he and the immediate family members knew what the amount was.

Well, the insurance agent would have known, and if he knew there were probably others that knew, MacArthur thought. After all, Wilcox is a small town. Most everybody knows everybody else's business. As it turned out, Howell and the Sprayberrys' insurance agent were actually very close friends.

As he walked into the station the dispatcher told him she had a message for him that just came in. "The lady did not give me her name, she said she would call again later," the dispatcher reported.

"Did she say what she wanted?"

"No sir, all she said was she needed to speak to you right away. No wait, she did ask if you had returned from school yet. I thought that was kind of strange."

MacArthur had a feeling that it might be one of the counselors he had just talked to. No one else but Rachel knew where he had been the last hour.

It has to be one of them, he guessed.

His phone was ringing as he entered his office.

The dispatcher reported, "Line two, Detective, it sounds like the lady that just called."

"This is Detective Nowlin, how can I help you?"

He recognized the voice.

"Detective, this is Teresa Ross. I didn't want to say anything in front of Ruth, but I have some information that you might want to hear. Ida and I were very close friends. We shared almost everything in our lives. I don't know if it has anything to do with her murder, but I felt I should tell you anyway."

"Ms. Ross, can you come down to the police station and we can talk about it here?"

"Detective, I'd rather not. I will meet you somewhere, it's just that I don't want anyone knowing that I am talking to the police. I will explain it later," Teresa Ross said, with fear in her voice.

"Fine, why don't we meet at the park, say around 4:00 this afternoon?"

"Ok, I'll be there. I'll be on the last bench in front of the small duck pond. Do you know where that is?"

"Yes, I'll see you then."

MacArthur wasn't sure what to expect from this secret meeting, but one thing was for sure, Teresa Ross was scared of something.

The park was very quiet with the leaves rustling in the trees, as fall was approaching Wilcox. It looked as though it might rain, with storm clouds forming over the hills. Pigeons had long abandoned the park without anyone being able to explain their departure. Squirrels played along the paths that formed between the huge oak trees.

It was almost 4:00 pm when MacArthur arrived at the park. He walked slowly towards the area adjacent to the small duck pond where he was to meet Teresa Ross. He approached the bench and sat down.

He was no stranger to this place. It was here that he and Marilyn spent some afternoons feeding the ducks and talking about nothing in particular.

As he closed his eyes, he could almost see Marilyn's black shiny hair falling all around her face. He could smell her sweet perfume. He could still hear her girlish laughter and feel her arms around his neck.

MacArthur was brought back to reality when he thought of Marilyn's unfaithfulness. This would be something he could never forgive her for. He chided himself for ever thinking she was the one he wanted to spend the rest of his life with.

"Detective Nowlin, I'm sorry I'm late. I got detained at school, just as I was leaving the office."

"That's fine Ms. Ross, I just got here myself," MacArthur replied as he stood up.

Teresa and Jimmy Ross had moved to Wilcox in 1999. Jimmy got a job at the county water system and Teresa started teaching English at Wilcox High School. While teaching during the day, she continued her education by taking night classes at nearby Liberty College in the neighboring county, getting a degree in high school counseling within two years.

Ida Sprayberry had been the one to recommend Teresa for the position of counselor in 2001. Although Ida Sprayberry was almost 20 years her senior, they developed a close friendship.

Teresa looked upon Ida Sprayberry as her personal mentor. She spoke of the problems she was having in her new job, as well as her personal life. Teresa and Jimmy's marriage wasn't coming along as smoothly as Teresa had hoped. The love was there, they both just had to learn to accept each other, and not try to change each other, Ida would say to Teresa.

As their friendship grew, Ida Sprayberry begin to open up to Teresa about things in her life that were not as they seemed. Teresa never felt at ease when Ida would later share some of her most private secrets. Because she was a trusted friend, Teresa would sit and listen, not quite sure if she should give advice, or if Ida was seeking any. Teresa felt that Ida just needed someone to listen.

"Now, Ms. Ross, exactly what is it you want to tell me?"

Teresa Ross began to tell MacArthur a very long and colorful story.

She said she began traveling with Ida Sprayberry in the summer months, when guidance counseling workshops and conferences were being held in parts of the state. These visits were part of the continuing education program required by the state board of education. Often times Teresa and Ida Sprayberry would share a room. It was very common for other members of the faculty to attend these conferences as well. After meetings all day; everyone would meet and have dinner and drinks. For many, this was the real reason for attending these conferences.

Ida's husband, Samuel used to go along, but the past summer, he never attended any of these conferences with his wife.

Principal George Howell usually attended these conferences as well. He kept to himself most of the time. He never joined the group for dinner and drinks. He must have sensed the group did not want to socialize with him. He was very difficult to get to know. He preferred his own company, as one of the assistant principals used to joke.

Teresa continued with her story as MacArthur sat listening, not sure what to make of it.

She told MacArthur she remembered on her first guidance counselor's state conference, she was sharing a room with Ida Sprayberry, when someone knocked on their door. Ida was in the shower, so Teresa opened the door and saw that it was Mr. Howell. He seemed very surprised and said he had asked

Mrs. Sprayberry to bring some paperwork and that he would get it from her at the meeting in the morning.

She said she told him Ida was in the shower, he said it could wait, and that he would get them from her tomorrow. Teresa told MacArthur she didn't think anything about this visit from the principal. When she told Ida Sprayberry about his visit, she quickly brushed it off and said she would give him the papers he was talking about tomorrow.

Several months later, Teresa would remember this seemingly innocent visit and reflect on what it actually meant.

"Well, Detective as you probably already know, Ida Sprayberry and I not only worked together, but we were very close friends as well. About one week before she and her husband were killed, she came into my office very upset. After she calmed down, she began to tell me how frightened she was. When I asked her why, she said she had made a terrible mistake and it was too late to make things right. I told her I didn't understand. Then she told me she was having an affair with George Howell, our principal."

"You are saying she admitted to you she was sleeping with the principal?" MacArthur asked.

"Yes, she said she didn't think her husband knew of the affair, but Harriet Howell, George's wife suspected something. He said that his wife was going to expose the whole sordid affair. I asked her how long she had been seeing Mr. Howell. She said it started about 10 months ago."

Teresa Ross caught her breath and continued with her story.

"She said that if this got out, her marriage would be over, as well as her career. She then began to get threatening messages on her cell phone."

"Did she say who was sending the messages and who she was frightened off? "MacArthur asked.

"Yes, Harriet Howell."

"What kind of threats did Mrs. Howell make?"

"Ida told me that Harriet warned her that she was not going to sit idly by and let her destroy everything she and her husband had worked for all of these years. Ida took that to mean that her life might be in danger."

"Ms. Ross, did you tell anyone about this conversation the two of you had?"

"No, not even my husband. I didn't know what to do. Then something strange happened. Two days later she comes into my office and tells me that she and Mr. Howell had ended the affair and his wife, Harriet was going to try and reconcile their marriage. She seemed extremely relieved."

"What happened next?" MacArthur asked.

"That same day she told me that she was going to tell her husband, and how she hoped he would forgive her and not leave her."

"Ms. Ross, forgive me for sounding indifferent, but what does all of this have to do with the murder of Dr. and Ms. Sprayberry?"

"Don't you see? Now both of them are dead. She must have told him, he snapped, and killed her, then himself," Teresa Ross said, with an accusing tone.

"That's some story, Ms. Ross," MacArthur said, shaking his head.

"Look Detective, I don't think you believe me, but what I have told you is the truth."

"Oh, I don't doubt that Ms. Ross. It's just that what you've told me doesn't prove Dr. Sprayberry killed his wife, then himself. In fact, there is nothing about this case that suggest a murder/suicide."

MacArthur could sense the frustration in Teresa Ross's voice.

"Ms. Ross, you mentioned to me earlier on the phone that you didn't want anyone knowing you were talking to the police. Why is that?"

"Because, I still work for Mr. Howell, and I don't want anything to jeopardize my future at the school. If he thinks I'm going around telling of his affair, it could cost me my job. Do you understand Detective?"

"Of course, I do Ms. Ross. No one has to know of our conversation here today."

"Thank you. I must go now, my husband will be getting worried about me if I'm late getting home."

As Teresa Ross walked swiftly back to her car, MacArthur thought she probably meant well, but she definitely was over reacting. Besides, if Dr. Sprayberry had found out about the affair, why would he kill himself after killing his cheating wife?

CHAPTER 24

It had been a long day. MacArthur decided not to go back to the office. He would pick up some Mexican, food and go home and try to get some much needed sleep.

He was about to unlock his apartment, when he noticed the door was not locked. He drew his weapon and walked into his apartment very slowly. He turned on the lights and began to search each room.

He still had his gun out, as he finished searching the last room. Whoever was in his apartment was gone. He began to look for items a thief might take during a break-in. To his surprise, he could find nothing missing.

Strange, why would someone break into my apartment and not take anything?

He decided not to report the break-in. As he was getting ready for bed, he came to the conclusion that the maid had come by and left the door unlocked. He reminded himself to give her a call in the morning. MacArthur fell asleep on the sofa while watching an old episode of *Columbo*. He woke up around 1:30, and stumbled to bed. As he tossed and turned in his bed, he tried to block out all the thoughts competing for his attention. The meeting with Teresa Ross was certainly interesting, but would the information be accurate? Even if it is, would it get him any closer to solving this case?

Thoughts of Marilyn lingered. Something about the principal he didn't like. He reminded himself he needed to get with Rachel first thing tomorrow morning.

He got up around 3:30 to get some tums for the indigestion he now had. Was it the stress or was it the nachos? Probably both.

When the alarm went off at 5:30, MacArthur felt as though he hadn't been to sleep at all. The shower was an instant relief. As the warm water ran down his face, MacArthur closed his eyes and reached for the shampoo. It was not in its usual place. Things like this pissed him off. Everything had its own place. He remembered he had used the last of the shampoo yesterday morning.

Was this a sign of what kind of day he was going to have? MacArthur had always believed in signs and omens. He never left for work without first checking his horoscope. Today's words of wisdom called for patience, honesty, and being a good listener.

What day didn't? MacArthur said, aloud as he threw the day old paper in the waste basket.

He shoved down a stale doughnut, and took his cup of coffee with him.

The drive to work gave him a chance to map out his plans for his workday. He knew it was time to go over his notes for the tenth time. There had to be something he was missing. Every crime scene told a story. Just what this story was, MacArthur hadn't figured out yet.

He checked for messages before going to his office. Chief Aldridge wanted to see him later this morning. He had been expecting this.

The Chief was getting pressure from city hall. The Sprayberry murders still had people on edge in Wilcox. Was this a random killing, or was someone living right there in Wilcox just waiting for their next victim? People who had never bothered to lock their doors before the murders, did so now

"Rachel, I almost forgot, did you get a chance to check out the neighbor's story about the night of the murders? You know the ones I'm talking about? What were their names?"

"I have their names written down somewhere in my notes. I'll take a ride back to the neighborhood later on this morning and talk with them again," Rachel told MacArthur as he was getting ready for his meeting with the Chief in 10 minutes.

"Thanks. Also, check out the original report written by the officer who took the call that night."

The Chief's secretary was buzzing MacArthur now, "MacArthur, the Chief will see you now."

"Tell him I'll be right there."

When he walked into Chief Aldridge's office, he found Mayor Hastings there as well.

The mayor spoke first. "Detective Nowlin, the Chief tells me that you don't have anyone in custody for the Sprayberry murders. Is that correct?"

"Yes sir, that is correct. We are working several leads at this time but ..."

"Leads, my ass, Nowlin. This case should have been solved by now. If you are not capable of doing the job maybe Chief Aldridge should get someone who is. I am tired of having the citizens of Wilcox asking why the murderers have not been found," the mayor said, sounding more and more disgusted.

"With all due respect sir, I'm just as anxious as you are to bring the killers to justice. But without enough solid evidence that would hold up in court; to make an arrest at this time would most likely be thrown out. The killer would walk for sure. We are doing all we can, we are working around the clock," MacArthur replied, feeling his face turning red. He didn't deserve to be talked to this way. It took all of his resolve to keep from telling the mayor to get someone else, and to go to hell. MacArthur may have had a short fuse, but he wasn't stupid. He kept his mouth shut.

Chief Aldridge spoke up and actually seemed to be defending MacArthur. He told the mayor the police were very close to making an arrest, which was a lie. Whatever the Chief's motive was for coming to MacArthur's aid, it did not go unnoticed by him. He would later thank the Chief for his support. Chief Aldridge told him he could thank him by finding the killer ASAP.

MacArthur understood where the mayor was coming from. The mayor answers to his voters, the chief answers to the mayor, and as the lead investigator he answers to the Chief. Everyone wants the same thing, the case solved and justice served for the deaths of Ida and Samuel Sprayberry. It was not personal, just business. However, that didn't stop him from wanting to punch out the mayor.

MacArthur stopped by the work room for his third cup of coffee, still fuming.

He called Rachel, and for the next hour they continued to go over the notes of the entire case.

"I think Teresa Ross' story would make for a good soap opera, but I can't see how it relates to the murders. We know for sure it was not a suicide/murder, so would Howell's wife go so far as to hire someone to kill Ida Sprayberry? No way."

"Do you think Teresa Ross may have had something to do with the murders, and maybe she is trying to steer us in another direction?"

"No, I don't think so, Rachel. Teresa Ross is not capable of murder in my opinion, besides what would she gain by the deaths of the Sprayberrys?"

"Yeah, you're right. That doesn't make sense," Rachel said, feeling foolish for suggesting it.

"I'll tell you what I do think. I think money was behind the killing, and who would benefit the most? Sean Sprayberry and his sister Susan Login, that's who. But, I think we can rule out the sister that only leaves Sean Sprayberry. No matter how hard I try to write him out of the picture, he just keeps coming back up."

"You know Rachel, when it comes to murder it's been said, if you want to catch a killer, follow the money."

MacArthur was headed out of his office to grab some lunch. He turned around to go back and get his coat when his phone rang.

This call would break the Sprayberry murder investigation wide open.

"Detective Nowlin, this is James Hinson. I'm with the state forensic lab, here in Columbia. We have just completed our testing on the partial palm print found at the Sprayberry murder scene. We ran it through our database and we got a match."

MacArthur could hardly control himself. This was the break he had been waiting for.

"Have you got a name?" MacArthur asked with excitement.

"The print we have matches that of Carlos Sanchez. A white male, 42 years old. He's got a rap sheet as long as my arm. It looks as though he's been in and out of prison since he was 20 years old. Armed robbery, extortion, and a host of other petty crimes. He was also arrested for carrying a concealed weapon, and discharging a firearm in a housing project. The list goes on and on."

MacArthur began taking notes as he asked, "What is the latest address you have on him?"

"There is one more thing Detective, it seems he has some ties to the Franco family. He may have been one of their soldiers at one time. He was arrested on suspicion of murder, but was acquitted when the only witness failed to show. They are one of the biggest crime syndicates in the Carolinas. His last known address was in Raleigh, over a year ago, 1190 West Haven Avenue, apartment 12 C."

"Got it, thanks Hinson." MacArthur could feel his heart racing.

He sat and stared at the phone. He told himself not to get too excited. Just because this man's print was found at the murder scene didn't mean he was the killer. He knew he faced an uphill battle just finding this Carlos Sanchez, then there was the matter of connecting him to the murder. The prints definitely placed him in the home of the Sprayberrys.

MacArthur was no longer hungry. He threw his coat over the back of his chair and placed a call to Rachel. In less than thirty minutes she appeared at his door. He looked up and motioned her to come in.

"It looks like we got our first real break. Just got a call from the state lab in Columbia. A James Hinson told me they had a match on that partial print we took from the door knob. Before you get too excited, we still have a lot of leg work. The first thing we do now, is find Carlos Sanchez. It was his prints that showed up. He has a long rap sheet and has been connected to the Franco family crime syndicate in North and South Carolina."

"Where do we start?"

"His last known address is in Raleigh. See what you can find out. It's a good chance he's back in prison again, or worse, dead." MacArthur tried not to think about the last possibility.

Rachel was already moving toward the office door when he told her there was more. She sat back down and took out her notebook. Until now, MacArthur had not told anyone about the key he removed from the back door on the night of the murders.

MacArthur pulled open his middle drawer of the desk. He took a small plastic bag out. Inside the bag was a key.

"I took this key out of the back door on the night of the murders. No one else knows about this key. I have a theory that the murderer gained access into the Sprayberry's residence by using this key. I believe whoever hired the shooter, gave him this key. How else could he have gotten in without forced entry, unless one of the Sprayberrys let him in? I don't think that happened."

Rachel wondered why MacArthur would not reveal evidence found at the murder scene, but now was not the time to ask him about it.

"Do you remember that Susan Login told me only she and Sean had keys to their parents' home? Well, it seems the next door neighbors, Mr. and Mrs. Dayton also had a key. The night of the murders, according to the records of the dispatcher here at the station, it was a neighbor that called in to 911 to report something wrong at the Sprayberry's home."

"Damn, how could I have overlooked that? I don't remember seeing that report. I asked you to get me a copy..."

"I did, but you said you would look at it later," Rachel interrupted.

"So it was the Dayton's that reported the shootings. Do you still have his statement?"

"Yes"

He asked Rachel to get it for him. She returned in minutes with the one page statement given by Sam Dayton on the night of the murders. As MacArthur began reading the report, he stopped and peered over his reading glasses and told Rachel to get started on tracing Carlos Sanchez. She nodded and left for her office.

According to the statement, Sam and his wife both thought they heard something like a firecracker go off next door. MacArthur immediately stopped, put the piece of paper down and picked up his 2 inch folder, filled with notes of the investigation. There it was! According to his notes, while interviewing some of the residents of the Sprayberry neighborhood, the Dayton's had said they had not heard anything that night.

As usual, in any investigation, there were conflicting statements whether or not shots were heard. Two sets of neighbors said they had not heard anything, but one other neighbor, who happened to be walking his dog, thought he heard something like a car backfiring in the direction of the Sprayberry's home.

MacArthur's next thoughts were, *Why would the Dayton's written statement be completely opposite of their onsite statement? After all, only an hour or two at the most had lapsed. Maybe they were confused in all of the excitement.*

MacArthur felt his adrenalin began to flow. Was it just a coincidence that the person calling 911 to report the murder was the same person that said he didn't hear any shots, but later in a written statement said he did hear shots? And, Sam Dayton later verified Sean's statement that he and his wife had a key to the Sprayberry home. He volunteered to give it to Detective Nowlin if necessary.

MacArthur's experience as a top investigator told him not to put too much emphasis on witnesses changing their stories. Unfortunately, that was all too common in this type of an investigation. Still, he wanted to have a talk with the Dayton's. MacArthur dialed their home phone, but no one answered. He decided to leave a message asking if Sam Dayton would give him a call.

Jo Kessler was on the other end of the line.

"Detective, this is Jo. I might have some information I think you'll find interesting. I've been doing some checking around like you ask me to and found out there are a few people who have some secrets."

"Kessler, I'm real busy right now…"

"Well, you better stop what you're doing; I think you'll will like what I have for you."

MacArthur knew the reporter well enough to know she wouldn't waste his time on something that was not of real interest.

"How about a cup of coffee? I'll meet you in 30 minutes at Sarah's café."

"I'll be there. Are you buying?"

MacArthur didn't bother to give her an answer. He was already putting his coat on and heading for the door. He hurried out of the station, and headed toward his car. He had to make one stop before he met the reporter.

Kessler and MacArthur's relationship was one of mutual respect. The one thing they both had in common was a determination to get the job done. They worked well together.

They both complimented each other. MacArthur knew that she needed him to stay one step ahead of her competitors. She knew only he could provide the information that enabled her to do so. Kessler knew he needed her and all of the resources she brought to the table. She could get information in ways that he couldn't.

MacArthur hoped that Kessler's involvement in this case would put him over the top in getting an arrest and conviction.

"You're late, you said 30 minutes. I was about to leave," Kessler said, knowing that was not true.

"No, you weren't," MacArthur said with a grin.

"You think the information you have will give you the lead to an exclusive story. You see, you do need me."

"Well, that works both ways doesn't it, Detective?" Kessler shot back.

"I suppose it does in this case. That is, if you have anything worthwhile."

"What if I told you the principal at Wilcox High School had problems keeping his pants up, if you know what I mean?"

"That's old news," MacArthur said, as he waited for something more important.

"Well, it seems Mr. Howell has other bad habits as well. What if I told you that the good principal is a big gambler and is hooked for a great deal of money? My source tells me he has been given a deadline by the "big boys" to come up with the money, or else."

"So?" MacArthur responded hoping there was more.

"There are two seniors on the football team at Wilcox High that will sign in division I. They are that good."

"What the hell does that have to do with anything, Kessler? I told you not to waste my time. Will you get to the point?" MacArthur protested angrily.

"Suppose the principal, Howell, bet on his own high school football games? With these two all-state players, Wilcox is expected to reach the finals of the state championship in November. However, if they were declared ineligible, due to failing grades, the prospect of winning goes way down. In other words, Howell is desperate. He has to have these two stars suited on Friday nights. That's the only way he can win enough to pay off the bookies. And how does he make sure these guys are eligible? You guessed it, by doctoring the grades."

MacArthur had a puzzled look on his face.

"Don't you get it? Ida Sprayberry was the chair of the guidance department at Wilcox High. She would have access to student grades. It seems the two players I'm talking about were not exactly top of their class. Actually, questions were raised to the validity of their passing grades in a particular class."

"So tell me, Kessler. How does all of this fit together?"

"That's just it, I'm not sure, but if you ask me, there's something rotten in Denmark. What we have here is a well-respected school official who happens to be a closet gambler who is in way over his head. He's being threatened by some very dangerous people who have given him a deadline to pay-up, or else. And you've got a dead guidance counselor, who was the only person besides the principal who had access to student transcripts."

MacArthur asked another question," Are you sure your information is reliable?"

"Oh, yeah. I would stake my life on it."

"You may be doing just that, Kessler," MacArthur replied.

"What's that supposed to mean?"

"I'm just saying, if there is something to this far-fetched story of yours, having knowledge of something like that could be dangerous. Have you spoken to anyone else about this?"

"No, only you, and of course my informant, who gave the information to me," Kessler answered, looking concerned for the first time since they sat down.

"Kessler, if you're right about what you just told me, you might better watch your back."

Jo thanked MacArthur for the coffee, although she didn't drink any. She told him she would be in touch. She walked out of the café and got into her Volkswagen Beetle. As she was about to start the engine, she had a strange feeling she was being watched. *You've been reading too many true crime novels,* she said to herself as she drove off.

MacArthur's head was reeling. On the drive back to the station, his mind was trying to fit all of this together. *Could Ida Sprayberry have been the one the shooter was after, not Dr. Sprayberry? The killer thought Dr. Sprayberry was out of town. He only intended to kill her. This case was becoming more confusing with the passing of each day*, MacArthur said, to no one.

It was almost 5:30. He checked his messages, there were none. He would give the Daytons another call in the morning. If there was still no answer, he was going to pay them a visit. MacArthur then made a phone call to the Raleigh

Homicide Unit. He asked to speak with Detective Jim Donald. He had met him a few years back while attending a training conference.

"This is Detective Donald."

"Jim, this MacArthur Nowlin with the Wilcox Homicide Unit. It's been a while Detective. How are things in Raleigh?"

"It's all good MacArthur. Can't complain. Nobody would listen anyway. How are you doing?"

"I'd be doing great if I could locate a man by the name of Carlos Sanchez. Have you ever heard of him?"

"Actually, I have. Sanchez is wanted for parole violation. We're trying to find him ourselves. This Carlos Sanchez runs with some very dangerous people. He's gone underground right now. I think it's just a matter of time before he shows up again. MacArthur, this guy is one mean *son of a bitch*."

MacArthur asked Detective Donald if he would send him a mug shot or picture of Sanchez.

He said he would get one out to his office today. He also told him that Sanchez's sister lived in Raleigh.

"Have you got an address or phone number?" MacArthur asked.

Donald said all he had was a name and telephone number.

"Thanks, Donald, you've been a big help. I'll be getting back with you soon," MacArthur said, as he hung up the phone. He was not about to wait until morning. As he dialed the number, MacArthur knew Sanchez's sister would most likely protect her brother at all costs. If he called and identified himself as a police officer, he felt certain she would not cooperate at all. He dialed the number and waited. Finally, after several rings, a female's voice answered.

"Is this Carlos' sister, Maria?"

"Who wants to know?"

"Maria, you don't know me, but your brother and I worked together for a while for a Mr. Belcher that lives in Durham. The reason I'm calling is to try and get a hold of Carlos. Mr. Belcher has some more work for us. Carlos told me a few months ago to call him if Belcher should want us back. He gave me his phone number, but I lost it. Do you have it?" MacArthur said, disguising his voice.

"Who did you say you are?"

"I'm Rolando Ramones. Do you got the number or not?"

"Carlos told me not to give anyone his number. I might get in to big trouble."

"Look Maria, Carlos knows me. I ain't no cop, if that's what you're thinking."

After a moment of silence, Maria said, "have you got something to write this down with? Oh, by the way, you tell him I want my money he owes me."

"I'll tell him, but that's between you and him. He's got a chance to make some good money if he'll go to Durham with me. Old man Belcher pays good," MacArthur said, still disguising his voice.

MacArthur decided he'd talked long enough to Carlos' sister. He didn't want her to become suspicious.

He dialed the number she gave him. He wasn't surprised to hear the recording, "no longer a working number."

He'd been hoping he could get lucky and trace Sanchez down, but he'd have to find another way. He was determined not to give up. He was going to find this key figure in his investigation no matter what it took. He realized it

M. HARMON HALL

was almost 7:00 pm. *It looks like I'm going to be here for a while.* He decided to walk around the corner and get a sandwich and soda. Within 20 minutes he was backs at his desk getting all of today's notes organized.

MacArthur began to do what he does best. He started to fit the pieces together one by one. If what reporter Kessler told him was correct then the principal Howell could have had something to do with the murder of Ida Sprayberry. It was a long shot, but people have killed or had people killed for lesser things.

He went back over the conversation he had with Teresa Ross. If Howell and Ida Sprayberry were sleeping together, it would make sense she would have knowledge of this and could have been in on the changing of grades on the two students' transcripts. Maybe Teresa Ross hadn't told him everything in his first interview with her. He made a note on his legal pad to call her tomorrow.

Near the bottom of his notes spread out on his desk was a small sheet of paper with only one line written. After closely examining it, MacArthur could barely make out the words. When he did, his eyes brows raised and the pupils of his eyes widened.

In his conversation with the other school guidance counselor, she had told him that Dr. Sprayberry was supposed to be going out of town to a conference on the day of the murders.

Ida usually went along with her husband on these conferences, but she had told her she was not going. The counselor told MacArthur the reason she remembered this detail was because she remembered thinking it was odd that Principal Howell was in Ida's office when Ida told her.

KEYS TO MURDER

That means Howell knew Samuel Sprayberry would not be home, leaving Ida Sprayberry alone for the weekend. The killer was not after Samuel Sprayberry, but Ida Sprayberry instead. MacArthur's hands began to sweat. His heart rate spiked and his mouth was dry. He needed coffee and lots of it.

He continued along this line of thought. *So that might explain why the key was left in the door. Why there was no forced entry. Did Ida leave the key in the door expecting Howell to let himself in? Or, since Howell knew the key would be there, arrange for the hired killer to enter the house through that door, go upstairs and shoot Ida Sprayberry?*

MacArthur was feeling good about his theory, but there was the matter of Dr. Sprayberry being shot while in the bed. After some wrestling with this, MacArthur came to the conclusion that perhaps the killer didn't expect Dr. Sprayberry to be there, so when the killer entered the bedroom, Dr. Sprayberry could have been asleep in bed.

He toyed with the idea that the killer shot him first, then went into the bathroom where Ida Sprayberry was taking a bath, and then shot her. He came back out and positioned Samuel Sprayberry's body to make it look as though he shot himself after killing his wife.

MacArthur thought, *it makes sense. The prints found on the door knob that led to the back door of the house belonged to Carlos Sanchez. Could Howell have hired Sanchez to carry out the hit?*

It just didn't seem possible that Howell was capable of murder. He had been the pillar of the community for almost twenty years. His reputation as a school administrator was one of respect. It had been rumored a few years back of his involvement with one of the younger teachers. That rumor mill faded when the teacher and her husband moved to another city.

MacArthur made a list of people he needed to talk with. That list included Howell, Sanchez, Ross, and Sprayberrys' neighbors, the Dayton's. He looked at his watch and was surprised to find it was almost 10:00 pm. He would try and get some sleep tonight, but thoughts of Marilyn's betrayal wouldn't leave him alone.

He missed her. He wondered where Killingworth was on her case. MacArthur didn't know it, but Killingsworth was quietly putting together a solid case against him.

New evidence would "show up" that would further incriminate him as Marilyn's killer. The noose was getting tighter and tighter, but MacArthur had no idea.

MacArthur was awakened with the ringing of his phone. As he listened to the caller he could hardly believe what he was hearing.

"Is she going to make it? How did it happen?" MacArthur asked the caller in a stunned voice.

The caller told him the doctors were giving her a 50/50 chance of surviving. The accident happened out on County Road 134, just outside the city limits of Wilcox.

MacArthur asked which hospital Jo Kessler had been transported to. He quickly got dressed and walked into the emergency room doors less than 30 minutes later. Reporter Kessler was still in surgery. MacArthur spoke to one of the doctors on call and asked about her chances of making it.

"Detective, if she lives through the night she may have a chance. She sustained several internal injuries and she lost a lot of blood at the scene of the accident," the young doctor reported.

MacArthur sat in the waiting room until the doctors had completed the surgery. He stood up and met the attending physician, asking him about Kessler. The doctor told him she made it through surgery, but was a long way from being out of trouble. He told him she was lucky to have made it this far. He said she was hemorrhaging and had a punctured lung. He repeated what the young doctor had told him earlier, if she made it through the night, she might survive.

MacArthur drank his third cup of coffee as he paced around the waiting room. His request for the police officers who worked the accident to call him was taking too long.

Finally, Officer Walton called him and told him it looked as though she ran a stop sign and was hit by a pick-up truck. The time of the accident was approximately 8:30 pm. He asked the officer where her vehicle was now. He told him it had been towed to the police department impound. MacArthur thanked him and hung up.

The driver of the pick-up truck had sustained some injuries that required hospitalization, but were not thought to be life threatening. He would later tell MacArthur, he never saw the car coming. After MacArthur's investigation of the site of the wreck, it appeared the driver was telling the truth.

The driver was identified as James Cook, a local painter. MacArthur could find no connection between him and Jo Kessler. Perhaps, it was just an accident. After inspecting Jo Kessler's car, he noticed the break line appeared to be severed. He felt that the line could have broken due to wear and tear of a

10 year old vehicle. But, the other side of that coin was that someone cut the line.

MacArthur's suspicious nature would not let him dismiss the idea this was no accident. *If it was not, who would have wanted Jo Kessler dead and why*? He thought.

The following day after the accident the toxicology report revealed that Jo Kessler's blood level indicated the presence of alcohol and a prescription drug that was most likely some form of muscle relaxer. The official cause of death was ruled an accident. The deceased had failed to stop at the stop sign and was struck by an oncoming vehicle. There were no charges brought against the driver, James Cook.

Later that same morning, MacArthur visited the high school to talk with the principal, Mr. Howell.

"What do you mean Mr. Howell is unavailable? This is a police matter and I want to see him now," MacArthur said with authority.

He waited outside the principal's office and was soon led to Howell's office.

"What can I do for you, Detective?"

"You can start by telling me about Ida Sprayberry, and don't bullshit me Howell. I've been up all night sitting in a hospital waiting to see if a friend of mine is going to live or die. I'm not in the mood for games. I don't have the time nor the patience."

George Howell stared at MacArthur as though he had lost his mind.

"You know, Mr. Howell, during the course of my investigation of the Sprayberrys' murders some interesting things have turned up. Things like, you and Mrs. Sprayberry playing doctor. Things like, student athletes suddenly passing a certain course although the teacher says both of them received a failing grade from her, back in May. And then there's that issue of a gambling problem."

"Detective Nowlin, I don't appreciate the fact that you come to my office and make false accusations about my…"

"Howell, I don't give a damn what you appreciate. You'd better start answering my questions, or we can go downtown, if you like, and you can answer them there."

"Look, Detective Nowlin, Ida Sprayberry was the head of our guidance counselor department. We did not have a personal relationship of any kind. I don't know where you got your information, but I suggest you check your source. As far as students' grades being changed, I can assure you that has not happened during my tenure here. At the beginning of the school year, we did have a situation where two of our football players attended summer school and were given credit for the class they took upon passing the final exam given. But, the grades were not posted correctly, and their student transcripts still were showing they both received "F's" in 11th grade English. The error was found, and the transcripts were corrected. End of story," Howell said.

MacArthur wasn't sure what to think at this point. His gut told him Howell was probably telling the truth, or some version of it.

"The gambling problem you are suggesting is also unfounded. My wife and I do occasionally go to the Indian Casino over in Butler County, but not very often."

MacArthur's insides were on fire. Howell's answers for his actions were spot on. Either he was the best liar he had ever heard, or he was telling the truth. It was too easy to find out the facts, for him to make up this story, MacArthur thought.

But what about Ross' story. Was she lying? Why would she? MacArthur thought. MacArthur told Howell that he would be checking out his story. He turned and walked out of the office and to his car.

MacArthur knew it was time to have another chat with Teresa Ross.

He drove by the hospital to see if there was any word on Jo Kessler's condition. The nurse at the station told him she would see if the doctor could talk with him now.

"Detective Nowlin, there hasn't been any significant changes in Mrs. Kessler's condition. Her vital signs are weak but holding steady for now. It's too early to tell if she's going to make it."

"Thank you Doctor, I'll stay in touch. If any changes occur, will you have your nurse call me?"

"Of course, Detective."

MacArthur felt that her "accident" was his fault. If he had not asked her to check around, maybe this wouldn't have happened to her. It seemed obvious to him, Jo Kessler knew too much, or got too close to something she shouldn't have. Or, could it be he was letting his imagination run away?

Reporter Jo Kessler was pronounced dead at 6:33 am the next morning. She never regained consciousness. The official cause of death was ruled to be from complications due to extensive internal injuries sustained in a vehicular accident on County Road 134.

MacArthur was notified within minutes of her death. He sat at his kitchen table trying to stay focused on what he had to do next.

Days later, the official police report stated it could not rule out the possibility of the break line of Jo Kessler's automobile being tampered with however, because of the condition of the 10 year old car, it was possible that the break line malfunctioned due to wear and tear.

MacArthur was convinced it had been tampered with. No matter, his priority was finding the killer of the Sprayberrys. He still held on to the notion that it was very likely that the person responsible for the Sprayberry murders was responsible for Jo Kessler's "accident" as well.

MacArthur finished his coffee and headed for the door. The weather man had been right, it was flooding outside. The wind was gusting with sheets of rain streaming. His umbrella was in the trunk of his car. He wished he had bought that raincoat Marilyn tried to get him to buy several weeks earlier.

In the short distance to his parked car, he got drenched. He started the engine of his Chevrolet Impala, but before he backed out of the parking space, he tested his breaks. *Can't be too sure in his line of work*, he thought.

He decided to drive out to the site of Jo's wreck. He wasn't sure why. He drove slowly, thinking about the fact that within six weeks he had seen two women in his life die. One was his friend and lover, and the other, a professional colleague with whom he had worked closely with. He didn't think this was a coincidence.

Rachel was waiting for him as he walked into the police station. She handed him a cup of coffee as she sat down across from his desk.

"I am sorry about Jo Kessler. I know you two were friends."

"Thanks, Rachel. It probably was just an accident, but the timing is a little suspect if you ask me. I looked at the break line and while I couldn't say 100% that it had been cut. Of course, my opinion doesn't really matter right now. They have ruled it an accident. I think she got too close to the truth, and paid for it with her life."

"So you think her accident is linked to the Sprayberry murders?"

"I don't know Rachel. Before I talked to Howell this morning I was convinced he might have had something to do with the Sprayberrys' murder. Now I'm not so sure. If his story about the student transcript error this summer is backed up, there would not have been any reason to cover that up."

"But, I thought they were having an affair?"

"They were, according Teresa Ross. Howell said it never happened, that their relationship was strictly professional. I plan to speak with her again today. I don't think she told me everything she knew the last time we met," MacArthur said, as he looked for her phone number. "Rachel, I need for you to interview the Dayton's again. You know, the neighbors and best friends of the Sprayberrys. It seems their stories about hearing shots fired that night have changed. See what you can find out about them as well. I called yesterday, but there was no answer. They still haven't returned my call. Take a drive over to their home this morning."

"I'm on it now," Rachel said, as she walked out of MacArthur's office.

MacArthur picked up his phone and dialed Teresa Ross.

"Mrs. Ross, this is Detective Nowlin. It's important that we talk again. There are some things I need you to clear up for me."

"Detective, I have already told you everything I know. I don't see any point in us going over what has already been said."

"Mrs. Ross, you said Ida Sprayberry was your friend, don't you want to find her killer?"

"Of course, I do Detective. It's just that …"

"With all due respect ma'am, I'm not sure you do," MacArthur said, trying to evoke a response.

"Look, just because she shared things with me that I wished now she hadn't, doesn't make me a killer."

"I'm not suggesting you killed her, Mrs. Ross. What I am saying is that I don't believe you have told me everything she told you before she and her husband were murdered."

After a long silence, Teresa Ross asked MacArthur when he wanted to meet.

"This afternoon, same place as before, around 4 pm."

She agreed to meet MacArthur under one condition, she wanted her name left out of the whole matter. He promised he would, if she came clean with him. Of course, he had no intentions of keeping her out of the case. Her testimony in court was going to be vital if what she was saying was true. Time was running out.

MacArthur went into the men's room in the station. As he was washing his hands, he looked in the mirror and saw someone he no longer recognized.

The man he saw in the mirror appeared to be much older. Signs of gray were creeping up along his temples. The lines in his face were much more pronounced. There seemed to be a general sadness about him. The man who had once prided himself in looking vibrant and alive was nowhere to be found.

MacArthur said to himself, *it's this damn job, maybe I've been doing it too long. Maybe I've gotten so careless that I can't see the forest for the trees.*

Maybe I should be working harder on trying to find out who killed Marilyn, instead of spinning my wheels on this damn case. He allowed himself a few minutes of self-pity, then cursed himself for being such a wimp. He was not going to let this bring him down. He was not going to give the killer the satisfaction of outsmarting him. If it was the very last thing he ever did, he was going to solve this case.

He dried his face with the last strip of a brown paper towel located over the sink. He tossed the used paper towel towards the waste dispenser, as though he was shooting a basketball. As he walked out of the restroom, his thoughts darted back to his high school basketball days and his terrible relationship with his coach. It seemed he just couldn't come to grips with the coaches' assessment of his skills. *"MacArthur you're just not as good as you think you are,"* his coached declared, for everyone to hear.

It was true that MacArthur spent more time on the bench than out on the floor. It was obvious to him, the coach lacked the ability to recognize talent when he saw it. MacArthur did concede many years later that telling the coach to "kiss his ass" didn't help to bridge the gap between the two of them. That episode in his life reminded him of his favorite line in the movie *Cool Hand Luke.* Paul Newman played the character of "Luke." The line was, *"what we've got here is a failure to communicate."* He remembered thinking; *I can relate*. After all of these years, he was not ashamed to admit he still hated the coach. Forgiving others was not one of his strong points. He admitted he held grudges and often times refused to let go of them. Forgiving himself came even harder.

Later that afternoon, MacArthur met with Teresa Ross for the second time. Their meeting place was the same as before. His hopes of getting Teresa Ross to come forward with information she had been withholding was soon dashed.

She recanted everything she had told him in their first meeting. She said that she had made the whole thing up because she was angry with the principal. He had failed to keep his promise to promote her to head of the guidance counselor department, replacing the deceased Ida Sprayberry. She also told MacArthur that the grade changing incident never took place. Oh, about the gambling thing, she said that was a lie also.

Teresa Ross said she was friends with Ida Sprayberry, but any affair between her friend and Howell was simply not true. She apologized to MacArthur and said she felt really bad about leading him on with such a far-fetched story. She assured him that her principal was not the kind of guy that would do such a terrible thing. What she didn't tell MacArthur, was that she and Howell were having an affair.

MacArthur angrily told her he could arrest her for giving false information to a police officer while investigating a murder. He had no intentions of doing so, he just wanted her to squirm for a while. He walked back to his car thinking how much time he had wasted following this lead.

He asked himself the question, *but what about the information that Jo Kessler had given him about Howell's gambling problems?*

The once promising theory had dissipated before his very eyes. Experience had taught him not to become "married" to a single theory. Leads come and leads go. It was back to square one, and square one began with the two children of the deceased parents. Regardless of the twist and turns in this case, they always seemed to find their way back to Sean and Susan. MacArthur thought, *the same question keeps coming up, who had the most to benefit from the deaths of Dr. and Mrs. Sprayberry?*

Rachel called and told him she had a talk with Mrs. Dayton, Ida Sprayberry's best friend and neighbor. She told him that Mrs. Dayton said she could not be sure that what she heard that night was a gun firing. She also said that the Sprayberry's had no enemies she was aware of. They were to have taken a cruise together two weeks after their deaths. Dayton's information was of little help in the investigation.

CHAPTER 25

There was an unusually heavy fog on the morning of August 18th, Officer Jack King could barely see the grey Honda Accord with North Carolina license plates. One of Jack's favorite spots to observe traffic was in the abandoned parking lot of Smiley's gas station.

On this particular morning, he was sipping his coffee when he saw a car approach the four-way stop sign. The car slowed down, but failed to come to a complete stop. He pulled in behind the vehicle and turned on his blue lights. The car pulled over on the shoulder of the road and came to a stop and Jack approached the driver.

Jack King came from a long line of police officers. His grandfather and father had served as distinguished police officers in Silver Creek, North Carolina. Jack could not remember a time when he didn't want to be like them and serve on the police force.

Jack King was only 5'6" tall. He weighed only 130 pounds; too small to be a police officer according to the manual. Throughout his life he had asthma as well as very poor eyesight. Most would agree that Jack was not police material. Most, except Jack King. What he lacked in physical stature, he made up in perseverance, toughness, and a lifelong dream of becoming a police officer.

He had graduated with honors from the Police Academy two years earlier. He still lived at home with his mother. He felt she needed someone to take care of her due to her failing health. She had suffered a stroke after his dad died, which was almost a year ago.

Jack was not a lady's man. He had never dated much in high school, always the shy one. He had just met the new librarian, Wanda Sanders, at the Silver Creek Public Library. They had become good friends. Jack was hoping it would turn into more than just friends. Wanda wanted the same thing, she just hadn't told Jack yet.

In the small town of Silver Creek, Officer Jack King was highly respected because of his genuine desire to help people. He always had a smile on his face and was quick to laugh. People felt at ease around him. He loved his job.

Jack radioed in the model and make of the vehicle, as well as the license plate numbers.

"Good morning sir, may I see your driver's license and vehicle registration?" Jack asked, as he walked up to the driver's side of the vehicle.

"What's wrong officer; I wasn't speeding was I?" The driver said with an accent that was not from around Silver Creek.

"You failed to stop at the four-way stop sign back there," Officer King said, with a friendly but authoritative voice, just as he had been trained at the academy.

"Officer, I'm sorry, but I left my license in my hotel room along with my wallet. I'll be more careful from now on," the driver replied, hoping the police officer would just let this slide.

"I'm sorry, sir, but I'm going to need some kind of identification. What's your name and social security number?" Jack asked, with a stern tone.

"Hosea Amentez. I don't know my social security number, I lost my card last year."

"Mr. Amentez, please wait here while I call in to verify," Jack instructed, as he walked back to his patrol car.

When he radioed the dispatcher back at the station, she alerted him that the license plate number indicated the car was stolen. Jack called for backup immediately, again just as he had been trained. But, for whatever reason, he chose not to wait for backup. He got out of his car and walked cautiously toward the stolen car, with his hand on his pistol that was still in its sheath. He observed the trunk to make sure it was closed completely, as well as determining if there were any other people in the vehicle. What he didn't see was the sawed off shotgun between the car door and driver's seat.

Carlos Sanchez had no intentions of being arrested this morning, or any other morning. He put his left hand on the sawed off shotgun as Jack approached. His window was still rolled down. Jack leaned over and with one hand on his weapon and the other on the door, he asked the driver to step out of the vehicle.

Without any words, Carlos Sanchez raised the shotgun and fired once into the face of Officer Jack King. He was dead before he hit the pavement. Carlos Sanchez sped off heading north on Highway 234.

When back-up arrived only minutes later, the officer found Jack lying in the middle of the highway in a puddle of blood. He reached down and tried to find a pulse, but there was none. Jack King was dead, shot in cold blood. His gun was still in its sheath. His face was beyond recognition. There would be no open casket.

Privately, his fellow officers murmured, if only Jack had waited for backup; he might still be alive today.

Jack's mother was called within the hour. She would never get over the death of her only son. Having lost a husband and now her only son within months, Jack's death proved to be too much for Sarah King. She died two months later.

The shooting had occurred around 9:00 am. Immediately, an APB went out extending to surrounding counties. Silver Creek's police force and state patrolmen were determined to catch the cop killer.

A State Patrol's helicopter was brought in to assist in the search for the fugitive. A Honda Accord matching the description of the fugitive's car was sighted near the small community of Lance, North Carolina. Within minutes, the helicopter spotted the Honda Accord driving east on county road 3344. A road block was set up, armed police officers, as well as state patrolmen were in place when Carlos Sanchez approached. He immediately stopped his car about a thousand yards from the road block and jumped out and fled into the woods.

Dogs were brought in track Sanchez as he ran through the dense wooded area. Within two hours, Sanchez was found hiding in an abandoned shack. When ordered to come out with his hands in the air, Carlos Sanchez replied by opening gun fire on the officers that had surrounded the small shack. The police officers and state patrolmen responded with a barrage of gunfire. In less than a minute, it was over. When the first wave of law enforcement personnel knocked in the door, they found Carlos Sanchez lying on the floor bleeding profusely. He would survive the assault.

Jack King's fellow officers openly admitted they were disappointed. They wanted justice served in that tiny run down shack where the cold blooded killer held up. Everyone there was amazed that this killer had survived the hail of bullets.

Carlos Sanchez, alias Hosea Amentez, was transported to the Humana Hospital in Silver Creek, where he was treated for two gunshot wounds. One to his right thigh and the other in his left shoulder. Although he had lost a great deal of blood, his wounds were not life threatening. He spent the night in the hospital and was released the next morning to the custody of the Silver Creek Police.

The gunman was identified as Carlos Anthony Sanchez. He was booked that afternoon for the murder of police officer Jack King. The following morning at the arraignment, Judge Simon Stokers ruled there would be no bond. Sanchez's court-appointed lawyer did not question the ruling.

When a fellow police officer dies in the line of duty, word spreads quickly. It would be the next morning, August 19th when MacArthur got the news.

"Could I speak to the person in charge, this is Detective MacArthur Nowlin with the Wilcox homicide division?"

"Detective Nowlin, may I ask what this is in reference to?" the person answering the phone asked.

"I am conducting a double murder investigation. The man who shot your police officer is wanted for questioning here in Wilcox."

"You'll want talk to Chief Manor, hold on I'll see if he's in his office."

"This is Chief Manor. I understand you are interested in the suspect we arrested for the murder of one of our officers yesterday. Just between you and me, Detective, we should have killed the bastard yesterday, and saved the trouble of having a trial. Of course, that's off the record," the Chief said, in a hushed tone.

"Of course, I would feel the same way if it was one of my men, Chief. This Carlos Sanchez's, if he is the same man, prints were found at the murder scene of a double homicide I'm investigating. I would like to come over and have a talk with him, with your permission, of course," MacArthur asked, with a sense of urgency.

"I don't have a problem with that, Detective, but let me warn you, he got all "lawyered up" this morning. Some big shot out of Raleigh I think. I wonder how this loser could afford it."

"My reports indicated he may be tied to the Gianni family," MacArthur replied.

"Oh well, that explains it."

"Chief, I have one more favor to ask. If he's not already, would you put him on suicide watch? If I'm right, his testimony in my case could be the clincher to getting an arrest and conviction."

"Already have Detective."

"I appreciate you working with me on this, Chief. And again, I'm sorry about that young officer," MacArthur said, with sadness in his voice.

"Thanks, he was a good man. You know, I've been in this for over 25 years and never lost an officer. I guess I've been lucky, but I still can't understand why things like this happen," Chief Manor shared with MacArthur, as his voice cracked up.

"Yeah, it's such a senseless killing."

"When would you like to come, Detective?"

"How about tomorrow Chief? Say, around 1:00 pm?"

"That'll work, see you then."

MacArthur hung up the phone and for the first time in this case, he felt everything coming together. He hoped that Sanchez would talk to him. He knew it was not a certainty. He knew he had to offer something in return for his cooperation. Chief Manor had told him of Sanchez's wife and daughter. MacArthur knew exactly what his offer was going to be.

Don't get ahead of yourself. Just because his prints were found on the door, that doesn't mean he's the shooter, MacArthur said to himself. He was counting on making Sanchez think he knew more than he did about his involvement in the Sprayberry murders. *Hopefully, Sanchez will admit to the murders. If Sanchez is not guilty, he will not consider making a deal. Why would he?* MacArthur said aloud as he poured another cup of coffee.

He knew the chance of the D.A. not seeking the death penalty for killing a police officer was zero. He would want the same thing, if it was one of his men.

He called Chief Aldridge and informed him that he and Rachel would be going to Silver Creek tomorrow to interview a person of interest. MacArthur told him of the print found at the scene of the crime and that it belonged to the man in custody over in Silver Creek. Chief Aldridge seemed pleased. After all, the mayor was putting even more pressure on his department to find the killer or killers.

MacArthur spent the rest of the day following other leads that came in, by way of phone. There was one call that he felt could have some merit. The caller identified himself as Carlton Packard. He told MacArthur on the night of the Sprayberry murders, he was waiting to use the pay phone at the 7 Eleven on Jefferson Street. He thought the man using the pay phone was Hispanic. Packard said the reason he remembered this was because when the man left the phone booth and got in his car, he accidently backed into his car. Packard told him the guy didn't even get out, he just drove off fast.

Before Packard hung up, MacArthur asked him, "Why are you so sure this was the same night of the murders?"

"Because I had gone to the 7 Eleven to get gas and some beer, I heard about the killings on the radio scanner."

"How can you be so sure of the time?"

"Because I was supposed to pick up my girlfriend at 8:00. I was running a little late, that's why I was going to use the phone, to call her."

MacArthur got his full name and address and asked if he had a problem testifying in court if necessary. Packard said he wouldn't have a problem at all. MacArthur thanked him and asked him to give him a call if he should remember anything else. When he hung up, he jotted down everything the caller had said. He then let his imagination take over.

Just what if the guy in the phone booth was Carlos Sanchez? And, if he was the shooter, that would give proof of his being in Wilcox the night of the murders. Along with opportunity, if Sanchez was hired to kill the Sprayberrys, this would also give him a motive; money. Why kill the Sprayberrys, if not for money? There didn't seem to be any connection with the Sprayberrys. He was hired to kill them. It was the only explanation. And the same question comes up again, who would benefit from their deaths? Sean and his sister Susan. MacArthur's pulse was racing by now.

If the caller, Packard, could pick Carlos Sanchez out of a line up, it would prove that Sanchez was in Wilcox on the night of the murders. This didn't prove he did it, but it did prove he had opportunity. MacArthur called Rachel and told her about the shooting and arrest of Carlos Sanchez, over in Silver Creek. He also told her of the trip tomorrow to visit him. He didn't tell her of the caller. He didn't want to get ahead of himself on this. He wanted more evidence before sharing his theory with her.

Carlos Anthony Sanchez came to the United States by way of crossing the Rio Grande. His mother, two brothers, and two sisters crossed the border near El Paso under the cover of darkness when he was nine years old. They lived with an aunt, on the outskirts of El Paso. They were enrolled in the local public school system using false information. Carlos was the only child that spoke some English, but this language barrier made school very difficult for him. His home life was worse. Carlos was old enough to know how his aunt and mother put food on the table. It was not uncommon to see men coming and going all hours of the night and day. His mother never apologized for her lifestyle, because she knew it was the only way to provide for her children, and not lose them to the state agency. One of her best "customers" was an official with the local government. That was the only thing that was keeping her and her children from being sent back to Mexico.

Carlos was constantly in trouble at school. In the beginning, it was minor infractions, but these soon escalated to more serious offenses. He started to run with a local gang. The last trouble that got him expelled from school, was beating a boy so badly that he was hospitalized. Carlos said the boy had disrespected his sister and he would do it again. He was 17 years old at the time of the expulsion.

He began to get involved in petty crimes with other gang members. One year later, Carlos was arrested for burglary. He was put on probation, but only one month later, he was caught stealing produce from the local market. He spent 9 months in the county jail. It was there that he met Tony Mentis. They formed a friendship that would last for many years. It would be his friendship with Tony that connected him to the Gianni family in New Orleans.

Six years after Carlos met Tony, Tony was killed while robbing a convenience store in Slidell, Louisiana. Before he was killed, he introduced Carlos to a friend of his that was a runner for the Gianni family in New Orleans. It wasn't long before Carlos was making money running errands for the family.

He was fearless, he moved up the ladder quickly. Less than a year, he became a "soldier" in the syndicate. He and his partner extorted money from local store owners promising protection. Carlos was an excellent moneymaker for the family.

Soon he graduated to carrying out hits for the family. He would later confess to killing three people who had crossed the family. When the order came down from the top to take someone out, Carlos knew not to question the decision, but to do his job. "It wasn't personal, just business" he liked to brag to fellow inmates.

However, he was acquitted in all three murders. It seems the witnesses had a change of heart when it came to appearing in court. He did serve four years in prison for extortion and money laundering. He was rewarded with a gift of $5,000 for remaining loyal to the family. When he got out of prison he would go through the money in weeks. Other than buying a couple of new suits, most of it went up his nose.

When Carlos reached the point where he could no longer function; his relationship with the family dried up. In fact, it was debated if he should "retire permanently". Although he wasn't in any condition to help the family anymore, his loyalty to the family had not been forgotten. The call for a hit on Carlos Sanchez was called off.

MacArthur felt he was getting close. The pieces were coming together. Of course, he knew he needed more than a gut feeling to make an arrest. He would soon get it.

"Rachel, why don't you go home, it's been a long day."

"Are you staying awhile? "Rachel asked.

"Yeah, I'm preparing some questions for tomorrow's meeting with Sanchez."

"What if he refuses to answer any question without his lawyer present?"

"That's possible, but all we can do is wait and see what happens. I need to find a reason for him to want to hear what I have to say. There needs to be something in it for him," MacArthur replied.

He sat at his desk and stared at the picture of Marilyn. The last few weeks had been a blur. He wished he could give her a call. If only things could be the same. There were some memories that continued to linger. He closed his eyes and pictured her covered with bubbles, sipping her red wine as he massaged her neck. He could still hear her sweet voice as she proclaimed her undying love and devotion to him. He could still smell the fragrance of her hair. He could see her flushed cheeks and full red lips. He could hear the sound of her laughter and feel the touch of her velvet hands. MacArthur found himself longing to hold her just one more time. Suddenly, he slammed his fist down on the desk and threw her picture across the room.

What the hell is wrong with me? It was all lies. How could have I been so stupid? She turned out to be just like all of the rest, a selfish bitch that couldn't be trusted. Why would I leave the only woman who ever really cared about me? Why did I ever leave Kelli?

In typical fashion, he blamed himself for his dysfunctional life. He had gotten exactly what he deserved. He believed his fate was sealed a long time ago. When he walked out on Kelli he had charted a course of emptiness and loneliness for the rest of his life. He could never forgive himself. His pride wouldn't allow him to ask her to forgive him either.

If only he could have known, Kelli would have taken him back years ago. If he had only reached out to her. There were times she was tempted to call him and tell him of their son. The son MacArthur never knew existed. The son that would have changed his life.

Human pride has a way of displacing happiness and fulfillment in people's lives. MacArthur's inability to admit he was wrong and to say he was sorry would be the source of a lifetime of sadness. His work would be all he had to sustain an otherwise empty and meaningless life.

MacArthur gathered his notes and turned off the lights to his office and walked slowly to his car. He could feel the wind blowing in his face and smell fresh bread baking at the bakery across the street. He thought about driving by Marilyn's old apartment, but decided against it.

As he walked into his lifeless apartment, MacArthur prepared himself for another lonely night. If not for the Ambien, sleep would be impossible. He showered and put on a clean t - shirt and jogging shorts. He didn't own a pair of pajamas. He thought that men who wore pajamas were wimps. His conclusion was based upon the fact that John Wayne would never wear pajamas.

He turned out the lights of the bathroom, walked into his bedroom, and picked up the TV remote. The Tonight Show was one of a few TV shows he watched. There wasn't anybody in particular he wanted to see tonight. It must have been around 11:45 when he dozed off to sleep. He woke at 3:10, got out of bed and went into the kitchen. He poured himself a glass of milk. Sleep never returned. He got up and showered and decided to go down to the all night deli and get some donuts and coffee.

As he sat and sipped his coffee, MacArthur wondered what Killingsworth was up to. He was confident that Killingsworth's crusade to have him take the fall for Marilyn's death would be short-lived. He had no way of knowing just how close he was of actually being charged with the murder of Marilyn.

Killingsworth's investigation was nearing a point where an arrest was eminent. It was just a matter of tying down some loose ends before an indictment would be coming down. MacArthur would soon become the sacrificial lamb.

MacArthur finished his donut and coffee and asked for another cup to go. The walk was only 15 minutes, but the early morning cool air and the thoughts of his worst nightmare, not finding the killer, made the trip seem longer. After getting back to his apartment he never went back to sleep. He got dressed and drove to the station.

Around 9:00 that morning MacArthur got a call from Chief Manor of the Silver Creek Police. He told him that the District Attorney said his office was pursuing the death penalty. There would be no deals, as far as he was concerned.

MacArthur thanked him for the heads-up.

He was not surprised at the stance the D.A. had taken. Politics was never far away from the mix. The D.A. had aspirations of climbing the ladder. The conviction of a cop killer would certainly add to his resume. He hoped what he was about to offer Sanchez was enough for him to talk.

He and Rachel left for Silver Creek around 12:00. MacArthur had asked her to drive. She thought this was strange, MacArthur always drove. Little was said during the 35 minute drive. Rachel sensed he was unusually nervous. She had never seen him this way before.

When they arrived, Chief Manor was notified that MacArthur and his associate were there.

"Chief Manor, I appreciate you allowing me to come today," MacArthur said.

"No problem Detective, I think we both want the same thing, to see this monster fry," the Chief said earnestly. He picked up the phone and directed the officer in charge to bring the suspect into the interrogation room. Within five minutes, Carlos Sanchez was seated in front of MacArthur and Rachel.

Sanchez looked smaller than he imagined him to be. He had tattoos covering both arms as well as his neck. His face gave away his past. He had a scar over his right eye, a crooked nose, with gold capped front teeth.

MacArthur also noticed his hands, the finger nails bitten down to the quick. The pinky on his left hand was missing. It appeared he hadn't shaved in days. Carlos looked much older than his actual age. Looking at him, MacArthur couldn't help but remember the old adage, "rode hard and put up wet."

This was not the first time Carlos had been inside an interrogation room. He surveyed the situation and asked for a cigarette. MacArthur motioned for the attendant outside to bring cigarettes. The cop killer asked for a light as he put the cigarette to his lips. He sucked in a long deep inhale, smoke oozed out of the corners of his mouth.

"You know Detective, they say smoking can cause cancer. Do you smoke? If you don't, I would suggest you don't start. It can be a real killer, if you know what I mean."

"I used to, but I gave up the habit. I've never been one to do things just because everybody else did. Some people are just followers, you know, can't think for themselves. I think you are one of those people Carlos. You just let people lead you around," MacArthur said.

"Don't waste your time trying to profile me. You're not the first two bit cop looking to break me. You see, Detective, I don't give a damn if I live or die. My whole life I've been going against the grain. I don't see the point in analyzing why I turned out the way I did."

"Nobody's trying to analyze you, Carlos. To tell you the truth, I don't give a damn what kind of childhood you had. If you pissed in your bed, or were cruel to animals or was abused by an uncle, I could care less. Killing that cop yesterday sealed your fate. Nothing I can do or say will change that."

"Then why are you here? You must want something," Sanchez asked.

"Your prints were found on the door knob of the home where two people were killed, execution style back in Wilcox on August 8$^{th.}$ I think you entered the Sprayberry home through the back door, went upstairs and shot and killed both of them. You tried to make it look like Dr. Sprayberry shot his wife then himself. Carlos, I'm here to offer you a deal that will keep your wife and daughter alive. You and I both know they will be hunted down and killed for your sins. You have a chance to do something good for once in your life."

"Why would my wife and child be in any danger once I'm gone? It's not like they know nothing, "Carlos responded, sounding confused.

"You and I know that, but some bosses of the syndicate don't. Carlos, you know the drill, they'll come after your wife and use your daughter as bait. They can't risk the fact that your wife has information that could bring down their organization. Your wife and daughter won't be safe anywhere. Don't waste my time lying about how you didn't kill those two people," MacArthur continued, not knowing if Sanchez would deny the murders. "You've got 15 minutes to tell me the truth about what happened that night in Wilcox. If you do, then I'll see that your wife and daughter are protected. Otherwise, I walk out of here and your wife and daughter die."

"If I did kill them two people, and I ain't saying I did, how can you protect my wife and daughter?"

"I can arrange to have them enter the federal witness protection program. They will disappear. Their identity will be changed as well as their location. It's the best I can offer."

"I don't know, let me think about it," Carlos said, as he motioned for the guard to escort him back to his cell.

Once Carlos left the room, MacArthur sat and thought about what would happen. Could he really protect Carlos' family? Was he making promises he couldn't keep? Would the D.A. cooperate?

Rachel asked, "MacArthur, even if Carlos gives us information, will it be enough to issue an arrest? If he did kill the Sprayberrys, will he give up the person or persons who hired him?"

"You're asking me questions I don't have the answers to. Carlos has to believe that I can deliver. If he thinks I can't he probably won't deal. I'm the only one that can make sure his wife and daughter are safe. That's our only real leverage."

Carlos sat in his cell thinking about what MacArthur had offered him. He knew his life was over, regardless of if he was put to death, or put away to rot in prison the rest of his life. He had killed people, he knew he deserved to die. But, his wife and daughter didn't. Carlos Sanchez never felt any sympathy for the victims or their families. He was incapable of feeling anything. To him, the people he killed were just objects. There was no remorse. The only thing he was sorry for, was the fact that he had gotten caught.

In less than ten minutes, Carlos asked to see Detective Nowlin. He was ready to make a deal.

Carlos Sanchez shuffled in with chains attached to his feet and hands. He sat down without speaking. Once the guards left, Carlos asked MacArthur to explain once again how he was going to take care of his family. He assured Carlos that his family would go into the witness protection program. He explained in detail how the program worked.

"Detective Nowlin, how can I know you are telling the truth?"

"How can I know you are telling the truth?" MacArthur countered.

"Look, what I'm going to tell you is the truth. I'm betting my wife and daughter's life on it."

"It better be, because if I find you are lying to me, the deal is off. Carlos, I have been straight up with you. I will see that your family is protected."

"Ok, let's get this over with," Carlos said, with a sense of relief in his voice.

MacArthur took out his tape recorder and checked to be sure the batteries were working.

"Carlos, I'm going to record our conversation. Is that ok with you?"

"Yeah, it's alright with me."

MacArthur and Rachel spent the next two hours with Carlos doing most of the talking. At times he would ramble on about some of his dealings with the "family". Even though MacArthur wanted to interrupt him and tell him to stick to the point, he didn't. His experience as an interrogator proved to be crucial in this case.

Carlos covered every detail of the murders. He explained how he remembered smelling the bath soap that Mrs. Sprayberry was bathing in. His face was dripping with perspiration as he continued his tale of destruction.

He asked for a soda after some 45 minutes into the interview. MacArthur turned off the recorder and found the nearest soda machine. After taking a short break the interview continued.

MacArthur asked him if he knew the name of the person who hired him to kill the Sprayberrys. Carlos said he didn't, because the contact person provided the address and weapon. He told of how he found out about the hit.

"One of my buddies I had done some time with called me. It was sometime around the end of June, no it was July. He told me he had a job that I might be interested in; $3,000 up front and $3,000 when the job was finished. He gave me the address but not the names of who was to be hit. There was supposed to be a man and woman. I was to take them out."

MacArthur stopped him and asked him what he meant by "hit."

"You know Detective, kill'em," he answered, without showing any emotion.

Carlos continued his story. He was enjoying being on center stage. His confession of killing two innocent people for money gave him a sense of power. At times, he almost sounded proud of his accomplishment.

Rachel sat without saying anything. She was only a spectator in the unbelievable drama unfolding before her eyes.

"I was supposed to meet my friend in the Walmart parking lot on a Wednesday night of the same week I shot them. He brought me a gun, a nine millimeter Glock that had a silencer. He also brought me a key. That's how I was going to get into the house, through the back door."

"What did you do with the key when you left?" MacArthur asked, checking to see if Carlos' story matched the crime scene.

"I think I left it in the door. I met my contact two days after the hit. He brought me the other $3,000. I gave him the silencer I used when I shot them. He said he was going to get rid of it. Then he asked for the key. I told him I must have forgotten it when I left, I didn't have it."

"Carlos, did you leave anything upstairs after you shot them?"

"Yeah, I was told to make it look like the man shot his wife, then himself. When I got into the house, I didn't see nobody downstairs. I walked over to the bottom of the stairs and saw some lights on. I walked up the stairs and when I got to the top, I could see a door open. I remember thinking, there were some people in there cause I heard voices. I walked towards the door and when I got there, I seen Mr. Sprayberry laying on the bed asleep."

Once again, MacArthur asked a question that only the shooter could have known, since Mrs. Sprayberry was in the bathtub when she was shot.

When he asked Carlos if he shot them both in bed, he said no. He said Mrs. Sprayberry was not in the room when he shot Mr. Sprayberry.

"I walked over to the bed and, like I said, I seen Mr. Sprayberry laying on his back. I put the gun to his left temple and fired. Then I listened to see if Mrs. Sprayberry was coming out of the bathroom. When she didn't, I walked over to the door that was shut and peeked in and I saw her in the bathtub. She was lying on her back with her eyes closed, she must have been asleep too. She never knew I was there. I shot her once behind her left ear.

"What did you do next?"

"I got the note out of my pocket and laid it on the table beside the bed. I was told to leave it there. I left the casings on the floor in the bathroom and the bedroom. I only used two bullets. I walked over to the bed where Mr.

Sprayberry was. I raised him up and turned him over on his side. I put the gun in his left hand," Carlos continued.

"What did you do then?"

"Well, I checked again to make sure they were both dead. Then I walked downstairs. As I was walking through the kitchen I stopped and looked in the refrigerator. I saw some beer, so I decided to sit down at the table and have myself a brew. I didn't think they'd care," Carlos said, with a cold blooded grin. "I must have been there about 10 minutes then I went out the back door."

MacArthur sat looking at Carlos with contempt, thinking how could someone kill another person and think nothing of it? What kind of monster is this?

"Carlos, you mentioned this "friend" several times. Does he have a name?"

"Yep, but I ain't giving him up. Besides, he was just the middle man anyway. He just set up the deal, it was somebody else that paid for the hit."

"Do you know who that was?" MacArthur asked.

"No, and I didn't want to know. The less I knew, the better. My friend told me he had met with the money man twice. Once outside Silver Creek, and once in the parking lot of Walmart. He said it was during the second meeting in the parking lot where he was given the gun with a silencer, the money, and a key to the back door. He did tell me that the person that hired me to kill them people must have known them real good. Hell, they could have been family.

"What makes you so sure the man that hired you to kill the Sprayberrys knew them?"

"Cause, somebody had to have a key to the house, and somebody had to know that they would be home. Damn, it don't take no genius to figure that out."

"Is there anything else you want to tell us, Carlos? Have you left anything out? Remember, if I find that you are lying to us today, the deal is off, and you can say goodbye to your wife and daughter."

"Detective, do you think I'm stupid enough to admit to killing two people if I hadn't done it? Look, I'm not proud of what I did, but it was just business. $6,000 bucks goes a long way. I'll sign something if you want me to. What I told you is the truth. Now, you just make sure you do what you say you will."

"Carlos, you know you're going to have to tell your story to a judge and jury. Once I find out, and I am, who hired you to kill those two people, your testimony is critical to putting them away."

"I understand, that won't be no problem."

MacArthur decided that he would wait until the next day to press Carlos for the name of the contact person. This was going to be the second provision in the deal he was offering Carlos in return for his family's safety. He was going to tell Carlos that if he didn't give up the contact's name, the deal was off.

MacArthur called for the guards. Carlos was taken back to his cell, while he and Rachel made their way back to his car. This time, he drove. He played the tape over again on their way back to Wilcox.

He told Rachel he believed Carlos' account of the murder. He knew if he could find the middle man who sat up the hit, it was just a matter of time before the mastermind behind the murders would be identified.

Some two hours later he was sitting in his office when the phone rang.

"Detective Nowlin, this is Chief Manor. I'm afraid I've got some very bad news. Carlos Sanchez was found dead, about 15 minutes ago. He was put back in general population by mistake right after you left. His body was found in the latrine with his throat cut."

MacArthur felt as though he had just been hammered with a stun gun. After some silence, he thanked the chief for letting him know and hung up.

His star witness was gone. How would he ever find the contact now that Sanchez was dead? He took a deep breath and got up and poured himself a fresh cup of coffee, this was going to be another long night.

What else can go wrong? MacArthur asked himself. *At least we have the confession on tape, but would a judge allow it to be admissible in court? Even with this damn tape, it still doesn't tell me who hired Carlos to kill the Sprayberrys.*

Because he had given Carlos Sanchez, a confessed murderer, his word, MacArthur planned to protect his wife and daughter, just like he had promised earlier today. Even though he was about to make a deal with the devil, he was still going to keep his word.

Within a week Carlos' widow and daughter were given new identities, and relocated to another part of the country. Carlos had hidden his blood money after the hit. He had told his wife where it was, in case something should happen to him. She and her only daughter disappeared into the night. Filed away in some federal office was an official document indicating their new location and names. No one would ever know.

MacArthur did the only thing he could do at this point, he started going over his notes for what seemed the one-hundredth time. He decided not to tell Rachel about the unfortunate turn of events until the following day.

MacArthur had no way of knowing it, but the hit on Carlos had nothing to do with his confession to the Sprayberry murders. He had stolen some money from the "family." When it came to stealing from family, the consequence was always death.

Around 9:30 pm MacArthur decided he was calling it a day. As he began to put away the stack of files and notes, a single page fell underneath his chair. He pushed his chair backwards and bent over to pick up the sheet of paper. He was about to put it in with the other double stack of files and notes, when he noticed something in the margin. After taking a closer look, there it was!

The contents of the lost note, along with a comment Carlos made during his confession, suddenly made it very clear who paid Carlos Sanchez to kill the Sprayberrys. With a sigh, MacArthur thought, *damn it was right in front of me all along.*

For the first time in weeks, MacArthur slept through the night. He followed his regular routine and arrived at the police station at 7:30 am. Chief Aldridge was not in yet, so he began to do the paperwork that he would need to present to the judge for an arrest warrant. The first order of business however, was to contact the District Attorney's office.

The D.A. sat and listened to MacArthur's account of what happened that fateful night. He then told him, based on evidence acquired through the investigation who he believed was behind the hit. The D.A. acknowledged he had a solid case, but most of it was circumstantial.

The D.A. said he needed more. He needed evidence that a jury can see, feel, and touch. He told MacArthur he was just as convinced as he was about the identity of the person behind the killings, but he wasn't willing to risk going to court and take the chance the jury might find reasonable doubt.

MacArthur understood, but was still disappointed.

He told the D.A. he would keep him informed about the status of the investigation. He went to the public restroom before leaving the courthouse. As he came out he noticed Killingsworth headed towards the D.A.'s office.

Wonder what that's all about, MacArthur thought.

The key! He still had the key in his desk back at his office. If he could prove who the key belonged to it might just lead him to the person that hired the hit on the Sprayberrys.

Rachel had arrived by the time he had gotten back from the D.A.'s office. "Rachel, you're not going to believe what happened after we left the interview with Sanchez. He was killed in the latrine, his throat was cut. Someone wanted to make sure he was silenced for good."

"No way! How could that have happened when he was in isolation?"

"He wasn't in isolation. The guards mistakenly took him back to the general population. All's not lost, maybe, I was looking through my notes and found where I had some notes during one of the interviews. Do you remember when Carlos told us yesterday he knew both Dr. and Mrs. Sprayberry would be home that Friday night?"

Rachel nodded her head, "Yes I do, but what has that got to do with anything?"

"It has everything to do with it. You see, Dr. Sprayberry was supposed to be leaving that Friday afternoon to go to a conference in Chapel Hill.

"But I don't …"

"Let me finish Rachel. Do you remember his flight was cancelled? He was going to have to fly out early Saturday morning? Well, how could the person that hired Carlos know that both of them would be there that night? After all, several people knew Dr. Sprayberry was going out of town. It had been on his public calendar for some time. I'll tell you how. Only two people knew he did not make that flight, Sean Sprayberry, and Ida Sprayberry. Remember, Susan said she talked to her mother almost every day. She told you she had spoken with her mother the morning of the day Mrs. Sprayberry was killed. She couldn't have known her father's flight had been cancelled because at the time she had spoken with her mom the flight hadn't been cancelled yet. That eliminates the sister."

Rachel sat without making a comment. It was becoming clear to her where MacArthur was going with this.

"Take a look at the note I made during the last interviewed with Sean Sprayberry and his attorney," MacArthur said as he handed her the note.

Rachel read what he had circled in red. A huge grin came over her face as she handed the note back to him.

"So Sean knew his father's flight had been cancelled, because according to his statement, he had spoken with his father around 4:00 pm."

"That just leaves one person who knew…"

MacArthur finished her sentence, "Sean was the only person to know his father would be there that night. I would also bet money that he gave the contact man the key that Carlos used to get into the house that night. Sean Sprayberry is our man Rachel. All we have to do is prove the key that Carlos used to enter the Sprayberry home belongs to Sean."

"And how do we do that?"

"I don't know yet Rachel, but I'll find a way," MacArthur replied.

Sean Sprayberry picked up the phone on his desk and dialed the same number he had called on the day his parents, were killed.

"Did you hear about what happened to Carlos yesterday?" he asked.

"No, I ain't seen or heard from Carlos since the night I met him in the Walmart parking lot, two or three nights after he made a visit to the address you gave me," the caller replied.

"Somebody killed him in jail. When you met with him, did he say anything about a key?" Sean asked.

"No, he told me he had forgotten to get it when he left the house. I didn't think that was a big deal," the voice on the other end said.

"Well, it's a big deal now," Sean said.

"Look, I did what you told me to do. I delivered the money and the gun. I ain't got nothing to do with no key. Besides, if Carlos is dead like you say he is, it don't matter about no key or anything else. It ain't like he's gonna talk."

Johnny Simmons wanted nothing more to do with this whole matter.

"Johnny, we need to meet and discuss this situation," Sean said.

Simmons answered sternly, "We don't need to meet about nothin. I told you, I'm done here."

Simmons was too street savvy to fall for a meeting that would most likely be for the purpose of getting rid of the only person alive that could connect

Sean Sprayberry to the murder of his mother and father. No way, Johnny Simmons was going underground.

"Don't call me again Sprayberry. I would hate to see the same thing happen to you that happened to your parents. This time I will do it myself. Do you understand?"

With that, Johnny Simmons slammed down the phone.

Sean Sprayberry's world was about to unravel, he just didn't know it yet.

KEYS TO MURDER

CHAPTER 26

MacArthur's mind was filled with excitement. He knew he was close. Sean Sprayberry had his parents killed so that he could get his share of the insurance money. He had no doubts about that. It was in the shower where he did his best thinking. As the warm water ran down his face he said to himself, *it might just work*. He finished drying off, shaved, and had his second cup of coffee. Within an hour, he was back at his desk at the station. He was counting on Sean Sprayberry's arrogance and sense of superiority to incriminate himself.

"Rachel, are you up yet?"

"Yes, but why are you calling so early Detective?"

"Listen, I think I may have found a way to connect the key to Sean. What time are you coming in today?"

"Well, since its Saturday, I hadn't planned on going in today, but I can," Rachel replied.

"I'm sorry, I forgot it was Saturday. Go on with your plans, I'll give you a call later on this afternoon," MacArthur said, apologizing once again.

"Really, I don't mind coming in."

"No, I'll call you this afternoon."

MacArthur hadn't worked out all of the details yet. If his plan worked, he would be able to prove the key found in the door that allowed the shooter in belongs to Sean Sprayberry.

KEYS TO MURDER

It was 8:45 am when Detective Tim Killingsworth asked Chief Aldridge's secretary if he was in. She nodded and motioned him to go in.

"Chief, I need to search MacArthur's apartment. A tip came in yesterday from a caller who said we would find Marilyn's phone in MacArthur's apartment. If it's there that would add to the evidence we already have. How could he explain having Marilyn's phone in his apartment?"

"Did the source give his name? How reliable do you think the information is?" the Chief asked.

"I would say, very reliable. If the caller is right, this will give us plenty to get an indictment on MacArthur. Before I try and get a search warrant, I'm going to ask him to allow us to search his apartment. I don't really think he'll give us permission, but it's worth a try."

"Make sure he's present when you search his apartment. I don't want his lawyer accusing us of planting evidence. Also Tim, when were you going to tell me about you and Marilyn?"

Tim Killingsworth was caught off guard by this question.

"Chief, I know I should have told you, but I thought if I did, you would take me off of this case. I'm sorry I didn't come clean with you before now."

"So am I Tim. Is there anything you should tell me?"

"No sir."

"Well, I should take you off of the case now, but I'm going to allow you to stay. Just make sure there aren't any more secrets I need to know," Chief said as he motioned Killingsworth to leave.

"Thank you sir. You have my word that I will keep you abreast of the entire investigation. Speaking of the investigation, I believe MacArthur killed her in a jealous rage, when he found out about us. I think that given the right situation, MacArthur could very well be capable of murder."

"I'm not so sure I agree with you, Tim. All I'm going to say, is that you better be right on this. If you follow through with an indictment, there will be no turning back."

"I know, Chief, if I wasn't so sure of his guilt, believe me, I would not go any further with the investigation. I am convinced he killed Marilyn and the evidence will support what I'm saying," Detective Killingsworth said, with complete confidence.

"What proof are you talking about, Tim?"

"I can prove he left the Sprayberry murder scene and had plenty of time to reach the cabin where she was killed. He and I were the only two people who knew she would be there. He said Rachel saw him that night at the station, but she says it was the next night. Why would she lie about that? I don't believe she did. I think he is lying. I know it's hard to believe one of our own could have committed murder, but Chief, like I said weeks ago, the evidence is there. And, if we do find her phone in his apartment that seals the deal."

"Ok, Tim, but just remember what I said about if you are wrong. Keep me informed with every detail from his point on."

"Yes sir, will do."

Chief Aldridge wasn't convinced MacArthur was capable of doing such a terrible thing. The idea that he killed Marilyn made him sick to his stomach. He prayed Tim was wrong.

Killingsworth decided today was as good as any to confront MacArthur and ask permission to search his apartment. He knocked on his door and walked in uninvited. MacArthur was pouring over his notes as he looked up.

"What the hell do you want, can't you see I busy?"

"I came to ask for your permission to search your apartment," Killingsworth said, waiting for all hell to break loose.

"You have a lot of gall coming into my office and asking to search my apartment. I take it you still don't have a suspect."

"Actually we do. Right now, you are considered a suspect. Look, MacArthur I have tried to do everything I can to prove you didn't have anything to do with Marilyn's murder, but the evidence is there. MacArthur, you know I can get a search warrant without your permission. It would be easier on everyone if you consented without us having to go through a judge."

MacArthur sat and stared at Killingsworth in complete silence. The tension in the office was stifling. The two men stared each other down as two gunfighters would in the middle of the street at high noon.

"So, what is it you expect to find? Do you think I would be dumb enough to leave something in my apartment that would incriminate me if I had killed Marilyn? You know what Killingsworth, maybe it was you who killed her. The only person that knew she was going to be there was you. I know I didn't kill her, so that just leaves you doesn't it? I'm about to get an indictment on the Sprayberry case. I don't have time for your stupid accusations. I tell you what, you jerk, let's go right now to my apartment, and you can search it all you want.

MacArthur picked up his car keys and walked out of his office.

In twenty minutes he was unlocking the front door and left it open as Killingsworth and two police officers followed him in.

The search began in the kitchen. Killingsworth headed toward MacArthur's bedroom. MacArthur followed him every step. When he was satisfied there was nothing of interest, Killingsworth made his way to the smaller bedroom. As the other two officers continued to search the apartment MacArthur took a seat at the kitchen table.

One of the uniformed officers then made his way to the bathroom just off of the master bedroom. Within moments he came walking out with a phone. It was not MacArthur's.

Both he and Tim Killingsworth knew exactly whose phone it was. MacArthur had no idea how Marilyn's phone ended up in his bathroom.

"It was in a drawer, beneath the sink, Detective," the young officer reported.

"I suppose you don't know anything about this MacArthur?"

"Look, Killingsworth, I don't know how that got here," MacArthur said, with a look of surprise on his face.

"Bag it officer, we'll take it down to the station and get it checked out. Do you know whose phone it is?"

"You know damn well whose phone that is, its Marilyn's."

"I think we're done here. I don't have to tell you how this looks. I suggest you…"

"You don't suggest a damn thing to me, Killingsworth. I don't know how that got here, but I'm going to find out. Unless you're going to arrest me, I want you out of my apartment. I don't know what's going on, but someone is trying to set me up."

MacArthur closed the door behind Killingsworth and the uniformed police officers as they exited the apartment. He sat down on the sofa and tried to make sense of what had just happened. It was clear to him that someone was trying to frame him for the murder of Marilyn, but why? It just didn't make any sense. He couldn't think of but one person that could behind this. That person was Tim Killingsworth.

As when other crisis had come into MacArthur's life, he had to give himself a pep talk, *I can't worry about that right now. I've got to stay focused on the task at hand, and that is to prove Sean Sprayberry had his parents killed.*

He needed to think. He needed to clear his head. He got in his car and drove. Before he realized it, he was turning on to the dirt road that led to the cabin where Marilyn was murdered. He parked his car in front of the small cabin that still had yellow bands across the entrance. The walk to the small pond behind the cabin took 40 minutes, or so MacArthur guessed. He walked over to the dam where he had seen marks of a vehicle going down the side and into the water. He still believed the car, when recovered, would be Marilyn's. MacArthur sat down on the embankment and stared into the dark, murky water. In spite of telling himself to forget about Marilyn's phone found in his apartment, he couldn't get it off his mind. He began talking to himself aloud, *alright MacArthur, you've got to man-up. So what if Killingsworth is trying to pin Marilyn's murder on you? If you ever believed in the justice system, now is the time. What have I got to worry about? I know I didn't kill Marilyn, and no one can prove otherwise. But who is trying to frame me?*

The wind began to blow leaves across the small pond. He could feel the cool air on his face. He knew what he had to do, press on, and get a conviction on Sean Sprayberry. Sam and Ida Sprayberry deserved nothing less. With a renewed determination, MacArthur played the entire scenario over in his head.

When he finally reached his car, he had that feeling he was being watched. He slowly placed his right hand on the handle of his pistol. Off to his right, he thought he heard shuffling of leaves, like someone walking. As he approached the overgrown bushes, suddenly a squirrel ran out and darted up the oak tree standing nearby.

Damn, MacArthur, get ahold of yourself, he thought.

MacArthur turned and walked back to his car and got in. He backed out and turned around and headed down the dirt road he came in on. He never saw the small motorcycle, nor its rider. Again, his instincts were right. He was being watched.

KEYS TO MURDER

CHAPTER 27

Back at the police station, Rachel was waiting for MacArthur. It was almost 1:00 pm when he walked into his office. She followed down the hall and knocked on his door.

"What's up Detective?" she said trying to sound cheerful.

"Someone planted Marilyn's phone in my apartment. This morning I let Killingsworth do a search and one of his officers found it in my bathroom. He's really flying high now. He thinks I took it from her on the night she was killed. Only one person knew she was going to be at the cabin that night, Killingsworth. I don't know how anyone else could have known, unless he told someone else. He says he did not. But, how in the hell did her phone end up in my apartment?"

Suddenly, MacArthur remembered the night his door was unlocked when he came home. Someone had been in his apartment, but who? He had never followed up to ask his maid Mrs. Horn if she had been in his apartment that day.

"I was there, remember? We had a pizza, and discussed the Sprayberry case," Rachel said, trying to lighten the mood.

"Somehow, that's not funny right now, Rachel."

"I'm sorry, you're right. I was out of line."

"Someone must have planted Marilyn's phone in my bathroom the day I found it unlocked. That would explain how her phone ended up in my apartment. You don't suppose Killingsworth would stoop so low as to have someone plant it in my bathroom?"

"Who knows, Detective? But, I do agree with you, it very well could have happened that way. Do you think he's trying to cover his tracks by framing you for Marilyn's murder?"

"That's certainly possible, but we've got to get Sean Sprayberry right now. I'll worry about Killingsworth once that is done," MacArthur declared.

MacArthur placed a call to Susan Login, Sean's sister. When she picked up the phone, MacArthur identified himself.

"I recognized your voice Detective Nowlin. Look, about the last time we talked, I was on edge, as I'm sure you can understand,"

"Of course, Ms. Login. It was a very difficult time for you, I certainly understand."

"It's been almost a month and no arrest, are you any closer to finding my parent's killer than you were the last time we talked?" Susan Login asked.

"Actually, we are Mrs. Login. That's why I called. I wanted to tell you that we have a suspect in custody who made a full confession to the murder of your parents. At this time, the details he has given us line up with what really went down."

"That is good news Detective. Did he say why? He wasn't going to disclose the fact that the confessed assassin was already dead. It was important that Susan Login think the case had finally been solved. More importantly, he needed her to think that he was no longer looking at her brother as a suspect. It was only a matter of hours before the story of Carlos Sanchez' arrest and death would be on every local station. MacArthur knew he had only a small window of time to carrying out his plan.

"Ms. Login…"

"Please, Detective, call me Susan."

"Susan, I'm sure you'll want to go through your parent's belongings. Now that we've got someone in custody, you and your brother are free to enter your parent's home whenever you would like. Thank you again, for your cooperation during this investigation."

"I'm just glad you caught the man. My husband and I can sleep better at night knowing the killer is no longer out there somewhere," Susan replied.

"I'm not sure how long it will be before this case comes to trial, but I'll give you a call once it's on the docket," MacArthur replied.

"Thank you again, Detective. Oh by the way, have you given Sean the good news yet?"

MacArthur was glad she had brought up his name first. He replied, "No, I have not, but I'm going to give him a call as soon as I hang up here."

Of course, he had no intentions of calling Sean so quickly. He wanted him to hear the good news from his sister. MacArthur was correct in thinking she would call her brother the moment after she hung up with him.

Just as in the case with his sister, it was important that Sean think that since the case was solved, he would no longer be considered a suspect. After finishing his conversation with his sister, Sean Sprayberry was relieved that the whole matter was over. He could go on with his life, without looking over his shoulder all of the time.

Sean knew that as long as the hit man could not identify him as the one who paid for the hit, he was in the clear. But, there was one loose end he needed to take care of. The key to his parent's home. The same key he had given to the hired killer.

Rachel picked up the phone and dialed Michael Benjamin's number.

"This is Michael. Oh, Officer Peavey how are you doing?"

Before Rachel had a chance to tell him he was no longer considered a suspect, Michael asked her how the investigation was going. He said he had been watching the news, but had heard nothing of it.

"Michael," Rachel interrupted, "I'm calling you to tell you that we have someone in custody. He has confessed to murdering Dr. and Mrs. Sprayberry."

She didn't tell him the same guy was killed, just yesterday. Rachel decided to let Michael hear of the murder of Carlos Sanchez on his own.

"That's great news, Officer Peavey. I know I was acting a little weird before, but to tell you the truth, I was scared out of my mind. Did the guy who killed them say why he did it?"

Rachel replied, "Right now it appears he was hired to kill them."

"Hired to kill the Sprayberrys? Did he say who hired him? I would think the guy would want to save his own skin by giving up the person who did," Michael asked, having his own theory of who might have hired the assassin to kill the Sprayberrys.

"No, but we have some really good leads on who did," Rachel replied.

Michael was quick to tell Rachel who he thought might have hired the hit man.

"I'll tell you, Officer Peavey, I think Sean Sprayberry was the one. I don't trust him, and I wouldn't put it past him to do something like this."

"Just because you don't like or trust the guy, it doesn't make him a murderer, Michael." Rachel was careful not to show her hand and give Michael the smallest inkling she agreed.

"Well, all I'm saying is, I sure would take a close look at him."

"You know what's funny Michael, he said the same thing about you earlier today," Rachel lied.

Rachel brought the conversation to an end by reminding Michael that he might be called as a witness in the future. She explained because of his relationship with Dr. Sprayberry he might be asked some general questions.

He assured her he would be glad to cooperate if needed.

Rachel hung up the phone and smiled. Michael Benjamin was one cool customer. He thought he was always one step ahead of the law enforcement. It was a game to him. She had to admit, he was pretty good. She had agreed with MacArthur, neither felt Michael Benjamin had anything to do with the murders. There was no real motive.

Rachel's phone rang, it was MacArthur. He sounded almost as though he was out of breath.

"Rachel, I just got a call from the FBI lab in Virginia. Remember when we interviewed Sean Sprayberry a second time a couple of weeks ago?"

"Sure, I do. I remember his attitude was totally different than when we first talked with him," Rachel replied.

MacArthur continued, with his voice getting higher and higher, "When I asked him if he wanted anything to drink, he asked for coffee. We took the prints off of the paper cup he drank out of along with the partial print we found on the back of the suicide note, and them along to the FBI lab in Virginia. The two sets of prints were a match. The prints off of the coffee cup Sean used matched the partial print found on the suicide note. We got him Rachel. We got him."

"Will that hold up in court?"

"Unless he has some miracle explanation as to why his prints would be on the suicide note, hell yeah it will hold up. You see, that proves he was the one who wrote the note that Carlos left on the bedside table after he shot both of them. The note establishes a connection between the hit man and Sean Sprayberry.

"You know, for a while I didn't want to believe Sean Sprayberry could have actually killed his own mother and father. It just goes to show, you can never underestimate the power of money," Rachel replied.

"It makes sense now. That's the reason Dr. Sprayberry's prints were not found on the suicide note. If he had written the note his prints would have been all over the sheet of paper. Sean made a mistake when handling the finished suicide note. If I had to guess, when he finished the suicide note, he took the sheet of paper from the copier. That's when he left his print on the back of the sheet."

MacArthur made the motions one would use to remove a sheet of paper from a copier.

Rachel was impressed.

MacArthur now had his hard piece of evidence that would bring an indictment against Sean Sprayberry for the solicitation for murder.

He spent the rest of the day writing a formal summary of the Sprayberry murder case.

MacArthur left the police station around 6:00 pm. He was exhausted and needed food. Because of all the excitement during the day, he just realized he hadn't eaten. A Pizza Hut pizza sounded good. He always got the "meat - lovers". He took a corner booth and ordered sweet tea. MacArthur had bought a paper and began reading it as he waited for his tea.

On the front page of the *Silver Creek Banner* was the entire episode of the brutal killing of Officer Jack King during a routine traffic stop. The story included the chase and eventual capture of Sanchez. Pictures of him being carried out of the cabin and put into the ambulance accompanied the well written article.

There was no mention of Sanchez's murder. *Probably a good idea,* MacArthur thought.

"How's it going Detective? Hadn't seen you in a while. You know, ever since we started to deliver, there are of lots people I used to see that don't come in anymore," Tammy said with a smile.

"It does make it easier when you can have your pizza brought to your front door," MacArthur replied jokingly.

"I suppose so, but that don't mean I have to like it. You want lemon in your tea? Your order should be out pretty soon."

"Thanks Tammy,"

As she walked back to the cooking area Tammie couldn't help thinking what a good mood Detective Nowlin was in. Not like his usual self.

The pizza was more than MacArthur could eat, so he asked for a to-go box. Earlier when he was talking to Tammy, he hadn't noticed the bruises on her cheek or that her right eye was swollen.

"Tammy, how long are you going to let him treat you like he does? You don't have to stay in that situation, you can get help if you would just ask,"

"Detective Nowlin, it ain't like you think it is. He just loses his temper sometimes. He's a good man. It's just that times are hard right now, since he lost his job at the saw mill. He's trying real hard to get on at the pallet plant over in Silver Creek."

"Tammy, he's going to hurt you or one of the kids one of these days, when he comes home drunk again. The backhands and pushing you down will only get worse. I don't want to have to come to your place and find you or one of your babies dead."

"I know you mean well, but I ain't got no choice right now. My sister up in Raleigh has offered to let us come and stay with her and her husband for a while. But, I can't leave Luke, he needs me."

"If you ever need me, call me at this number," MacArthur said, as he handed her one of his cards.

He paid his ticket, left Tammy a ten dollar bill on the table, and slowly made his way to his car.

Sadly, MacArthur knew how that was going to end. He had seen this before. The wife feels guilty for provoking her abusive husband and refuses to leave. He makes her feel sorry for him and the next minute, he is beating the hell out her. Like any addiction, it only gets worse as time goes by. The real victims are the innocent children. MacArthur wished he could convince Tammy, but she had made up her mind. There was nothing he could do.

Few people knew that side of MacArthur Nowlin. The side that always pulls for the underdog. Because he kept his guard up all the time, the compassion he had for the down and out went undetected by those around him. He preferred it that way.

MacArthur had driven about two miles when he noticed he was being followed. He continued at the same speed, keeping his eyes in the rear view mirror. Whoever was following him was not very good at disguising it.

At the light, he made a sharp right and headed for Lowe's parking lot. He looked to see if his guest was still following him. Three cars behind, he saw the silver Ford sedan.

MacArthur pulled into the parking lot and sat for a moment pretending to look at his notebook. He could still see the car. It had parked four lanes over and turned off its lights. He only saw one person in the front seat. It appeared to be a male, with a baseball cap on. MacArthur got out of his car and started walking towards the entrance of Lowe's. Before he went in, he stopped and pretended to be looking at the line of riding lawn mowers on display outside of the main entrance. Through the reflection of the big glass doors, he could still see his stalker. After looking at the lawn mowers for less than a minute, MacArthur walked through the big glass doors and went inside.

He immediately took a left and walked towards the garden center. Making sure he was not seen, he slipped out of the side exit. Keeping his eyes on the silver Ford sedan, MacArthur circled around the huge parking lot and came up from behind. The man was sitting in his car smoking a cigarette with the driver's side window down. Before the stalker had a chance to react, MacArthur closed in on him pointing his gun at the stranger.

"Slowly get out of the car and keep your hands up where I can see them."

The man in the baseball cap did just as he was told. He immediately dropped the cigarette in his hand. MacArthur pushed him forward onto the hood of the car and pulled both of his arms behind his back. As he was trained to do a long time ago, He snapped the cuffs around his wrists and locked them into place. He walked the man around to the passenger side of his car. He opened the door and told him to get inside. Once inside, MacArthur told him to slide over to the driver's side. MacArthur sat on the passenger side, while he kept his gun drawn and pointed at the man with the baseball cap on.

"Who the hell are you, and why are you following me?"

"Detective Nowlin, I..."

"How do you know my name?"

"Because I've been reading and watching TV. I read your name in the paper as the Detective in charge of the murders they been talking about for weeks. You know, the Sprayberrys."

"What's that got to do with you following me?" MacArthur asked.

"I have some information I think you will be interested, in but I didn't want to go to the police station to talk to you. I'm not real comfortable in police stations."

"Do you have some ID?"

"Yes, my driver's license is in my wallet in my left back pocket."

MacArthur reached around and took the wallet out and found the driver's license.

"Is that your real name?"

"Yes, it is. Will you please take these cuffs off of my wrists? They are hurting me."

"No, not until you tell me what you want."

"I've already told why I was following you. I swear on my mother's grave, it's the truth," pleaded the man with the baseball cap.

"It says here your name is Johnny Simmons. Is that supposed to mean something to me?" MacArthur asked.

"I came to make a deal Detective."

"You are in no position to make any deals, Mr. Simmons, if that's really your name."

"Why don't we go and get a cup of coffee and I'll explain. Just hear me out. I have information as to who hired Carlos Sanchez to kill the Sprayberrys."

MacArthur began to think this guy might be telling the truth. How could he have known about Sanchez being a hired gun?

"You drive," MacArthur instructed.

"Are you going to take these cuffs off first?"

MacArthur warned his, soon to be informant that he would not hesitate to shoot him, if he tried anything.

Simmons assured him he would not.

He unlocked the cuffs and ordered Simmons to keep both hands on the steering wheel.

The café was six blocks away. Still leery, MacArthur told Simmons to walk in front of him as they entered. The place was almost deserted. One man sat near the entrance staring at his coffee and the only other person in the small café was standing at the old juke box looking for a song to play.

He reminded Simmons to keep his hands on the table at all times.

"You know, you should try to be more trusting. Besides, if I was going to do anything to you, I would have already done it. I've been watching you for two days. You really ought to get out more. All work makes Jack a dull boy," Simmons said, as he toyed with MacArthur.

"I don't have time for your cute jokes, get to the point, or I'll take you in for stalking a police officer." Both men knew that was not going to happen.

"First, I have to know what's in it for me. If I give you information that will lead you to the person who hired Carlos, of course I want something in return. You see, I'm a wanted man. But, not by who you think. I have been associated with, let's say, a family business that once you are in, there is no such thing as retirement. It seems that some money has come up missing and they think I have it. They take it very serious when money is missing.

"Get to the point Simmons."

"I need protection."

"Why come to me for it?"

"Because you can get me in the federal witness protection program. That's the only way I'll survive. I won't last a week on the streets. They have a huge network that stretches over the entire East Coast. There is nowhere to hide."

MacArthur felt for the first time, Simmons was telling the truth.

"I'm listening."

For the next hour, Johnny Simmons shared facts with MacArthur that only someone on the inside could have known. For instance, the fact that Mrs. Sprayberry was shot in the tub as well the two bullet casings that were found.

Finally, when MacArthur was convinced Simmons was somehow involved, he asked the one question that would bring about closure to this case.

"Who hired Carlos Sanchez to kill Dr. and Mrs. Sprayberry?"

"I've been straight with you, right? I've got to know that you're going to be straight with me about getting me into the protection program. I've got to know you can deliver what I'm asking for. Well, can you?"

Before MacArthur answered him, his mind flashed back to the conversation he had with Carlos Sanchez. He did not want to run the risk of losing another witness that could put Sean Sprayberry on death row.

"As I see it, Simmons, you don't really have a choice. If the feds say no, and you refuse to give up the name, you still end up in a box somewhere off of Chesapeake Bay. In other words, I am your best hope of surviving. But, you already knew that didn't you Simmons? You wouldn't be talking to me now, if you didn't think I could help. Here it is, you help me and I'll give you my word I will try everything within my power to get you in the program. I not going to sit here tonight and make a promise that I can't keep. If you knew anything about me at all, you would know that my word is my bond."

Simmons sat without talking, while MacArthur waited for his answer.

"I need to go the bathroom," he said.

"Fine, I hope you don't mind a little company," MacArthur said, with a boyish grin.

"I thought we were past the trust thing. I really like going to the bathroom alone. But, since I think you might get a thrill out of it, no problem."

When the two men returned to their booth, Simmons was first to speak.

"Detective, I guess you're right. The way I see it, I don't have anything to lose. I can hide just so long before they find me. Back in July, I got a call from an old friend who I had done time with up in Richburg, five years ago. He said he knew someone who had asked him about setting up a hit. He gave Sprayberry my phone number and two days later he called me. He said he had a situation that needed taking care of. I asked him what he meant by "taking care of." He suggested we meet and talk about it."

MacArthur interrupted him by asking Simmons if he had known Sean Sprayberry before the hit.

"Let me finish, Detective. I think it was about a week after our conversation that Sprayberry called again. The meeting was to take place in Silver Creek out on Highway 32. He said to meet him the next day at the abandoned feed and seed store just past mile marker 42. We met, and he told me he wanted me to find someone who could kill two people. He said they were man and wife and that it needed to happen within the next seven days. He didn't say why he was in a hurry, and I didn't ask. He gave me an envelope with $5,000 in cash in it. He said he would pay the remaining $5,000 once the job was done. He wanted it to look like the man had killed his wife and then turned the gun on himself. He said it was very important that the killings appeared to be a murder/suicide.

I told him it might take me longer than seven days to set this up. He insisted on no longer than seven days. He said if I couldn't get it done, he would find someone else. I figured he was bluffing, but I was broke and needed the money. I couldn't take a chance and miss such easy money. I told him I would get back with him in two days. He said he would give me the details then."

Simmons paused and asked for more coffee. MacArthur was surprised how calm he was as he told his story. He continued, "I knew a guy by the name of Carlos Sanchez. He had carried out some hits for the family a couple of years back. We met at Lou's Bar and Grill located outside of Silver Creek. He agreed to take on the job. I told him he would get $3,000 up front and $3,000 when it was done. I know that didn't add up to $10,000 but since I was the broker I figured I deserved the extra $4,000. Besides, Carlos didn't know what

Sprayberry was putting up, anyway. In fact, Carlos would never know the name of the man paying him for the hit. Sometime around July 28th, I remember that date because that it's my mother's birthday. Well, anyway, I met with Sean Sprayberry for the second and last time. He had his father's nine millimeter Glock pistol. He said he wanted this gun used in the hit. He also said make sure the casings are left on the floor so they could be found easily. He reminded me again that he wanted to make sure it looked like a murder/suicide. He had written down the address and what time the hit should take place. He also gave me a suicide note that the shooter was to leave on the bedside table. The last thing he did was give me a key that he said went to the back door. It was to be used to get into the house."

MacArthur interrupted Simmons and asked where the shooter was supposed to leave the key when he left.

"Sprayberry said for the shooter to take the key with him and return it to me. Then I was supposed to mail it back to him, since we were not to have any more contact after the hit was carried out. Later on, after looking at the address where the hit was supposed to take place, I realized he had ordered a hit on his own mother and father. What a cold bastard! He told me to have my man ready. It would probably be a very short notice when the hit was supposed to take place. I got the call Friday afternoon around 4:30."

MacArthur asked Simmons if Sprayberry asked about the key days after the hit. He said he did ask about it and was upset that he hadn't gotten back his key.

"Oh yeah, he was pissed alright. He told me to get that key, no matter what it took. I told him Carlos didn't give me a reason why he didn't return the key back to me."

KEYS TO MURDER

Simmons finished his story by telling MacArthur he met with Carlos a week after the killing and gave him his final payment of $3,000. He said that was the last time he saw Carlos.

MacArthur believed he now had a way to connect the key he had taken from the back door on the night of the murders to Sean Sprayberry. However, he would need the help of Johnny Simmons to carry out his plan.

He asked him if he still had Sean Sprayberrys' phone number. He said he did.

MacArthur's new and revised plan called for Johnny Simmons to call Sean Sprayberry and tell him Carlos had told him he had decided to hide the key when he left the house. Simmons was supposed to tell Sean that a couple of days later, Carlos called him and told him once he got the rest of his money, he would tell him where the key was hidden.

The success of MacArthur's plan depended on Sean taking the bait. That is, if Sean went looking for the key where Carlos said he had hidden it, this would prove it was his key. This would also prove his guilt. Why else go to the trouble of recovering a key he said he no longer had?

Johnny Simmons agreed to make the call.

It was getting late, he and MacArthur rode back to Lowe's parking lot where MacArthur's car was parked. The call was to take place the next morning. He couldn't be sure Simmons would follow through with his plan. There was always a chance he would change his mind over night.

The next morning MacArthur was relieved when the dispatcher buzzed him and said a Johnny Simmons was calling.

"Detective Nowlin, have you talked to anybody this morning about our deal?"

"I've put in a call to the District Attorney's office, but he hasn't returned my call yet. Are you ready to make the call?" MacArthur asked.

"Yeah, let's do it. Tell me again what I'm supposed to say to him."

After going by the Sprayberry residence earlier this morning on his way to work, MacArthur had seen a small statue of a life-size rabbit in the flower bed near the back door entrance. This was the same door used by the gunman to enter the house.

MacArthur instructed Simmons; "Tell Sprayberry you remembered Carlos telling you he put the key under the cement rabbit. Before you hang up just causally mention that as far as you know, it's still there. Don't arouse his suspicions by talking too much about the key."

"What if he asks me why I told him earlier I didn't know where the key was?" Simmons asked anxiously.

"Just tell him you had been drinking the night you last talked with him; and you later remembered what Carlos told you."

"Where do you want to make the call?"

"At my apartment." He gave Simmons the address and told him to meet him in 30 minutes. MacArthur would later question if it had been a good idea to give Johnny Simmons his address.

Rachel knocked on his door, as he was hanging up the phone. He signaled her to come in.

"Rachel, it's about to go down. I'm meeting Simmons in 30 minutes. He's going to make the call to Sean I told you about early this morning. Let's hope he takes the bait and goes looking for the key."

"Do you need me to go along?"

"No, I need you to have a chat with the Chief's secretary to see if she's heard any details of Killingsworth's investigation. Didn't you tell me once you could trust her?"

"Yes, she and I have been friends for over a year," Rachel replied.

MacArthur got in his car and drove the long way to his apartment, making sure he wasn't being followed. When he arrived, he saw Simmons sitting in the silver Ford sedan smoking a cigarette.

"Those things are going to kill you."

Johnny Simmons threw down what was left of the Winston and twisted his foot on it, making sure it was out. He was wearing the same baseball cap, pulled down on his forehead. He had sunglasses on, even though it was cloudy, threatening to rain any minute.

"Let's rock and roll," Simmons chanted, as MacArthur unlocked the door to his apartment.

Simmons's hands were shaking as he took him the phone.

MacArthur saw the humor in the fact that this man, who had been the contact person that would lead to the murder of two innocent people, was nervous about making a simple phone call.

The phone rang six times before the voice on the other end picked up.

"This is Simmons, I ...."

Sean Sprayberry cut him off and shouted, "What are you doing calling me at this number?"

"Hey, you want to know about that damn key of yours or not?"

When Sean didn't hang up immediately, Simmons knew he had his attention.

"Where are you calling from? How do I know this call is not being recorded?"

"Do you really think I would be stupid enough to go to the cops? Think about it!"

"What about the key? You told me you didn't know where it was," Sean said, clearly interested now.

"I guess you heard about Carlos? He called me the day before he shot that policeman and wanted to borrow some money. I asked him what he had done with the money I had just given him three weeks ago. He said he lost it in a crooked poker game. Well, I told him you might could help him out, if the key should turn up. He said he had lied about leaving it in the door. He said he hid it for insurance, if I ever double crossed him."

MacArthur was listening to every word Simmons was saying. He was impressed with his ability to bullshit so well. *He probably would have made a good cop*, he thought.

"Did he tell you where he hid it?" Sean asked, impatiently.

"Yeah, after I promised to get the money from you."

"Well, where is the damn key?" Sean Sprayberry said, sounding desperate.

Simmons was actually beginning to enjoy this game of deception. After all, his whole life had been based on deception. Always trying to con someone out of something.

"It's under the concrete rabbit, in the flower bed near the back door."

MacArthur was motioning him to end the conversation now. He closed by telling Sprayberry he was headed west and would give him a call once he had settled in. Of course, Simmons never expected to see the additional money.

The trap had been set. Would Sprayberry take the bait and go looking for the key?

He then instructed Simmons to check in at the hotel just outside of town. He also reminded him not to use his real name when checking in. MacArthur also told him to stay there until he contacted him.

A meeting was set up within the hour. MacArthur and Chief Aldridge met with the District Attorney Sanford. MacArthur laid out the entire course of his investigation. He told the D.A. of Carlos Sanchez's confession, but explained he was now dead. He told of the plan to try and catch Sean Sprayberry going after a key that he had left for the assassin. Lastly, he told him of Johnny Simmons, the contact man, was willing to testify that it was Sean Sprayberry who gave him $10,000 to have his parents killed.

The D.A. still had reservations. He questioned if a jury would believe Johnny Simmons.

The D.A. stood up and looked directly at MacArthur and said, "I know you don't want to hear this, but it's possible his lawyer could convince a jury that Sean's print could have been on the sheet of paper prior to the time his father used that particular sheet of paper to write the suicide note. Look, I know that sounds far-fetched. I want to put this monster away just like you

MacArthur, but we can't afford to make any mistakes that would allow him to walk. We have to convince a jury that he's guilty of murder beyond any reasonable doubt. Give me something more. I promise you we will get this guy.

There was nothing MacArthur could say, he knew the district attorney was right. As MacArthur and Chief Aldridge were walking out of the office, the Sanford stopped MacArthur.

"You and I both know that in every homicide, the killer always makes at least one mistake. Find that mistake MacArthur, and we'll nail this bastard. That's a promise," the district attorney said, shaking MacArthur's hand.

An hour later, MacArthur sat at his desk with a fresh cup of coffee. He could think of but one more card to play. The key. From the very beginning of this investigation, MacArthur knew solving this case and finding justice for Dr. and Mrs. Sprayberry somehow rested on that damn key. He kept thinking about what the district attorney had said about killers making mistakes. Sean Sprayberry was about to prove that time tested theory.

MacArthur turned around and walked back to the District Attorney Sanford's office.

"Sir, if I can catch Sean Sprayberry with the same key that was used to let the killer in his parent's home the night they were killed, wouldn't that be enough to bring charges of against him?"

"What do you mean catch him with the key?"

"I mean, set up a surveillance team to case out the Sprayberry's home. If my guess is right, Sean will come looking for the one thing that could connect him to the murder of his parent's, the key that belonged to him."

The district attorney leaned back in his chair and thought about MacArthur's plan. There was total silence in the room. After, what seemed an eternity to MacArthur, he spoke.

"If he does as you suspect, and if this contact person, Simmons is willing to testify that he got the key from Sprayberry, I think we have a case that will stand up in court. But, the taped confession of Sanchez is still in question as to whether a judge will allow the jury to hear it. We can't rely on that piece of evidence alone."

"Mr. Sanford, I can deliver both of the things you're asking for," MacArthur replied quickly.

It didn't take long for Chief Aldridge to grant MacArthur's request to put together a surveillance team made up of a pair of two plain clothed officers to case out the Sprayberry home around the clock.

Of course, MacArthur was going to be there. He and Rachel took the night watch, thinking Sean would use the cover of darkness to retrieve his key. His assumption was correct. The first night came and went without Sean Sprayberry.

Just after 11:00 pm on the second night of the surveillance Sean Sprayberry, with his lights off, eased down the paved driveway of his parent's home. MacArthur was careful to remain out of sight, as he lay in the thick bushes that bordered the Sprayberry's home. Sprayberry got out of his car with a flashlight in his hand and walked around to the back of the house. Once there, he walked straight to the flower bed where the cement rabbit was located. It was exactly where Simmons had told him it would be. Carefully, he picked up the rabbit and moved it a foot or so. He turned his flashlight on and immediately spotted the key. He returned the rabbit to its original spot and stood up.

On MacArthur's cue, floodlights lit up the backyard. Sprayberry was blinded momentarily. MacArthur moved quickly and was standing beside him as his eyes made the adjustment to the sudden burst of lights pointed at him.

"Find what you were looking for Sean? What do you have in your hand?" MacArthur asked, as he reached for the key.

"What's this all about? I came to my parent's home to pick up a few items. I was just about to go in when you and your swat team descended on me like I was some kind of criminal," Sprayberry replied, pretending to be offended.

"Sean Sprayberry, you are under arrest for the solicitation of the murders of Dr. and Mrs. Sprayberry." MacArthur had been waiting for this moment for almost two months.

"You've got to be kidding. Is this some kind of sick joke Detective?"

"Put him in the car officer and take him in," MacArthur ordered.

He was read his rights on the way to the police station. MacArthur followed the black and white unit back to the station.

Sprayberry made his one phone call. He told his wife to call Maurice. He explained to her this was all just a misunderstanding. He would get everything straightened out by morning. She did as he asked, Maurice Penn was on the way.

MacArthur wanted to question Sprayberry without his lawyer. But, he knew the law, and hoped he could get him to answer his questions before Penn could get there.

MacArthur had Sprayberry placed in an unoccupied cell, for the time being. He set up a suicide watch immediately. Thirty minutes later, he was led into one of the two interrogation rooms in the Wilcox Police Department.

The room was very small, only 12 feet by 10 feet. An old table sat in the middle of the floor. The walls were painted a dull gray. There were no portraits, nor any other comforts of home. Three metal folding chairs were placed around the table. Two chairs were on one side and the other across the table.

MacArthur was counting on Sprayberry's inflated self-confidence and arrogance to agree to waive his right to have an attorney present during questioning. He didn't disappoint.

MacArthur began with the obligatory statements, "You know, you don't have to answer any questions without your attorney being present? If you agree to answer questions without your attorney present you will be exercising your right to waive your Miranda rights?

"I haven't done anything wrong. I don't have anything to hide. Go ahead, ask your questions."

With the tape recorder on, MacArthur began by asking him what he was doing at his parent's home. He gave him the same answer he had given him when first arrested at the house.

"I was going into my parent's home to get some personal things of theirs I knew they would want me to have. I don't see why the key is such a big deal, after all its mine. I always keep the key under the rabbit.

"Look, Sprayberry, I'm going to be perfectly honest with you. We know you hired Carlos Sanchez to kill both of your parents. Why don't you give it up? The time has come to tell the truth," MacArthur said.

"I'm telling you Detective, I didn't have anything to do with the deaths of my parents. Besides, what reason would I have to kill my own parents?"

"How about 800,000 reasons? We also know about your financial problems. We know you're about to lose everything. Probably your wife and the kids as well, once she finds out you haven't been making mortgage payments for the last four months. I already know the truth, but I need to hear it from you.

"Oh, and just so you'll know, the District Attorney is going to ask for the death penalty. This might be you're only opportunity to save yourself from the silver needle and get life without the possibility of parole."

Sean Sprayberry was trapped and he knew it, but he still believed he could outsmart the police and somehow get away with murder.

"I think I've answered enough of your foolish questions. I don't have anything else to say without my attorney."

"That's probably a good idea. Take him back to his cell officer," MacArthur replied.

The interview was over.

The arraignment was scheduled for 10 am the following morning. It had been exactly six months since the murders of Samuel and Ida Sprayberry.

MacArthur was mentally drained. It had been one hell of a day. He drove slowly back to his apartment. He was spent. He made a ham and cheese sandwich and went straight to bed. He slept very little. Not because of the usual problems, but because of the excitement he felt knowing it was just a matter of time before Sean Sprayberry would pay for the deaths of his parents.

He was up early and arrived in his office before 7:00 am. He was going to interrogate Sean this time with his lawyer present. He knew that Sean's lawyer, Maurice Penn, was going to be very selective when it came to Sean answering his questions. His goal for this meeting was to introduce enough evidence for his attorney to agree to a deal. Maurice Penn was no fool. Saving his client from a lethal injection would be his only option, once he heard the facts.

Penn and his client could plead not guilty and go to trial, but the risk was too great that if found guilty he would get the death penalty. In fact, because of the heinous nature of such a crime in which a grown child willfully plotted and carried out the murders of his parents, a jury was sure to ask for the death penalty.

District Attorney Sanford III was being pressured by city hall and everyone else to seek the death penalty. Reluctantly, he agreed to take the death penalty off of the table. If Sean Sprayberry pleaded guilty to the murders of his parents he would serve a life sentence without the possibility of parole. Not everyone in the D.A.'s office was pleased with his decision.

Milford Sanford III realized how expensive a long and drawn out trial would be for the taxpayers. Wilcox would be inundated with media from all over the state. This quiet, sleepy town didn't need that kind of exposure. Emotions ran high, but Sanford knew in his heart he was doing what was best for his town and its citizens. Sean Sprayberry would rot away in prison for the rest of his life.

Sean Sprayberry and his attorney, Maurice Penn had agreed to a "sit-down" at 8:30, an hour and a half before they were to appear before the judge to enter a plea.

Sean and his attorney were already seated at the small table in the interrogation room when MacArthur entered the cramped room. He didn't mince his words. He began by telling Penn that his client would be proven guilty of murder if this went to trial. MacArthur reminded him of the overwhelming evidence against him. He strongly suggested that his client's best bet was to accept a deal and plead guilty. This would take lethal injection out of the equation. He would serve life without the possibility of parole. At least his client would live.

It was clear that they were not prepared for a plea of guilty. Penn was not going to throw in the towel so soon. He began by pointing out that his client had a right to visit his parent's home and to take anything there. After all, he and his sister were now the owners of the property. He continued by saying that his client did not know Carlos Sanchez, the confessed shooter. He believed that his client was being framed for something he didn't do. He explained how much Sean loved his parents and how close he and his father were.

MacArthur sat patiently not interrupting. Finally, when he had heard enough, he stopped Penn and made the following statement.

"Mr. Penn, I would like to ask your client a question about a key."

Penn looked at Sean and nodded.

"Sean, last night, when we arrested you at your parent's home, you told me you were about to go in and get some personal items. Is that correct?"

"Yes, that's exactly what I was doing."

"Detective, where are you going with this? I'll say it again, my client had every right to be on the property of his parent's home."

"Sean, didn't you tell me in our first conversation that it had been almost a month since you had last visited your parents prior to their deaths?"

"That's right, I remember telling you that. We had a birthday party for my mom at my parent's home. Her birthday was July 2nd. My sister and her husband were there also."

"Sean, how were you planning on getting into your parent's home last night?"

"I was going to use the key that is hidden under mom's cement rabbit that sits near the back door. My parents keep that extra key there in case they should lock themselves out. My sister and I are the only other people that know where it is hidden."

"How long would you say that key has been hidden in that location, several years, a year …?"

"Detective, I can't say for sure. I don't remember the first time it was put there, but it's been there a long time. Maybe three years or more."

"I believe you told Officer Peavey and me the first time we talked that you had lost some keys and that your parent's house key was one of them. You also told us you had not replaced it at the time."

"Why all the questions about a damn key? Look, I lost it and some others that were on the same key ring a few weeks ago. Big deal. That doesn't make me a murderer Detective."

"Actually it does Mr. Sprayberry."

With that statement, Sean Sprayberry had just sealed his fate. This was the answer MacArthur was hoping to get from him.

"Mr. Penn, your client couldn't have been using that key under this particular cement rabbit. In fact, he couldn't have known about the rabbit at all. The reason is because Mrs. Dayton, the Sprayberry's neighbor and close friend stated in a written deposition that she and Mrs. Sprayberry had been shopping the week before Dr. and Mrs. Sprayberry died. She stated that Mrs. Sprayberry bought a cement rabbit at Lowe's. We have records of the purchase. I asked Sean's sister yesterday if she knew anything about the existence of a cement rabbit at her parent's home. She did not. She said the first time she heard about the rabbit was during a phone conversation with her mother just three days before she was killed. She said her mother told her she had bought it when she and Mrs. Dayton had gone shopping the week before.

Mr. Penn, your client is lying about the key. In fact he is lying about several things. When I asked him if he knew a guy by the name of Johnny Simmons, he said he did not. However, we have a recording of a phone conversation three days ago between Johnny Simmons and your client. The reason Sean Sprayberry was looking for that key the night he was arrested was because Simmons told him he could find it under the cement rabbit."

"Just because my client was looking for a key under the rabbit proves nothing. This Johnny Simmons could very well be lying as well," Penn replied.

"Mr. Penn, how can you explain why your client was looking for a key that didn't exist," MacArthur countered.

"He was looking for a key to get into his parent's house."

MacArthur stood up and asked, "How did he know to look under the cement rabbit for the key? After all, your client didn't even know about the rabbit until the conversation with Simmons."

MacArthur continued, "You see, the key was the only thing that could connect Sean Sprayberry to the murder of his parents. Johnny Simmons is prepared to testify in court that Sean Sprayberry paid him $10,000 to have his parents killed."

Maybe you can explain how your fingerprint ended up on the suicide note that was supposedly written by your father."

MacArthur was closing in on the kill.

"Suppose you tell your attorney you were the only one that could have known that both parents were going to be home the night they were killed. When you spoke to your father that Friday afternoon he told you that his flight had been cancelled. He told you that he was taking an early flight out the next morning. You ordered the hit that Friday night, because you knew they both would be home."

"That's enough Detective," Maurice Penn said, as his face lost all color.

"Here's the deal, if your client enters a plea of guilty to first degree murder, the District Attorney has agreed to take the death penalty off the table. We have that in writing, but this deal is on the table for 30 minutes, starting now."

MacArthur did not wait for a reply as he got up and walked out.

"What do you think? Will he take the deal?" Rachel asked MacArthur, as he poured himself a cup of coffee.

"He's crazy if he doesn't. He'll get the needle if this things goes to trial."

MacArthur had finished only half of his coffee when Maurice Penn stuck his head out of the door and motioned him in.

"Detective, my client agrees to the District Attorney's offer, but we want it in writing before we enter a plea of guilty."

"We'll have the paperwork drawn up in twenty minutes."

MacArthur rose from his chair and said to Sean," You are a despicable human being."

There would be no trial. The judge accepted the District Attorney's recommendation. Sean Sprayberry pleaded guilty to the solicitation and murder for hire of his mother and father. He was transported to Holder Prison in upper state North Carolina, where he would spend the rest of his life.

A week later, MacArthur met with Susan Login because he felt he should. For some strange reason, he thought it would bring closure to this terrible ordeal. He was surprised when she opened up about her and Sean's life as children. He was shocked when she revealed that she and Sean were adopted when she was six years old, and Sean was eight. Before that, they had lived with two different foster parents. It seems that Sean had some hidden anger that he could never suppress. Susan admitted that he had made threats over the years towards his adopted parents. No one took him seriously. Perhaps, someone should have, Susan said with tears streaming down her face.

MacArthur's conversation with Susan only reminded him of how a family that looked so normal on the outside, could be so dysfunctional behind the perfectly manicured lawns and white columns. He took a deep sigh, he understood this much better than she could have ever imagined.

Susan would never forgive her brother for the unspeakable act he had masterminded. She refused to visit him for the rest of her life. She would tell friends later, "I don't have a brother, the one I knew is dead."

Cathy Sprayberry, the wife of Sean Sprayberry continued to defend him. On his behalf, she worked on numerous appeal efforts for over three years. Finally, all of her options dried up.

The letters and visits to the prison became fewer and fewer. Four years after her husband's conviction, Cathy Sprayberry filed for a divorce.

She and her two children moved to Birmingham, Alabama and started a new life.

CHAPTER 28

MacArthur decided to do something he had never done. He was going to take a couple of weeks off and try to relax. He made plans to spend a few days at Myrtle Beach. Then he planned to head over to Gatlinburg and hang out there.

He had no real agenda. He was just going to take each day, one day at a time. He knew this vacation would not erase what had happened over the last five months, but maybe it would help get his mind off of it for just a few days.

What he didn't know, was that Killingsworth was interviewing Sonny Barrett, the very same morning he was to leave for his two week vacation.

On the morning of January 10th, 2006, Tim Killingsworth would get a phone call that would bring him closer to making an arrest for the murder of Marilyn Hampton.

The dispatcher buzzed Detective Killingsworth around 9:00 am. There was a man on the phone who said he had information about the woman in Wilcox that was killed back in August. Another routine call, Killingsworth guessed. However, this call would be anything but routine.

"Is this Detective Tim Killingsworth?"

"Yes, it is. How can I help you?"

"I've got some information about that woman that got killed back in August there in Wilcox."

"Who am I talking to? Killingsworth asked.

"I'm Howard Molder, a friend of Sonny Barrett's."

"Is that supposed to mean something to me?"

"Well, it should since he told me he killed that woman".

Molder now had Killingsworth's attention.

"Me and this Sonny Barrett fellow was drinking in a bar two nights ago and he told me he had killed a woman for money," Molder said, sounding very sure of himself.

"Did he say why he killed her?"

"He said she had screwed him over, and made a fool out of him about two years ago. He said he planned to get even with the bitch."

"Did he tell you the name of this woman he supposedly kill?"

"Naw, he didn't say her name, just that he killed this woman he used to know," the caller replied.

Tim Killingsworth asked Molder if he would come in and give a written statement.

"Look Detective, I can tell you where to find him, and then I'm through with this thing. I ain't getting involved. Just being around a jail cell makes me nervous."

"Go on."

"Well, we were in this bar on the west side of Memphis the other night, and we were drinking and then decided to take some girls back to Sonny's motel to smoke some pot. After we got there, he started talking about all kinds of crazy things. You know, about what a football hero he had been, and how he had owned his own gym and made lots of money. Well, I didn't really pay much attention to what he was saying since I knew he was a blow hard. But, when he said he had killed a woman for money, I started to listen more.

By the way, Detective am I going to get a reward for this information?"

"Just continue, we'll talk about a reward later," Killingsworth snapped.

"Like I was saying, he was bragging about making a lot of money for killing this woman. He said he was paid $4,000 up front and had another $4,500 coming after he killed her. He said he never got the $4,500, but he was going to get it one way or another."

"Mr. Molder, why are you coming forward at this time? You could have called sooner, but you chose to call today. Why?"

"I lived in Wilcox for about six months last year, while I was with a construction crew painting the water tower. I used to hang out at some bar called Charlie's, or maybe it was Sam's, anyway I met Sonny then and we became friends.

Then, a couple of weeks ago, I ran into him at this bar I was telling you about. We have been hanging out ever since. I thought if what he was saying was true, somebody ought to know about it. Besides, I got to thinking since he knew I knew about the murder, and if he was telling the truth, he might want to get rid of me. This crazy bastard needs to be off the street, if you know what I mean."

Killingsworth asked Molder where he could find Sonny. He told him he had seen him last night.

"I believe he's been staying at a motel called *"Sleep Over"*, yeah that's the name of it, *Sleep Over*. His room number is 307. It's not far from *Shakey's Bar* on 5th street. That's where we hang out most every night."

"Mr. Molder, I appreciate you calling in and giving me this information. I'm going to ask that you don't mention this phone call to anyone, until I get back with you, it could affect your reward," Killingsworth lied. There was no reward. "What's a number I can reach you at?"

"Detective, you ain't got to worry about me saying nothin to nobody. I hope I don't see that fool again," Molder ranted, ignoring the request for his phone number. After hanging up, Killingsworth remembered about the restraining order signed against Sonny Barrett. He also knew that Sonny had made threats towards Marilyn Hampton months before she was killed.

Killingsworth began to play the scenario over and over in his mind. Could there be a connection between Sonny Barrett and MacArthur? After all, it was MacArthur who Marilyn went to for a restraining order against Sonny. It would definitely not be a stretch for MacArthur to play on Sonny's hatred for Marilyn and to coerce him a sizeable amount of money. Especially now, due to Sonny's state of mind. That way, none of the attention would be pointed in MacArthur's direction, instead it would be aimed at a man who had, on more than one occasion, told others he was going to make Marilyn pay for making a fool out of him. That man was Sonny Barrett.

Killingsworth now believed that MacArthur could have lured Sonny into making the hit, not only for revenge, but for the money. He believed that MacArthur very well could have used Sonny's prior threats to strengthen the case of him killing Marilyn.

Howard Molder was anything but a law abiding citizen. He had been convicted of armed robbery, a parole violation, and accused of child abuse. He was never convicted on the latter charge. Molder was not exactly the kind of witness you wanted on the stand. Killingsworth knew that Molder would be picked apart by the defense in a courtroom. His credibility as a witness would certainly be exploited by the defense.

If Detective Killingsworth was going to make a case, he was going to have to prove that MacArthur had some kind of connection with Sonny Barrett. Better yet, Sonny Barrett was going to have to implicate MacArthur in the murder for hire, that is, if Sonny committed the murder.

He was determined to use every resource at his disposal to locate Sonny Barrett. Three days after Molder's call, Barrett was tracked down and found in a rundown motel on the western side of Memphis. He was arrested without any resistance. There were outstanding warrants for his arrest on charges of possession and distribution of controlled substances back in Wilcox.

Sonny was put in the back of a squad car and transported downtown Memphis. Upon arrival, he was taken to one of the interrogation rooms downstairs. Sonny stated he would not answer any questions unless he spoke to Detective Tim Killingsworth of the Wilcox Police department in Wilcox, North Carolina. When asked why, Sonny told them he had information about a murder back in Wilcox last year. Detective Killingsworth was notified by the Memphis Police Department. He said he would catch the first flight out, and be in Memphis the next morning.

Killingsworth's plane touched down at the Memphis International Airport at 9:50 am the following morning. A black and white unit was waiting for him. He arrived at the Memphis Police Station within 20 minutes. Sonny was brought in by two guards wearing hand cuffs and a chain around his ankles. He sat down at a small table in the middle of the cramped interrogation room. Killingsworth entered the room and took a seat directly across from him. He made small talk for a few minutes, then asked Sonny if he wanted something to drink. He said no, but he would like a cigarette.

Sonny was all too eager to reminisce about the good old days. He talked about being recruited by most all of the SEC teams, as well as the University of Texas and Clemson. Of course, none of this was true, but in Sonny's world he was the "man."

Killingsworth asked him about his relationship with Marilyn Hampton. Sonny told him that they had dated for several months and he had broken off the relationship. He said Marilyn was very upset over this. Of course, this was another lie, they dated for almost three months before she broke up with him.

"Sonny, you and I both know that's a lie. The truth is, Marilyn Hampton ditched you. Your temper and jealousy was too much for her to handle. She told you it was over and you couldn't handle it, so you got even by killing her."

"That's not true. Yeah, we broke up, but I moved on. I didn't need the bitch anyway."

"Didn't she file a restraining order against you?"

"She said she did, but I never saw it. Besides, I didn't want anything else to do with her by then."

"How can you explain your prints found in the cabin where she was murdered?" Killingsworth bluffed.

"I don't know nothing about prints or a cabin and I damn sure didn't kill her. Ok, I made some threats, but I never intended on going through with them. I only wanted to scare her."

"You did more than just scare her. You surprised her at that cabin and raped her several times before you stabbed her and then cut her throat."

Sonny started shaking and asked for some water. After a few minutes, he regained his composure and continued to deny any involvement in the murder.

"Sonny, I don't think you killed her on your own. I think someone else talked you into it. They agreed to pay you a lot of money. I think you planned to leave the country, maybe even go to Mexico."

"That's bullshit. I don't even like Mexico, man. Look, I ain't killed nobody. You're trying to blame this on me just because I dated her and some cop believed her when she said I threatened her. Detective, I hate to say this with her dead and all, but that was one kinky bitch. She liked to …"

"Sonny, we can go round and round if that's what you want to do. So you are saying you were not in Wilcox on August eighth?"

"Yeah, that's right. I was in Memphis, with my girlfriend. There's no way I could have killed her. The reason I remember that date is because my girlfriend's birthday was the next day," Sonny said with everyone in the room knowing this was a lie.

"What if I told you I have proof you were in Wilcox that night? You were not only in Wilcox, you were less than two miles from the murder scene around the time of her murder?"

"I'd say you'd be wrong, Detective."

"Do you remember stopping at the 7 Eleven that night and getting a cup of coffee? Well, the camera that covers the entrance remembers you,"

This information had come from an anonymous caller weeks earlier. At the time, Killingsworth didn't think anything of it.

Sonny's face suddenly had no expression. He stared at Killingsworth as a deer would stare at the headlights of a car.

Killingsworth suggested they take a break. He wanted to let what he just told Sonny sink in. He was hoping Sonny would break. Twenty minutes, later when the interview continued, Sonny had a meltdown.

He was brought back into the interrogation room where Killingsworth was already seated. His demeanor was much more subdued. He had the look of a beaten down man. He had decided it was all over. He decided to the truth. Well, maybe not all of the truth.

"I'm just going to come clean. This has been eating at me like a cancer. I can't sleep at night, I have nightmares, and I hear voices. You're right, I murdered Marilyn."

"Could you repeat what you just said?" Killingsworth asked.

"I said, I killed Marilyn."

Sonny Barrett spent the next hour going over every grisly detail of the abduction and murder. He left nothing out. Twice during his confession, Sonny sobbed and was asked if he wanted to take a break. He declined and continued. He described just how scared Marilyn had been and how she begged for her life. However, he didn't tell Detective Killingsworth what he did after she was dead. There were just some things not meant for others to know.

He told of his and Marilyn's break up, and how devastated and angry he was. He describe the cabin where she was raped and murdered. He told Killingsworth he had not planned to kill. He told where he had hidden her car, and that her personal items would be found in a bag, in the trunk of her car.

The most interesting information Sonny gave, in Killingsworth's opinion, was how he knew Marilyn was going to be at the cabin that night. He said he received a call around 9:10 that night, telling him he could find her there.

Sonny gave other details of the murder that only the killer could have known. Killingsworth had no doubt Sonny was telling the truth.

"Sonny, you say you received a call around 9:10 that night? Who called?

Sonny continued telling his story, totally ignoring Killingsworth's question.

"Detective, you've got to believe me when I say I never meant for her to die. I loved Marilyn. I was drunk and wasn't thinking clearly. We struggled and she ripped off the mask I was wearing over my face. Once she knew who I was, I had no choice, but to kill her."

"Why did you wait so long to come in?"

"I was scared."

"Are you willing to write out a full confession for the murder of Marilyn Hampton?"

"Yeah, I just want all of this to be over. I don't care what happens to me now. I wish I could undo what I have done, but I can't, so I'll just live with it."

"I ask you a few minutes ago who called you and told you Marilyn would be at the cabin."

"I'm just not ready to say right now," Sonny said, with a reason in mind.

Detective Killingsworth asked him if he had acted alone. His answer stunned everyone listening.

"Do you mean, was there somebody else with me when I killed her?"

"Did anybody else have any part in Marilyn's murder?" Killingsworth asked, making sure he understood the question.

Sonny Barrett was not as dumb as he pretended to be. He knew the only way to avoid the death penalty, was to cut a deal with the prosecution. He had counted on the state going after the person who hired him. That's why he was holding back the name of the caller. He was using this as leverage for a plea bargain.

"Detective, I haven't told you the whole story. What if I told you that someone hired me to kill Marilyn? The person that called me that night was the same person that hired me to kill her."

"Was it MacArthur Nowlin?" Killingsworth asked anxiously.

"If I give up the name of the person who paid me $8,500 to kill Marilyn, can you promise me life without parole, instead of the needle?"

"I don't have the authority to do that Sonny. The District Attorney is the only one who can make that call."

"I ain't saying who hired me, until you can promise me a deal."

"Look, Sonny, don't waste my time or the D.A.'s if you aren't telling the truth."

"If the District Attorney will deal, I'll give you the name, Detective."

Killingsworth told him it would take some time to get in touch with the D.A. An hour later, he had District Attorney Sanford III on the phone. Sanford told him he would have an answer by the next day.

Sonny was taken back to his cell. He stared at the four gray walls and wondered what went wrong with his life. He thought about killing himself, but didn't have the guts to do it. In reality, Sonny Barrett was nothing but a coward. He had hidden behind drugs and alcohol for so long, he no longer knew who Sonny Barrett was.

I never once ever got a real break. People were always putting me down. Nobody really understood me, Sonny said to himself as he sat in an eight foot by eight foot jail cell bargaining for his life. Sonny Barrett, the home town hero, with the world at his fingertips was about to spend the rest of his life behind bars. He slept very little that night. He hoped they would buy what he was selling.

District Attorney Sanford III called Killingsworth around 9:00 am. He had made the decision to agree to the deal. He made it clear to Killingsworth that if any of the information given by Barrett was false, the deal was off. Detective Killingsworth said he understood and thanked him.

Killingsworth was waiting when Sonny was brought in to the same interrogation room that they had met in the day before. Sonny agreed to the provisions handed down by the District Attorney. He said he wanted everything in writing. Killingsworth agreed. Sonny had not gotten a lawyer.

"MacArthur Nowlin is your man. He hired me to kill Marilyn. He told me he thought she was cheating on him."

"How did he set this up?" Killingsworth asked.

"I got a call from a friend that told me word was out that someone wanted a woman in Wilcox taken out. He asked me if I thought I might be interested. Well, I ain't never killed nobody, but what the hell. The next day I got a call from a man saying he had a project he needed finishing. I asked him what he was talking about, he said he was willing to pay a lot of money to have this person go away. I asked him if he meant killed. He said yes.

We planned a meeting two days later at the Walmart parking lot over in Silver Creek. I told him what kind of car I would be driving, so he would know it was me. I'm sitting there smoking a cigarette and having a beer, when suddenly Detective Nowlin opens the passenger door and gets in. I think, oh shit, I'm busted, you know. He tells me to calm down, that he has a job for me. That's when I realized he was the man on the phone. He told me he knew all about how Marilyn had dumped me and how she was going around telling everybody I was some kind of freak.

I'm thinking about now, what the hell. Then he says he is willing to pay me $8,500 if I will ice her. I said, you mean kill her? He said, exactly. Well, I'm thinking he is setting me up, but I thought I'd go along with it for a while. He pulls out a brown envelope and hands it to me. He told me to take a look inside. There was $4,000 in there. By now, I'm thinking he was serious. He told me he would set me up at the *Wayward Inn*, that's just outside Wilcox. When the time was right, he would call me and give me the details. I told him I'd do it, but how can I be sure he was on the up and up. I asked him what would keep him from turning on me once the hit was made. He said we both had too much to lose to rat on the other. What he didn't know was that I had a camera on the back seat of my car. I watched him get in his car, but before he pulled off I took a picture. You know, for insurance."

Detective Killingsworth sat mesmerized. He couldn't believe MacArthur could mastermind such a terrible thing. He was thinking, no way anyone could make up such a story. He was certain Sonny was telling the truth. When Sonny told him how MacArthur had found out about Marilyn having a secret affair, there was no longer any doubt that MacArthur was guilty.

"Do you still have the picture?"

"No, the damn camera didn't work."

Killingsworth was disappointed, but he thought he still had more than enough evidence to indict MacArthur.

"He told me that as head of the homicide department, he would decide who worked the murder case of Marilyn once her body was discovered. He said he would be leading the investigation, and that he would make sure I would not be a suspect. If he had kept his word, I wouldn't be sitting here today. On the night of the murder I got a call telling me that Marilyn would be at the cabin around 9:30. You know the rest of the story."

Two days later, after being extradited back to Wilcox, Sonny stood before Judge Henry. He pleaded guilty to first degree murder and would serve life without the possibility of parole. As part of the deal, Sonny agreed to testify for the prosecution at MacArthur's trial, if there was to be a trial.

Sonny was transported the next day to Holman Prison in the northern part of North Carolina.

Killingsworth was ecstatic. He thought all along that MacArthur killed Marilyn. *I've finally got that son a bitch*, he said aloud, as he drove home.

Up until now, the state's case against MacArthur was based solely on circumstantial evidence.

With only four days of his get-away behind him, MacArthur packed his bags and returned to Wilcox. As he explained it to Rachel, it just didn't feel right. Out there somewhere was Marilyn's killer. He could not relax and enjoy himself until the killer was behind bars.

MacArthur had gotten home late Thursday night and decided to wait and unpack his things the next morning. He was tired and planned to sleep in late. He couldn't remember when he had done that. He was surprised how well he slept, only getting up once throughout the night.

KEYS TO MURDER

He woke around 7:30 am, and lay there for a few minutes, then decided to make a fresh pot of coffee before he showered. Dripping with water from the shower, MacArthur searched for his old green bathrobe. It was his favorite. He remembered how Marilyn had hated it, and had threatened to throw it away and get him a new one.

He walked into the kitchen and turned on the small TV sitting on the counter. The news this morning was similar to the news every day. Murder, robbery, assault, ugly divorces, etc. He kept telling himself he was going to stop watching the news. He got to see firsthand how people can do horrible things to other people, he didn't need to be reminded about such terrible things. He was convinced mankind was innately evil.

He thought he heard some noise outside. It was probably his neighbor looking for their lost cat again. He once considered taking that damn cat for a one-way ride out in the countryside. He might have, if he thought he could have gotten away with it. He was not going to harm the cat, just relocate him. MacArthur had always compared women to cats. Both were moody and unpredictable.

When his doorbell rang, he was prepared to tell his aggravating neighbor, like so many times before, he had not seen his cat.

Opening the door to his apartment, with his green robe wrapped around him, MacArthur found Tim Killingsworth standing in his doorway.

"MacArthur Nowlin, you are under arrest for the murder of Marilyn Hampton."

Outside, there were two police cars with their blue lights flashing, while four uniformed officers stood beside them. Neighbors were already peeking outside their apartments, curious as to what was going on this early on a Friday morning.

"MacArthur, get dressed, we're going for a ride downtown," Killingsworth said with a smirk on his face.

He motioned for one of the uniformed officers to follow MacArthur as he walked to his bedroom.

"You worried I'm going to come out shooting?" MacArthur asked sarcastically.

Killingsworth didn't respond.

Five minutes later, MacArthur, followed by the police officer, came out of the bedroom.

"Aren't you going to read me my rights? You do know the procedure don't you Detective?"

"They'll be read to you on the way to the station, MacArthur." Killingsworth replied.

"Cuff him."

MacArthur voluntarily put his hands behind his back and waited for the officer to carry out his duty. Afterwards, the three of them walked outside and MacArthur was placed in the police officer's car. The officer put his hand on top of MacArthur's head so that he wouldn't hit it as he bent over to get into the back seat. MacArthur had performed this same procedure a hundred times. In his wildest dreams, he never thought he would ever end up in the back seat of a black and white unit. Reality was slowly setting in.

The ride didn't take very long. On the way, MacArthur said nothing. The driver of the police car said, "Detective, I'm sorry I've got to do this. For what it's worth sir, I don't think you are guilty and I don't think you should have been brought in like this. You deserve better, sir."

"Thank you officer, I understand, you're doing what you're supposed to in the line of duty. I have no hard feelings toward you."

MacArthur was read his rights, the same rights he had read to others so many times before. All of this was so surreal. It was like it was not happening, yet, here he was in hand cuts sitting in the back of a police car arrested for murder.

Once at the station, MacArthur knew the routine. Soon he would be wearing an orange jump suit. He hated orange. He was fingerprinted and a mug shot was taken. The usual questions were asked, name and address. A complete waste of time, MacArthur thought. This process took almost an hour. When it was completed, he was granted a phone call.

MacArthur called Jake Rhymes, an old friend who was an attorney in Raleigh.

"Jake, this is MacArthur. It seems I'm going to need your services."

"What the hell for MacArthur? You must have beat the hell of one of your prisoners?"

"Actually, Jake it's a little more serious than that. I've been arrested for the murder of Marilyn."

Jake remained silent for a moment, internalizing what he had just heard.

"I'll be down there in three hours. I know I don't have to tell you this, but don't say a word."

"Thanks Jake, I'll be right here when you get here," MacArthur said, trying to ease the tension by making a joke.

"Very funny MacArthur. You know, if you had followed your real calling, becoming a comedian, you probably wouldn't be in the mess your in."

MacArthur was led back to his jail cell. He laid down on the cot. It reeked of old sweat and vomit. Looking through the bars of a jail cell from the inside was something he thought he would never see. It was frightening to say the least.

Somewhere in the back of his mind, ever since Marilyn's phone had been found in his apartment, he knew it might come to this.

MacArthur tried, as he had for days, to think of who would want to frame him for murder.

Was Killingsworth capable of this? MacArthur thought.

There were so many questions he had, but he had no one to give him answers.

Rachel heard the news from one of the officers in the coffee room.

Chief Aldridge's secretary called and told her he wanted to see her.

"Come in, Officer Peavey. I'm sure you've heard the news by now."

"Yes sir, I have."

"I'm going to be up front with you, Peavey, I just don't want to believe MacArthur killed this woman. However, the evidence Killingsworth has gathered says otherwise. Marilyn's phone found in his apartment, an hour and a half unaccounted for the night of the murder, and the fact that she had been carrying on an affair with someone else would definitely provide a motive. It doesn't look good for him right now. Still, my gut tells me he couldn't have done this."

Chief Aldridge looked directly at Rachel and asked, "Do you think he's capable of doing what he has been accused of? You probably know him as well as anyone on the force. I know you two worked very closely on the Sprayberry murders. Officer Peavey, has he ever indicated in any way he was involved?"

"Chief, I have a great deal of respect for Detective Nowlin. To tell you the truth, I don't know what to believe anymore. No, I don't think he did it, but if the evidence shows he did, then it is what it is. Sometimes we may think we know someone, but we could be wrong. Right now, it looks like I may have been wrong about Detective Nowlin."

"Peavey, I appreciate your honesty. Whatever happens, I believe the truth will come out," Chief Aldridge said with conviction.

"Yes sir, I agree. The truth will definitely come out."

Rachel excused herself and walked out of Chief Aldridge's office.

That was not the response I expected to get from her. Did she just throw him under the bus? The Chief thought, as he lit a cigar.

Jake Rhymes, MacArthur's attorney arrived around 4:00 pm and went straight to MacArthur's jail cell.

"Good to see you again, my old friend, although I wished it was under different circumstances."

"It's good to see you too Jake," MacArthur replied.

MacArthur went through the details of Marilyn's murder and all of the circumstances surrounding it. He explained how Detective Killingsworth has suspected him from the beginning. He also told Jake why Killingsworth was so close to this case. MacArthur even discussed, as painful as it was, how Marilyn had been cheating on him and with whom.

"Well, MacArthur, the first thing we've got to do is get you out of here. The arraignment is set for tomorrow morning at 8:30."

Jake asked MacArthur if there was anything he could get him before he left for his hotel. "How about a cheeseburger and fries?"

Jake Rhymer and MacArthur became friends in their freshman year of college. Jake and his family lived in Raleigh while MacArthur grew up in a different part of North Carolina. During Jake's first year of college, he and MacArthur had a couple of classes together. Both were majoring in criminal justice.

They met on Sunday nights in the library to share notes and to quiz each other as they prepared for next week's test. Jake would get frustrated with MacArthur because he wasn't as serious about his grades as Jake was. Jake had always wanted to become a trial lawyer, while MacArthur wanted to be a detective and then work for the FBI.

MacArthur always benefited more than Jake from their study sessions because he was almost never prepared. Jake tolerated him, because there was something about MacArthur he admired. No, he was not a scholar, but Jake had no doubts, MacArthur would be successful one day.

Jake wished he could be more like MacArthur. He just didn't seem to sweat the small stuff. MacArthur had a knack for cutting away the fluff and getting to the core of any situation.

At the beginning of their third year of college, they moved into an old house with two other guys, only three blocks from campus. The other two roommates would often refer to Jake and MacArthur as the "odd couple."

The reasons were obvious. Jake was studious, kept his room immaculate, and was always well dressed. On the other hand, MacArthur studied just enough to make average grades, his room was always a mess, and his attire consisted of two pair of worn out jeans and sweatshirts.

But, like opposites often do, they became best of friends.

MacArthur thought that Thursday night was the official party night. When nothing was happening anywhere else, Jake and MacArthur's place was "rockin." Music could be heard blocks from their house. Once, campus police raided their party finding several underage girls drinking beer. The parents of the underage girls were called down to the station to pick them up. Jake made sure this didn't happen again. But, this didn't stop MacArthur from having other parties, but with girls of legal drinking age.

Jake didn't always attend these parties. He would beg off, if he had an exam coming up, or if he just needed to spend a little extra time studying. MacArthur's philosophy was very simple, let tomorrow take care of itself.

Jake graduated with honors, and MacArthur was just lucky to graduate at all. Jake was accepted to law school at North Carolina State University. The two remained friends and kept in touch on a regular basis. After getting his law degree, Jake took a job with a small law firm in Chapel Hill. He quickly climbed up the ladder and in his sixth year, was made a partner. His easy manner in the courtroom and his acquittal rates were soon noticed by some of the larger firms around Chapel Hill. But, Jake chose to stay where he was.

Life was good, and over the next few years, he married, and his wife gave birth to a beautiful baby girl they named Chloe. Jake doted over his little girl, and made no apologizes about spoiling her. Chloe had just celebrated her third birthday when she began to have coughing spells. The doctors said it appeared she had allergies. When the test results came back they confirmed she was suffering from leukemia.

Jake took her to every specialist in North Carolina as well as Virginia. The specialists were consistent with their prognosis. Chloe was given three to six months to live.

When the end came, Jake was holding her in his arms. He could feel his sweet baby girl struggling for every breath she took. As she slipped in and out of consciousness, Chloe would look up at her daddy and try to smile.

Jake Rhymes' life, as he knew it, ended with the last breathe of his beloved Chloe.

The next few years, he and his wife talked about having another baby, but the strain of such a loss had taken its toll on their marriage. Jake and his wife divorced after nine years of marriage. Jake remained in Chapel Hill, and continued to practice law with the same firm he had been with since graduating from college.

His colleagues noticed a change in Jake. He had become reclusive, seldom attending any social functions. His quick wit and contagious smile had all but disappeared. Counseling had been suggested by one of the partners. Jake agreed to see a counselor, but after two visits, he invented reasons or conflicts that would prevent him from attending the sessions. Within a couple of months, the visits stopped altogether.

MacArthur had attended Chloe's funeral one year earlier and had seen Jake's marriage coming apart. He felt helpless. He wanted so badly to help his one and only true friend.

Jake's doctor gave him a prescription for something to make him sleep at night. It wasn't long before Jake was asking for samples for other made-up ailments. Jake was starting to think he couldn't get though the day without his pills. As with any addiction, the dependence upon the pills became more apparent. When one doctor would cut him off, he would just find another who would prescribe what he needed.

Jake's life was spiraling out of control. His partners suggested he take a month off, just to relax. Jake was in denial of his growing addiction to pain killers and refused. His position with the firm was in jeopardy, but Jake was clueless.

It wasn't until he was issued an ultimatum that he realized he needed help. He called his best friend, MacArthur. The two of them spent a weekend at one of his client's lodges near Pigeon Forge. Jake agreed to get some help. MacArthur made him promise that he would call someone Monday morning. Jake never made the call.

MacArthur didn't hear from Jake for over two years. It seemed that after he got fired from the firm, he just vanished from the planet.

Then, early one June day, Jake called MacArthur from a hospital somewhere in Maryland. He had survived a suicide attempt after taking a bottle of pills. He had no one to turn to but MacArthur. Three days later Jake returned to Wilcox with MacArthur. He had lost almost 40 pounds and had become so weak he could hardly walk. MacArthur nursed him back to health. He enrolled him in a group therapy class where he went three nights a week.

Clean and sober, Jake left Wilcox five months later. Through a contact of MacArthur's, Jake got a job with the Locke County Court House. He was assigned to represent clients that had no representation. He became a court appointed lawyer.

Through the years, Jake never forgot how MacArthur had saved his life, as well as his career. By the time MacArthur had called him to come and represent him, Jake had once again become a well-respected and highly sought after defense attorney.

Jake told MacArthur he would take the case only if he agreed there would be no charge for his services. When MacArthur protested, Jake looked him and said, "You saved my life once, this is the least I can do for you."

Friday morning seemed as though it would never come. The tiny cell MacArthur now called home made him appreciate the steamy motels he had stayed in over the years. Of course, he got very little sleep. He had never noticed the different sounds one could hear in a jail cell.

The arraignment was scheduled for 8:30 am. Judge Seymour would be presiding. Judge Henry had recused himself due to a conflict of interest.

"Mr. Nowlin how do you plead?"

"Not guilty, Your Honor."

The assistant district Attorney agreed when the judge allowed MacArthur to be released from custody on his own recognizance, until a trial date was set.

Jake thanked the judge and the assistant district attorney.

MacArthur spent the rest of the day going over the events of the night Marilyn was murdered. He had no idea who might want Marilyn dead. Killingsworth was the only person he could connect to her murder. In only a matter of a few days, he and Jake would learn that the state had a star witness. A witness that claims he was paid $8,500 by MacArthur to have Marilyn Hampton killed.

Jake came by around 7:00 pm with a pizza and cokes. He asked MacArthur to try and remember the last conversation he had with Marilyn.

"I can't remember every word Jake, but she was mad. She said something about my lack of commitment and how I loved my job above all else. I did tell her I was sorry."

"Did she mention another man or that she was going to break up with you?"

"No, when I was told of that, I was totally surprised. In fact, I thought we might take our relationship to the next level. You know, maybe even get married." MacArthur paused and then said, "Wait, I do remember her saying, we need to talk?"

Within a few days, a grand jury was convened and held that there was enough evidence for the case to go to trial. Neither he nor Jake was allowed to be present, which was consistent with the law.

MacArthur Nowlin would stand trial on April 4, 2006, for the murder of Marilyn Hampton.

M. HARMON HALL

CHAPTER 29

"Who in the hell is Sonny Barrett?" Jake asked.

"He grew up here, was a local football hero. He's never been worth a damn, Jake. He fooled Marilyn for a while. The two of them dated until she saw what a piece of crap he was. That's how I met Marilyn. She came to the station to file a restraining order against him. He had made some threats but no one, including me, thought he would ever carry them out."

"Why is he fingering you?"

"That's what I can't figure out. I don't have any history with this loser. I've never arrested him or anything like that. I did handle a restraining complaint against him filed by Marilyn just after they stopped dating."

"We're going to have to discredit him as a witness on the stand. We've got to show that he can't be trusted to tell the truth."

"Jake, I know where Marilyn's car was hidden. I'm sure it's in a small pond behind the cabin where she was killed. I used to go there for some duck hunting."

"Does anyone else know?"

"No."

"There might be something in her car that could prove your innocence."

"Like what?"

"I don't know right now; let me think about this for a while. I'm not sure if disclosing where her car is hidden will be beneficial to your case. It could make things worse. Let's sit on this for a while, MacArthur," Jake reasoned.

M. HARMON HALL

    MacArthur had been placed on administrative leave until the result of the trial was determined. Of course, he had to turn in his badge and gun. His nephew, Waddell would come by from time to time. He tried to keep him informed on what Killingsworth was up to. MacArthur went to the local basketball games a couple nights a week. When he would go to the post office or grocery store, the people's faces said it all. MacArthur often thought, *so much for innocent until proven guilty.* He had never felt so alone in his entire life. There was no one to talk to.

    Rachel proved to be a "fair weather friend" who no longer called him. He wanted to call Marilyn's mother to tell her he didn't kill her daughter, but Jake advised against it. In rare moments of light-heartedness, he would joke with Jake that he knew how Charles Lindberg must have felt on his solo flight across the Atlantic.

    Time seemed to stand still for MacArthur. He had too much time to reflect upon his life. There were certainly some things he would have done differently. Maybe he should have tried to express himself in a more personable way. Perhaps, he could have learned to be more trusting. Maybe he should have been more diplomatic in his dealings with others. But, his biggest regret and worst mistake of all was walking out on Kelli.

    It wasn't going to prison that bothered him the most. He could learn to adapt. It was the thought that people would label him a cold blooded killer. MacArthur didn't really care if people liked him, maybe he should have, but he did care about his reputation. He took pride in the fact that he was known as an honest, hardworking man that stood for what was right. To be sent away to prison as a disgraced law enforcement officer was something he couldn't bear.

KEYS TO MURDER

His contempt for Killingsworth was as strong as ever. He blamed this witch hunt entirely on him. Although, Chief Aldridge and District Attorney Sanford could have stepped in and put a stop to this madness, he knew the evidence presented by Killingsworth was convincing. He didn't really blame the Chief and D.A. After all, they were just doing their job.

Part of Jake's strategy was to introduce several witnesses that could attest MacArthur's good character. The biggest problem he faced, Jake believed, was explaining how Marilyn's phone turned up in his apartment. According to the phone records, she had called her mother that night as well as Killingsworth, Rachel, and MacArthur in that order.

When Jake asked MacArthur about it he swore that after making the call around 7:45 that night he did not talk with Marilyn again. He explained to Jake that he called then to tell her their weekend getaway was off.

"MacArthur, think hard. There has to be an explanation as to this phantom call according to the prosecution. Could you have spoken to her during the investigation and not remember?" Jake asked.

"Jake, I didn't talk with her again. If I had, I would remember, because I knew how pissed she was."

"Was there a time when you didn't have your phone with you? I mean, could someone else have taken the call without you knowing about it?"

MacArthur sat quietly for some time thinking back to that night. He retraced his actions from the time he got to the Sprayberry's until he went to bed. He went back over the time when he entered the police station. He checked his messages and went to the bathroom. That's it!

"Jake, I remember leaving my phone on my desk before I went to the restroom. The reason I remember is because I never take my phone with me when I am going to-well, you know. It's possible, she called while I was in the restroom and when I got back I didn't notice I had missed a call. That can be the only explanation I can think of. Rachel used to fuss at me for not checking my messages sometimes and just deleting them without ever looking at them."

"That's very possible. Because, the records show that the call lasted only 12 seconds. Let's just hope the jury believes it," Jake said, as he changed the subject.

CHAPTER 30

Finally, April 4 arrived.

The trial began like most do. Both sides went back and forth during the "striking of the jury" phase. It took the better part of a day to complete the process. The 12 jurors and two alternates were selected and were instructed by the judge as to their responsibilities. The jury selected a foreman and notified the bailiff they were ready.

MacArthur and Jake were seated at one of two tables in the front of the courtroom. They sat at the table on the left side of the courtroom while the prosecution sat on the right side.

The atmosphere was like that of a carnival. Those who could not find a seat, stood outside. This event had all of the trappings of a circus that had come to town. The media was present, although Judge Seymour would not allow cameras inside the courtroom.

MacArthur leaned over and told Jake, this must be what it feels like when lambs are led to slaughter. Jake didn't find the humor in it, considering MacArthur's life depended on his ability to convince the jurors that his best friend did not kill Marilyn Hampton.

Marilyn's mother had made the long trip from California to see that justice was served. Several police officers were stationed at different points around the courtroom and outside as well. Most of them believed MacArthur was innocent regardless of how things might have looked. Detective Killingsworth felt the isolation in the months leading up to the trial.

M. HARMON HALL

The Bailiff told everyone to rise as Judge Wyatt Seymour approached the bench. Once everyone was seated, Judge Seymour asked if both sides were ready. He looked at Assistant District Attorney McKinney and told him to begin with his opening statement to the jurors.

Assistant District Attorney McKinney was a striking man, standing over six feet tall. His features resembled those of an athlete. Big shoulders and lean; it was clear he took care of his body. His red hair was cut short, and he was dressed in a conservative grey suit. He stood up and slowly walked toward the jury box.

"Ladies and gentlemen of the jury. First, I want to thank each one of you for doing your civic duty by serving here today. Your task is really very simple, and yet extremely important. You must decide if this man, MacArthur Nowlin, was involved in any way that led to the death of Marilyn Hampton. In the next few days you will be provided with evidence that will show beyond a shadow of a doubt that MacArthur Nowlin hired someone to kill Marilyn Hampton. We will show that MacArthur Nowlin's motive for murder was one of the oldest known to man, jealousy and resentment from being rejected by a woman he loved. You will hear the testimony of the man that has admitted to committing this brutal murder. You will hear that same man, with nothing to lose, testify under oath that MacArthur Nowlin hired him to kill Marilyn Hampton. I am confident after all of the evidence has been presented, there can be only one verdict, that is, guilty. Thank you."

McKinney smiled at the jury and walked back to the prosecution's table. Confidence radiated from his round face.

Judge Seymour then instructed Jake to proceed with his opening statement.

Jake got up slowly with his yellow legal pad in his right hand. He smiled at the jurors as he approached the jury box. His demeanor resembled that of a man about to tell a story. He took his coat off and rolled up his sleeves. He removed a handkerchief from his back pocket and wiped his brow then his mouth. One jury member would later say he looked like *"Matlock."* Some of the younger jurors wouldn't have known who *"Matlock"* was.

"Ladies and gentlemen of the jury, I'm not going to try and impress you by presenting several theories as to why my client, MacArthur Nowlin is innocent. In fact, I am going to let the prosecution do that for me. Why? Because there is not one shred of evidence that links MacArthur Nowlin to this terrible crime. But, you will hear testimony from a man that has confessed to raping and stabbing Marilyn Hampton 35 times, slicing her throat, causing her slow and painful death. The prosecution is basing their entire case on the testimony of this confessed rapist and killer. I ask you, ladies and gentlemen, is that the kind of person you put your trust in to tell the truth? What the prosecution won't tell you is, this confessed killer was offered a deal. For his testimony, the death penalty would be removed for a life sentence instead. I know you will do the right thing, find MacArthur Nowlin, not guilty. Thank you."

Jake smiled at the jury and walked slowly back to the defense table. He had already begun the task of discrediting the key witness. MacArthur thought his remarks to the jury were excellent.

"Mr. McKinney you may call your first witness."

"Thank you, Your Honor."

"Your Honor, the State calls Detective Tim Killingsworth to the stand."

Detective Killingsworth entered the courtroom dressed in a beige suit with a blue tie. He walked with his head held high and his shoulders back. He was sworn in and took a seat.

McKinney began by asking, "Detective Killingsworth, are you employed by the Wilcox Police Department?"

"Yes, I have been a homicide Detective for eight years."

"Detective, did you know Marilyn Hampton?"

"Yes I did."

"What kind of relationship did you have with Ms. Hampton?"

"We were involved in a romantic relationship I guess you could call it."

"So, Detective, you are admitting you and the deceased had an intimate relationship?"

"Yes, you could say it was intimate."

"How long had this affair gone on?"

"I would say about one month," Killingsworth replied.

"Detective, did you ever tell MacArthur Nowlin about your affair with the deceased?"

"Yes, I did. I told him I was not proud of what had taken place, but after several calls from her after they argued…"

"Objection, Your Honor, this testimony is nothing more than hearsay."

"Overruled, you may continue Detective Killingsworth."

"We met for coffee and she would tell me how she had become afraid of him…"

"Objection, Your Honor, we have no way of knowing what she said to the witness, or what she was implying," Jake stated boldly.

KEYS TO MURDER

"Your Honor, the State is merely trying to establish a pattern of the defendant's behavior towards the deceased in the days leading to her murder," McKinney interjected.

"Overruled Counselor, but Mr. McKinney you're on thin ice here."

"Thank you sir."

"Detective, I know this was not easy for you to come and testify here today. Your open admission to having an affair with the deceased has ultimately resulted in a separation between you and your wife, has it not?"

"Yes, like I said before, I'm not proud of what I did. I never intended for our relationship to go that far, it just happened," Killingsworth testified, as he lowered his head.

"Detective, how would you describe your relationship with the defendant?"

"I guess you could say we were never buddies. We got along ok at work."

"How would you describe Mr. Nowlin's temperament?"

"Objection, Your Honor, this witness has not been identified as an expert. He is not qualified to make such a determination," Jake interrupted.

"Sustained, the witness will not answer that question."

"Thank you, Your Honor."

"Mr. Killingsworth have you ever been witness to the defendant using excessive force in the line of duty, as a police officer of the law?"

"Objection Your Honor, this witness has not been recognized as an expert on the definition of what is excessive force?" Jake interjected.

"Sustained, Counselor I fail to see the relevancy in your question. Move on," Judge Seymour instructed, giving McKinney a stern look.

"We have no more questions at this time, but ask the court permission to call this witness at a later date, "McKinney said, as he returned to the prosecution's table. He smiled at the jury as he sat down.

"Does the defense wish to cross examine this witness?" Judge Seymour asked.

"Yes, Your Honor."

With his yellow legal pad in his left hand, and his glasses on top of his head, Jake approached the witness stand.

"Detective Killingsworth, you just told the court that you and the defendant were not exactly buddies, but you two got along ok at work. Isn't it true that you hated the defendant? Isn't it true you told several co-workers you detested MacArthur Nowlin?"

"Like I said, he and I were not what you would call friends. I mean, we didn't hang out together," Killingsworth answered.

"I guess not. You were too busy hanging out with his girlfriend."

"Objection Your Honor, that last statement is uncalled for," McKinney protested.

"Sustained. Mr. Rhymes, is there a question in here somewhere?" Judge Seymour asked, sarcastically.

"Yes, Your Honor."

"Detective Killingsworth, is it possible, because of your disdain for the defendant, you became too personally involved in your investigation? Is it possible you could not be objective while carrying out this investigation?"

"No, while I don't care for the defendant, the facts of this case are what they are," Killingsworth replied.

"So, it would be safe to say today, under oath, your hatred and jealousy of this decorated homicide detective could in no way compromise your ability to be objective throughout the investigation?"

"Objection, Your Honor, Mr. Rhymes is suggesting this sworn officer of the law would deliberately skew the facts of this case simply because he didn't care for the defendant."

"Sustained." I think you've made your point Mr. Rhymes, please move forward.

"Detective, you stated earlier in your testimony that you told the defendant, MacArthur Nowlin, about your affair with Marilyn Hampton, did you not?" Jake asked

"Yes, that is correct."

"When did you tell him of the affair?"

Killingsworth looked over at the prosecution's table as if he should answer, or not. His gaze did not go unnoticed by some of the jurors.

"Detective, do I need to repeat the question? "Jake pushed.

"I don't know exactly what day it was."

"Was it before or after Ms. Hampton was killed?"

Killingsworth was backed into a corner, he realized what was coming next. He stared at Jake for several seconds.

"Forgive me Detective, this really is not a difficult question. When you admitted for the first time to the defendant, MacArthur Nowlin, was it before or after Marilyn Hampton was killed?" Jake pressed.

"I believe it was after Marilyn's death," Killingsworth answered, reluctantly.

"Could you repeat your answer Detective?"

"I said, it was after Marilyn's death."

"So, the defendant was not aware of your affair with Marilyn Hampton at the time she was killed?"

"I can't say for sure. He might have heard it from someone else, I don't know," Killingsworth replied, showing signs of nervousness for the first time.

"But, you didn't tell him, did you Detective?"

"No."

"Did you tell anyone else you were having an affair with Marilyn Hampton?"

"No, I don't believe so."

"I'm sure you would agree with me Detective Killingsworth, based on your testimony just now my client's motive for killing Ms. Hampton no longer exists. That is, prosecution has suggested that the one and only motive that MacArthur Nowlin had for killing Marilyn Hampton was because he was jealous and wanted revenge for her unfaithfulness. I ask you Detective, if he didn't know anything about the affair between you two then why would he want to kill the same woman he was about to ask to marry him?"

"Mr. Rhymes, all I'm saying is..."

"Thank you Detective, no further questions Your Honor," Jake said, as he cut Killingsworth off.

When Jake had finished cross examining Killingsworth, McKinney came back to ask him one more question.

"Detective Killingsworth, is it possible that the deceased could have called MacArthur Nowlin the night she was killed? In other words, it is possible he could have known?" McKinney asked, trying to minimize the damage done."

"Yes, in my opinion, it is."

"Objection Your Honor, the court is not interested in his opinion," Jake stated, as he rose from his chair.

"Sustained."

"That's all of the questions I have for this witness Your Honor."

"You may be excused Detective Killingsworth, Judge Seymour said as he announced a 20 minuet recess.

Jake had done what he intended to do, he had put some doubt in the juror's minds. The notion that MacArthur's motive for having Marilyn Hampton murdered was jealousy and revenge was now certainly in question.

Regardless of this setback, the prosecution was sticking to its game plan. That is, Sonny Barrett's testimony would be the last thing the jury would hear from the prosecution.

"All rise, the court is now in session with the Honorable Judge Seymour."

"Mr. McKinney you may proceed," Judge Seymour stated, as he was seated.

"Your Honor, the State calls Sally Hammonds to the stand."

Jake whispered to MacArthur, "What's her story, who is she?"

"She worked with Marilyn at the beauty salon," MacArthur answered.

Sally Hammonds was sworn in and took a seat.

"Ms. Hammonds, what was your relationship with Marilyn Hampton?"

"I worked for her at the beauty salon."

"Would you say you two were good friends, as well as co-workers?"

"Yes, Marilyn and I talked a lot and we would go to dinner, movies, and we went shopping on some occasions."

"Did she ever mention MacArthur's name when you two were together?"

Sally Hammond spoke in a soft nervous tone. It was clear she was very uncomfortable on the witness stand. McKinney was aware of this, as well. He didn't want to keep her up there very long.

"Yes, she didn't at first, then she would tell me things they would argue about, and how mad Detective MacArthur…"

"Objection Your Honor, this is nothing more than hearsay."

"Objection overruled. You may continue Mrs. Hammond."

"Like I was saying, Marilyn would tell me about their arguments and how she was becoming afraid of him."

"Mrs. Hammond, did she ever tell you she was seeing someone else and that she was going to break up with the defendant, Mr. Nowlin?"

"Yes, she did. She told me she had been seeing someone else and that she thought she was falling in love."

"Objection Your Honor, I fail to see what this has to do with the defendant."

"Overruled, you may continue Counselor."

"Ms. Hammond, did the deceased ever mention the defendant becoming violent?"

"Objection Your Honor, this is nothing more than hearsay," Jake replied.

"Overruled. You may answer the question Ms. Hammond."

"I don't recall her ever mentioning that he hit her, but if he did I don't think she would have told me"

KEYS TO MURDER

"Thank you Ms. Hammond. That's all the questions for this witness Your Honor."

"Mr. Rhymes, do you wish to cross examine this witness?"

"Yes, Your Honor."

Jake stood up and walked toward Sally Hammond and looked her straight in the eyes.

"Ms. Hammond, you told the court that the deceased told you about Mr. Nowlin's temper, did you not?"

"I said, Marilyn told me how mad he would get when they argued."

"I see, Ms. Hammond have you ever seen the defendant, MacArthur Nowlin display anger or appear to be upset the times you were around him?"

"Well, Marilyn said…"

"Ms. Hammond, I'm not asking you what Marilyn said, I'm asking you what you saw or heard."

"No, I have never seen him get mad, but I hadn't been around him very much."

"Ms. Hammond, I believe you stated a few moments ago that Ms. Hampton had told you of her affair. Is that correct?

"Yes, I believe I said that."

"Ms. Hammond, did she tell you she was having an affair with Detective Killingsworth?"

"No, actually she said that she was thinking about breaking up with Detective Nowlin."

"Ms. Hammond, in your earlier testimony, could you have been mistaken or even confused when you said she was having an affair with anyone?"

"Well, I guess so, but I assumed that what she meant."

"But, she never actually told you she was having an affair."

"Mr. Rhymes, what I meant to say was…"

"Thank you Ms. Hammond, no further questions Your Honor," Jake turned, and walked back to the defense table.

It was almost 4:25 pm. Judge Seymour rapped his gavel on the bench and declared. "We will reconvene these proceedings tomorrow morning at 9:00 am sharp."

Jake and MacArthur picked up some burgers and fries and went back to his apartment. There was not really much to discuss. Both knew tomorrow would be a big day in the trial. The prosecution would call Sonny to the stand.

"Jake that was a piece of work with Hammond today. She was so confused, you had her about to confess she could have been having an affair." MacArthur laughed.

Jake soon left for his hotel room. MacArthur decided he would watch the *Tonight Show*. It wasn't very long before he was asleep on the sofa.

He woke up around 2:30 and got in his bed. He was surprised he slept as well as he did. He showered and got some early breakfast at the Pancake House, located near the courthouse.

MacArthur didn't know that Jake was planning to put Kelli on the stand. Jake didn't tell him, because he knew he would not agree to it. Jake was surprised when she agreed to make the long trip and testify on behalf of the man who had walked out of her life.

Kelli had arrived in Wilcox on the afternoon of the first day of trial. She checked in at the Hampton Inn. The next morning, she waited outside of the courtroom where Jake had asked her to meet him. She hadn't planned on seeing MacArthur.

When MacArthur walked up the long row of steps leading to the entrance of the courthouse, he spotted Kelli. She was seated on one of the benches just outside of the entrance.

"What are you doing here Kelli?" he asked, surprised to see her.

"Jake called me and asked if I would come to testify on your behalf. I'm not sure if this was a good idea. Just so you will know, I did this for Jake, not for you," Kelli said, as she stared at MacArthur.

"Well, I didn't know. If I had known, I wouldn't have allowed it."

"That's exactly what Jake said."

There was a long pause with neither saying anything. The tension between the two was most evident. MacArthur finally spoke.

"How have you been?" he asked, realizing how insincere it sounded.

"MacArthur we're not going to play this game. I'm here for one reason only, and it's not to reminisce about the old times we had. I promised Jake I would come…"

"Yeah, yeah, you told me that already," MacArthur said, using the same tone he had used so many times before.

"Some things never change, do they MacArthur?"

"I suppose not."

There was total silence again. Neither knew what to say. So much was going through both of their heads. Both wished Jake would hurry and get there to relieve this agony.

She was determined not to let him know how much she had missed him. How much she still loved him. And, she certainly wasn't going to tell him about the son he never knew about.

If he would only put his arms around me once more. If he had known I had forgiven him a long time ago. I want to tell him so badly how much I still need him, how much I still love him.

MacArthur wanted to tell her how much he had missed her. How his life had never been the same. He wanted to tell her she was still as beautiful as the day he met her. He wanted to hold her hand and touch her hair. Most of all, he wanted to tell her what a terrible mistake he made years ago when he walked out.

"Kelli, I don't think it's a good idea for you to be here. I'll explain to Jake that you changed your mind and went home." MacArthur stood up and without saying goodbye disappeared into the courthouse.

Kelli sat there for a while and then quietly got up, tears now running down her face, and walked back to the hotel. She slowly packed her things and walked downstairs to check-out. Within minutes, she was on her way back home where her son waited for her.

MacArthur cursed himself. *I'm such a dumb, selfish asshole? Why didn't I go after her and tell her what I'm really thinking? What good will that do, besides where I'm going it doesn't matter anyway.*

"Sorry, I'm running late. I had problems taking a shower this morning, there was no hot water."

"I told you not to stay at that dump, but you're so damn cheap you thought you could save a few bucks," MacArthur said laughing. "I thought you had skipped town."

"I thought about it," Jake joked. "You know MacArthur, I've got a good feeling about today. I don't know why, I just do."

"I hope your right, Jake."

Where is Kelli? Jake thought.

As they walked into the courthouse, MacArthur told Jake about his conversation with Kelli. He told Jake he suggested she go home. Jake was not surprised. But, he was sorry he didn't get a chance to see her and thank her for coming;

The second day of trial was rather routine. Witnesses were called to testify that Marilyn and MacArthur had been seen arguing in public places. Some said they saw her crying, while others testified that they had seen them at different places and both of them seemed very happy together.

Jake's rebuttal was simple, just because two people argue in public doesn't mean one kills the other. In his cross-examining, Jake asked each witness if they had ever quarreled with their boyfriends or husbands. His point was made, every couple argues at some time, but that doesn't lead to murder.

Tomorrow, the third day of the trial, Sonny Barrett would take the stand. It was no secret why he would be called back to testify.

Court was adjourned at 4:30 pm. Judge Seymour instructed the courtroom that the trial would continue beginning at 9:00 am tomorrow.

CHAPTER 31

Everyone had been anticipating this day. Sonny Barrett would be called by the prosecution to testify against MacArthur. Sonny was expected to testify it was MacArthur who hired him to kill Marilyn, on the night of August 8th, 2005.

The courtroom was filled to capacity. Marilyn's mother, son, and her grandmother were seated two rows behind the prosecutor's table. Assistant District Attorney Charles McKinney and his assistant, Randal Holliday, had the look of a tiger about to finish off his quarry. Both had displayed an air of extreme confidence throughout the trial.

At the defense table, MacArthur and his attorney, Jake Rhymes sat without talking.

MacArthur was dressed in a blue suit, white shirt, and wearing a red and black tie. The stress of all of this had taken a toll on him. Over the past three weeks, he had lost almost 10 pounds, as his face appeared to be drawn.

Throughout the trial, MacArthur never seemed to know what to do with his hands. He was either clasping them together or rubbing them. They were dry and some said they even noticed a slight tremor in them. His hair was combed neatly, but appeared longer than usual.

MacArthur felt the coming of a perfect storm. During the trial proceedings, he often watched the jury's reaction while different witnesses testified under oath. MacArthur was not confident at all.

He had seldom shown any emotion during the trial with the exception of when pictures of Marilyn's body were introduced as evidence by the prosecution. MacArthur's eyes had shown a sadness that no one around him had ever seen before.

Some would speculate this was just for show, others believed he was grieving for the loss of Marilyn.

Throughout the trial Assistant District Attorney McKinney tried to convey the idea to the jury that they shouldn't be fooled by the outward appearance of the accused. Jurors heard, through the testimonies of hostile witnesses, MacArthur had a history of lacking empathy for anyone he had ever come in contact with. McKinney made efforts to portray him as a professional law enforcement officer that had been trained to disguise his true feelings and emotions.

Just as expected, this trial had attracted outside media sources, as well as the local media. Today, would be no exception. Judge Seymour had not allowed cameras in the courtroom from the very beginning. Outside, the trucks of the largest TV stations in the surrounding area were poised to be the first to cover the main attraction, the testimony of Sonny Barrett.

Everyone rose, as Judge Seymour entered the courtroom. As he had every day of the trial, Judge Seymour instructed the people in the courtroom to remain silent, and if there were any outbursts they would be removed.

"Counselors, are you ready to proceed?" the judge asked, as he looked at the defense team of lawyers and then the prosecution's team.

"Yes, sir, Your Honor," both replied.

"Mr. McKinney you may call your first witness."

"Thank you, Your Honor. The prosecution would like to call Sonny Barrett to the stand."

Sonny Barrett was escorted into the courtroom through the side entrance. He was wearing orange overalls issued by the prison. He was clean shaven, his hair combed from back to front, and his "jewelry" consisted of chains on both his feet and hands. A large tattoo covered the entire right side of his neck and several others on his arms and legs which were hidden by the long sleeve shirt and trousers he wore.

Long gone was the athletic body of Wilcox's high school football hero. Instead, a burned out, overweight man, showing the evidence of a fast and hard life. The once piercing blue eyes had turned to glazed, reddened eyes of a man that had too many sleepless nights and drank too much alcohol. Many of the older people sitting in the courtroom did not recognize him.

How could Wilcox's "golden boy" fall to such depths as this? The world was at his feet and yet he threw it all away with drugs and alcohol.

The death of Marilyn Hampton was not the only tragedy revealed in this trial.

Sonny gazed around the courtroom as though he was the star of the show. In his mind, he was. He smiled at the bailiff, as he made his way to the witness chair. After raising his right hand and placing his left hand on the Bible, he was sworn in. He repeated the time honored oath and then sat down.

If he was nervous, he didn't show it. He was going to enjoy his 15 minutes of fame.

McKinney approached the witness as he would an old friend, smiling and asking him how he was doing. In a moment of mental lapse, he asked him to tell the court his name and where he lived..."

"My name is Richard Samuel Barrett. I am currently residing in the state penitentiary up in Lineville," Sonny said, smiling as some in the courtroom found this to be humorous.

McKinney realized just how stupid the second question was, but he couldn't do anything about it now.

The fact was, Sonny Barrett had pleaded guilty to first degree murder of Marilyn Hampton over a month ago, before Judge Henry. He had entered a plea bargain with the district attorney's office and he was sentenced to life without the possibility of parole. His testimony today was the leverage he needed to keep from getting the death penalty.

"Mr. Barrett, are you here today on your own free will?"

"Yes, I am."

"Mr. Barrett, it is a matter of record that on May 6rd of this year, you pleaded guilty to the murder of Marilyn Hampton on the night of August 8th 2005. Is that correct?" McKinney asked.

"Yeah, that's right."

"And, is it also true that while you admit to this terrible crime, you did not act alone?"

"Objection, Your Honor, the witness is being led by this type of question."

"Overruled, Mr. Barrett you may answer the question."

"You mean did someone hire me to kill her?"

"Yes, that's what I'm asking you. So you committed this unspeakable act after being contacted and offered money to kill Ms. Hampton?" McKinney stated, making sure the jury understood that this was a murder for hire.

"I was approached and offered $8,500 to kill Marilyn," Barrett stated, coldly without any remorse.

"Mr. Barrett, did you ever receive any money for the murder?"

"Yes, I got $4,000 up front, and was supposed to get the rest after I killed her, but I never did get paid."

"Your Honor, that's all the questions I have for Mr. Barrett for now," McKinney said, knowing he would put Sonny back on the stand to identify MacArthur as the person who hired him.

He also anticipated the defense to cross- examine the state's key witness. The state's strategy was to drop the bomb shell at the very last possible minute, for the jury to get the full force of Sonny's damning testimony.

Jake stood up slowly with his ever present yellow legal pad in his left hand. As he approached the witness stand, Sonny didn't make any eye contact with him.

"Mr. Barrett, over a month you confessed killing Marilyn Hampton. Is that correct?"

"Yes, I did"

"Mr. Barrett, you say you came here today to testify because you chose to do so, no one made you. Is that right?"

"Yeah, that's right. What I did was wrong, but I shouldn't be the only one to pay for this. After all, someone else was in on it too."

"Mr. Barrett, that's down right commendable of you," Jake said, sarcastically for the entire courtroom to hear. "Let me get this straight, Mr.

Barrett. A human life is going for around $8,500 these days," Jake said, trying to discredit the witness. "Mr. Barrett, I think it's safe to say, that's not the real reason you are here today. Is it not true that the D.A's office agreed to reduce your sentence from death by injection, to life without parole? That is, if you testified as to who hired you to kill Marilyn Hampton? What else did they promise you?"

"Objection Your Honor, Mr. Rhymes is suggesting this witness has been coerced by the state."

"Overruled." You may answer the question, Mr. Barrett."

"What was the question again?"

"Were you offered a deal if you came and testified today?"

"Yeah, Mr. McKinney told me that if I testified in court and told who hired me to kill Marilyn, I would be spared the needle."

"I assume "being spared the needle" means your sentence would be reduced to life in prison rather than the death penalty?"

"Yeah, that's what I mean."

"Mr. Barrett, if they hadn't agreed to reduce your sentence, would you have come forward on your own?"

"Yeah, sure I would've."

"So you contacted Mr. McKinney's office, rather than them contacting you to testify here today?"

"If you mean I called them first, no. Mr. McKinney came to see me and told me what he would do."

"Mr. Rhymes, where is this going? I think the court gets it," Judge Seymour interrupted, showing a lack of patience.

"Your, Honor I'm trying to show that Mr. Barrett's appearance here today may have been brought about with the prodding of the prosecution," Jake replied.

"Continue, Counselor, but be careful,"

"Mr. Barrett, is it not true that three years ago, in this very same courtroom, you were found guilty of perjury?"

"Objection, Your Honor, what happened three years ago has no bearing on today's trial. The defense is reaching."

"Overruled, you may answer the question Mr. Barrett."

"To tell you truth, I don't remember what you're talking about," Sonny replied, acting as though his memory had failed him.

"So, you are so accustomed to lying, you don't know when you are telling the truth and when you're not? The facts are clear, you were found guilty of lying during your testimony. How can we be sure that you are not lying today?"

"Objection, Your Honor, the defense is making an assumption that has no substance."

"Overruled."

"Mr. Barrett, were you ever involved romantically with the deceased?"

"Do you mean did we date?" Sonny asked, trying to sound as though he was confused.

"Yes, were you two romantically involved for a short time?"

"We went together for about two or three months, I believe sir."

"After those two or three months the deceased ended the relationship. She told you she was no longer interested. And, isn't it true you threatened her. She must have taken your threat very serious because she went to the police seeking and getting a restraining order against you?"

"Yes, but I never laid a hand on her."

"Didn't you tell her that she would live to regret leading you on and making a fool out of you?"

"I don't remember saying that," Sonny shot back.

"Well, whether you remember or not, you were heard by witnesses threatening the deceased. Mr. Barrett, I suggest to this court you acted out of revenge completely alone. No one hired you to kill Ms. Hampton. You planned the whole thing yourself. Mr. Barrett, you have lied in this same courtroom before, and I think you are lying here again. I submit to this court that Ms. Hampton saw you for the loser you are, and wanted nothing else to do with you. You couldn't handle the rejection, so you got even.

"Objection, Your Honor, Mr. Rhymes is making statements that are conjecture in nature and is badgering the witness," McKinney blurted out, as he rose from his chair.

The courtroom began to buzz.

"Order in the court. I will not have these outbursts. I will clear this courtroom, if this continues," Judge Seymour said, in an attempt to gain control of the proceedings.

"Overruled." Answer the question, Mr. Barrett."

"That's not true. Yes, I killed her, but it was not my idea." Sonny retorted.

"Mr. Barrett, help me to understand, you came here today to testify for the sole purpose of carrying out your duty as any good citizen would?" Jake said, dripping with sarcasm.

"I came here today because…"

"You came here today because you are trying to save your own ass."

"Mr. Rhymes, I will not tolerate that kind of language in my court, do you understand?"

"Yes, sir Your Honor, I apologize and I assure you it won't happen again." No further questions at this time.

"We will take a 20 minute break," the judge declared, as his gavel came crashing down.

Jake and MacArthur walked outside. Jake smoked a cigarette while MacArthur sat quietly.

"I didn't know you smoked?"

"I don't, just started today," Jake said, laughing, trying to ease the tension that surrounded them like a cloud.

"Jake, no matter what happens, I appreciate you being here for me these past months. You're the only true friend I have."

"You would have done the same thing for me, MacArthur," Jake replied, putting his arm around him.

"You're not going kiss me, are you?" MacArthur joked, in an effort to ease the tension that was mounting.

The two of them walked back to the courthouse without speaking. There was nothing left to say at this point.

"All rise, the court is now in session, the Honorable Judge Seymour presiding," the bailiff announced.

"You may call your next witness, Mr. McKinney," Judge Seymour stated, as he motioned to one of the police officers standing near the bench.

Before McKinney raised from his chair to answer, Judge Seymour whispered to the police officer to get him a bottle of water. He knew this day was far from being over.

"Your Honor, the State would like to recall Mr. Sonny Barrett to the stand." McKinney deliberately waited until the very last minute to have Sonny drop the bombshell and testify under oath, that MacArthur had hired him to kill Marilyn.

As Sonny was ushered back into the courtroom, he never looked at MacArthur. They both knew the truth.

Sonny was sworn in again and sat nervously as Assistant District Attorney McKinney approached the bench. Before he reached the stand, he stopped, turned around, and took his coat off and placed it on the chair he was sitting in.

All eyes were focused on him now as he moved toward Sonny.

"Mr. Barrett, you have stated here in this courtroom today that you killed Marilyn Hampton on the night of August 8, 2005. Is that correct?"

"Yes sir, I did."

"Under oath, you also stated that you were hired to kill her for a sum of money. Is that not correct?"

"Yeah, that's right."

"Mr. Barrett, is the person that hired you to kill Ms. Hampton in this courtroom today?"

"Yes."

"Would you please stand and point out the person that hired you to kill Marilyn Hampton on the night of August 8, 2005."

Sonny Barrett rose from the witness chair with drops of sweat forming on his forehead. The air of confidence he had displayed throughout his testimony was now gone. He stared at the defense table and slowing raised his right arm.

The courtroom was completely silent. Sonny's heavy breathing could be heard by those close to the witness. All eyes were darting back and forth between Sonny and MacArthur, as though they were watching a tennis match.

MacArthur's mind was racing. He was angry. He was about to be accused of something he didn't do. His future was about to be decided by a cold blooded killer. His only hope was that the jury would not believe Sonny Barrett's testimony.

Who had put him up to this?

There were so many questions, but at this moment MacArthur knew in his heart, that really didn't matter. He was a marked man. He knew that as a former officer of the law, he would not last very long in prison.

MacArthur's whole life flashed before him. *Maybe I do deserve this after all,* he thought. No, he didn't kill Marilyn, but he was responsible for ruining Kelli's life. He thought of the father who he had never known. Thoughts of the shame he was bringing to his mother and sisters flooded his mind.

So this is what it has come to? The very same legal system that I had risked my life for as I tried to protect and find justice for other victims is about to put me away for life.

Sonny Barrett raised his hand and pointed in MacArthur's direction.

McKinney turned and faced the defendant's table as he asked Sonny, "Mr. Barrett, are you telling this court that the defendant, MacArthur Nowlin hired you to kill Marilyn Hampton?"

From that vantage point, it looked as though Sonny was pointing directly at MacArthur. To everyone's surprise, he was not.

"No, it was not Detective Nowlin; it was her! It was Rachel Peavey."

Rachel Peavey had been seated only a few feet behind MacArthur throughout the trial.

"Rachel Peavey hired me to kill Marilyn Hampton. I'm sorry Detective Nowlin. I should have told the truth to begin with," Sonny said, as he lowered his head.

The entire courtroom was in a state of shock. Tim Killingsworth sat without any expression on his face. He could not believe what just happened. He knew immediately, his career was over in Wilcox.

Judge Seymour was pounding his gavel on the bench, demanding order in his courtroom. No one heard him.

Slowly, Rachel Peavey rose from her seat. The scene was similar to an old *Perry Mason* TV episode. That's when the guilty party stands up and confesses. As some of the people near her saw what was happening, they began to get quiet. In moments, the entire courtroom was silent.

The scene was unforgettable.

Finally, Rachel Peavey slowly stood up and spoke with a soft controlled voice. Her eyes never leaving MacArthur.

"I waited for eight years to see that you got what you deserved, for what you did to my father. MacArthur Nowlin, you ruined my life, as well as my entire family's life. Eight years ago you falsely accused my father of a crime he didn't commit. He was found guilty because you testified against him. He kept trying to tell you he was innocent. You had the wrong man, but you didn't care. It was just another closed case and life moved on. Well, it didn't move on for my father. One week later my father hung himself in his prison cell. My mother never got over this terrible injustice. She died four months later. MacArthur Nowlin, you killed both of my parents, just as if you had put a gun to their head and pulled the trigger.

So, why did I have Marilyn killed? Because, I wanted you to know how it feels to lose someone you love. I wanted you to feel the pain each day you wake up. I wanted you to feel as though your whole world is falling in all around you. Sonny Barrett is right, I did hire him to kill Marilyn Hampton, and you want to know something? I'd do it again. Going to prison doesn't bother me. I don't have a life anyway, thanks to you. Do you realize how hard it was pretending to be your friend? Working beside you every day. I should have put a bullet through your head the day we were out behind the cabin. And I would have, except that death would have been too easy for you. I wanted you to suffer and live the rest of your life without hope. I hope you rot in hell."

As quietly as she had risen from her seat, Rachel Peavey sat down.

Jake jumped to his feet and in a very loud voice said, "Your Honor, on the basis of this testimony I move that all charges against my client be dismissed."

"Mr. McKinney does the State object to the defense's motion of dismissal?" Judge Seymour asked, looking directly at the prosecution table.

McKinney stood and replied, "Your Honor, in light of circumstances witnessed here today the State has no problem with the defense's motion to dismiss all charges against MacArthur Nowlin."

"Bailiff, please take Ms. Peavey into custody at this time," Judge Seymour decreed.

MacArthur sat stunned. He never saw this coming. No one saw this coming. Jake sat back down and put his arm around MacArthur and said in a quiet voice, "It seems that legal justice system you are always defending proves you were right. Justice was served here today."

In the days that followed, MacArthur remembered that Rachel was in his apartment that night to share a pizza and go over the Killingsworth case. He also remembered that she had gone to the restroom and had taken more time than she should have.

That's when she planted Marilyn's phone in my bathroom. It was all beginning to make sense. She was secretly helping Killingsworth build a case against him, without Killingsworth knowing it. It was Rachel who made the call to Killingsworth telling him where he would find Marilyn's phone. It was suspected, other anonymous calls to the station were made by Rachel as well. She knew Marilyn was planning to meet Tim Killingsworth that fateful night because Marilyn called her after she had arranged to meet Detective Killingsworth. Rachel immediately called Sonny, who was staying at the *Budget Inn,* just outside of Wilcox. Rachel had been supplying Sonny with drugs to sustain his habit. That way, she had control over him. The drugs she furnished him came from drugs confiscated on police raids, over the past few months. To make sure Detective Killingsworth never arrived for the interlude that night, Rachel called Detective Killingsworth, telling him his wife had called the station and she sounded upset. He needed to go home immediately. This would insure he would not go to the cabin that night.

Sonny Barrett explained that Rachel Peavey threatened to kill his parents if he didn't point the finger at MacArthur as the one who hired him. The district attorney agreed to keep his end of the deal even though he had been lying about who hired him. Justice was served, was the reason given by the district attorney's office.

MacArthur was reinstated as lead detective in homicide for the Wilcox Police Department. District Attorney Sanford and Chief Aldridge issued public apologies for the ordeal MacArthur had to endure the past several months. He responded by saying he harbored no ill feelings toward them.

During her arraignment, Rachel stated the only regret she had was not killing Sonny Barrett. She pleaded guilty to the charges of murder for hire, and was convicted and sentenced to 25 years to life. After serving 16 months of her sentence, Rachel Peavey died of colon cancer.

MacArthur actually felt sorry for Rachel. She was filled with so much hatred, her total existence was nothing but a façade. Her only purpose in life was to seek revenge. He considered visiting her in prison, but never did. In spite of his earnest attempts, he could never forgive her for killing an innocent victim just for revenge. Marilyn didn't deserve to die.

Two days after the trial, Chief Aldridge called Tim Killingsworth to his office.

"I told you when you came to me accusing MacArthur of murder that you damn sure better be right. Well, you weren't. I want your ass out of here today. Because you're my sister's child, I will write a letter of recommendation. After that, don't expect me to help you again. You almost cost a man his life, because of your blind hatred and jealousy. Don't bother telling me how sorry you are. There's nothing you can say or do that will make this right. Now, get the hell out of my office."

One month later, Tim Killingsworth's wife filed for divorce.

MacArthur resisted the urge to confront him, but decided he was not worth it. Their paths would never cross again.

He never apologized to MacArthur.

Over the next several months MacArthur's life slowly returned to normal. On the first Monday in October, the station looked and sounded like it usually did after a long weekend of DUI's, domestic disturbances, and public drunkenness. MacArthur was having his second cup of coffee and checking his messages when the dispatcher buzzed him saying he had a call on line one. He asked her who the caller was, she said she wasn't sure. The connection was not very good. But, she thought the caller's name was Kelli.

Made in the USA
Lexington, KY
27 March 2015